Praise for Bern

The Godsend

'A splendidly readable and creepy story'   *Sunday Express*

'Bernard Taylor writes with grace ... a shocker ... I enjoyed every horrid word of it'   *Daily Telegraph*

"An excellent, chilling first novel"   *Boston Sunday Globe*

Sweetheart Sweetheart

'The best ghost story I have ever read ... a potential classic'
     Charles L. Grant

'This is a novel of great power, engrossing and immensely moving'
     British Fantasy Society

'Reaches its horrifying climax with seductive grace'   *Library Journal*

Mother's Boys

'Never again will you take the sweet smile of a child at face value!'
     Sunday Times

'Chilling plot, masterfully handled'   *Yorkshire Post*

'Some of the nastiest domestic chills ever produced ... a brilliantly constructed conte cruel'   *City Limits*

'One of the best chillers you are likely to read this year'
     USA Daily News

The Reaping

'Taylor works wizardry again'   *Publishers Weekly*

'Taylor weaves a web that grows tighter with each turn of the page'
     Booklist

'A deftly-woven horror story'   *ALA Booklist*

Bernard Taylor is an award-winning author of several suspense and horror novels, among them *The Godsend* and *Mother's Boys*, both of which were adapted for the big screen. He is also the author of non-fiction true crime accounts, including *There Must Be Evil*, about the notorious murderer Elizabeth Berry, and *Perfect Murder*, for which he won the Crime Writers' Association Gold Dagger Award (with Stephen Knight). He has also written for stage, television and radio.

Also by Bernard Taylor

NOVELS
The Godsend
Sweetheart, Sweetheart
The Reaping
The Moorstone Sickness
The Kindness of Strangers
Madeleine
Evil Intent
Mother's Boys
Charmed Life
Since Ruby

NON-FICTION
There Must be Evil: The Life and Murderous Career of Elizabeth Berry
Perfect Murder: A Century of Unsolved Homicides
(with Stephen Knight) – Winner of the CWA Gold Dagger Award
Cruelly Murdered: Constance Kent and the Killing at Road Hill House
Murder At the Priory: the Mysterious Poisoning of Charles Bravo
(with Kate Clarke)

THE
COMEBACK

BERNARD TAYLOR

Duckworth Overlook

First published in the UK in 2016 by
Duckworth Overlook

LONDON
30 Calvin Street, London E1 6NW
T: 020 7490 7300
E: info@duckworth-publishers.co.uk
www.ducknet.co.uk
For bulk and special sales please contact
sales@duckworth-publishers.co.uk

978 0 7156 5117 9
Typeset by Charlotte Tate
Printed and bound in Great Britain

This is for F.E.F

...not for all the rice in China

......ONE

With the sound of the drapes being drawn, followed by the clink of china, Rosemary came out of her sleep. Opening her eyes, blinking at the light, she saw Carrie standing at the bedside.

'What's up?'

'Nothing's up,' Carrie said. 'I just came to wake you.'

'Great.' Rosemary gave a sigh. 'I open my eyes to see the light of day and find you standing there like some dumb waxworks reject. What time is it? I told you I wanted to sleep.'

'I did let you sleep, Rosie,' Carrie said. 'It's almost eleven. I brought your coffee – and the mail.' Carefully, she poured a cup of coffee. 'And it's a beautiful morning.'

'What day is it?'

'Friday. You know it's Friday. Come on, sit up.' As Rosemary pulled herself up in the bed Carrie adjusted the pillows at her back. 'You ready for your coffee?'

'I guess so.'

Rosemary's grudging tone came as no surprise. After all, the dinner party at the Davisons' hadn't broken up till almost twelve. 'You want some aspirin?' Carrie asked. 'Seltzer?'

'What? No, just the coffee – and a new head.' Rosemary reached for the small hand mirror on her bedside table, and looked at her reflection. She gave a groan. In no fit state for trivialities after last night's party, she had done a less than thorough job of removing her make-up before falling into bed. Now, hours later; her wide mouth was smeared with traces of lipstick, while the remains of the foundation that she had so carefully applied before setting out was now grimed into her skin, settled into the lines that ravaged her once attractive face.

Setting the mirror back down, she said, 'You know something? Queen Elizabeth – the first one, that is – she had the right idea. From the age of fifty she banned every looking glass from the palace. Yep. And from then on she just relied on what her ministers and all the other hangers-on told her as to how she looked. That was one smart lady. She probably went to the end of her days thinking she looked like Miss World.'

Carrie laughed. 'Rosie, you look fine, really you do. Here – take your coffee.' She held out the cup of coffee and Rosemary took it and sipped from it. Carrie watched her for a moment, then moved to the window. 'I'll let in a little more light.'

'Not too much.'

As Carrie adjusted the drapes, Rosemary winced, screwing up her eyes. 'Don't go mad now. You Texas girls are never satisfied unless the whole damn world looks like wide screen Cinerama.'

Carrie, standing at the window, looked out over the shining waters of the Hudson. On the far shore the buildings of Tarrytown were unusually clear. 'The river looks so calm today,' she said.

'It's *always* calm.'

'And the humidity's low.'

Rosemary snorted. 'Thank God for that. I don't care how long I live here, I'll never get used to this bloody climate.'

'Oh, *I* see,' Carrie said, turning, moving back to the bed, 'it's going to be one of those days, is it? Nothing's going to be right, right?'

Rosemary nodded. 'You got it.'

'Just so long as we know.'

'Hand me a cigarette, will you?'

Carrie took a cigarette from the packet on the bed-side table and passed it to Rosemary. She watched while she lit it, then said, 'So – how was the dinner party? Was it fun?'

'Fun?' said Rosemary. 'It was the Davisons, for Christ's sake. The same old faces. Same old gags, same old memories. Jesus. It had its moments, but *fun* I wouldn't call it.'

'You stayed late enough.'

'Yeah, well, we live in hope.'

'I guess so.' Carrie pulled the small chair closer to the bed and picked up the few items of mail she had brought in on the tray. 'You want to look at the mail?' She took up a letter-opener, slit open the envelopes and placed them on the coverlet at Rosemary's side.

Rosemary set down her coffee and put on a pair of spectacles. 'Bills, bloody bills,' she said. 'Why are people so damned unoriginal?' She looked at a piece of paper, groaned and tossed it aside. 'I can't deal with this crap.'

'Rosie, it's a final demand,' Carrie said. 'Come on now. We can't be without the telephone.'

A deep sigh along with a dismissive wave of the hand. 'Okay, so pay it.'

Carrie nodded, then extracted a letter from an airmail envelope. 'And here,' she said, 'is something from England.'

'From England? What are they chasing me for?'

Rosemary took the letter from Carrie's outstretched hand, unfolded it and began to read. 'Well,' she said, coming to the end of the letter, 'they *did* it. Well, what do you know!'

'What is it?' Carrie detected a new note in Rosemary's voice. 'You got some good news?'

Rosemary gave a laugh, flicking the letter with a scarlet-tipped finger. 'They did it.'

'What are you talking about?'

'My records!'

'What?'

'My records, my old records – can you believe that?'

'Your records?' Carrie didn't understand. It had been years since Rosemary had recorded anything. It had been years since she had even attempted to sing. All that was long in the past. 'What are you saying?' she said.

'It's from Amberlight, my old record company in the UK,' Rosemary said. 'They've taken some of my old records and put them out on a CD.' She added on a sharper note, 'And not before time, either.'

'Hey,' Carrie said, 'that's good news! That's wonderful.' Then, with an ironic little smile: 'We could certainly use the money.'

Rosemary nodded. 'We certainly could. Unfortunately, though, there won't be much. They're only doing a small pressing. It might just buy us a hamburger.' She handed the letter to Carrie. 'Here, read it for yourself.'

Carrie took the letter, studied it. 'That's great,' she said. 'And they say all the tracks are going online, too. Hey, that means they'll be everywhere. And they say they're sending you some samples of the CD. That'll be nice.'

'Yes – yes, it will.'

Carrie studied the letter a few moments longer, then said, 'Did you know about this, Rosie – the CD and everything?' She tapped the letter. 'They go on like you knew all about it.'

Rosemary hesitated before answering. 'Well, yes, sweetheart, I did,' she said. 'But it's no big deal. There was nothing definite. And nothing's going to come of it anyway.'

'Oh, no – don't say that.'

'It's true.' Rosemary held out her hand and Carrie handed her back the letter. 'You wait and see – they'll bring out the CD and it'll sell a dozen copies and that'll be it.'

'Oh, *you*,' Carrie said. 'Don't be so pessimistic. I think it's terrific. Just think – those old records of yours getting a new lease of life – it's brilliant. To think they'll be out there again – all your songs – all sounding fresh and new. I think it's wonderful.'

'Yeah, well, maybe.'

Carrie frowned. 'I don't get it. I'd have thought you'd be thrilled.'

Rosemary looked down again at the letter and shook her head. 'I don't know. When they first brought it up, the idea – I hoped so much that it would happen – but now – I don't know. In a way I wish it had never come.'

'But – but why?'

'Well, it – it just stirs everything up. And it only makes me dissatisfied.'

'Dissatisfied? What do you mean? You should be *glad*. I mean, other stars have had it done, and I doubt they're complaining.'

Rosemary jabbed a finger at the letter. 'Yes, I know that, but that part of my life is over. They bring this up and you start looking back at all the mistakes – all the things you should have done differently and – oh, what's the point in dragging it all up again?'

'What are you saying?' Carrie said. 'It doesn't have to be like that.'

Rosemary was silent for a moment, then she said, 'No – no, maybe not. I don't know. It's strange – you think you're totally forgotten, and then you find out that you're not. Yes, and maybe you're right – people are going to be buying my records again.' She gave a harsh little laugh. 'My God, can you believe it? Suddenly you learn there might be some people out there who *care*.' She sat for a moment, then, crumpling the letter, she tossed it onto the carpet. 'Ah, but so what? It's over. It's *over*.'

Carrie bent and picked up the letter and smoothed it out. 'I don't know why you say it's over,' she said, 'because quite clearly, it's not.'

'Carrie, honey, I made those records over forty years ago.'

'So?'

'Well, times have moved on, for Christ's sake. You need to get real.'

Carrie gave a little nod. 'Okay, if you say so.'

'I mean it,' Rosemary said. 'You want to try looking at some of the new TV shows instead of all those crappy old movies you insist on watching. They're doing things differently now, you know. Have you watched any of those talent shows they have on TV? They're full of kids who can't sing. They can't sustain a note for longer than two seconds and they can't hold a melody. Yet they all get told they're star material. Sure. And every kid up there gets to tell everybody he's on some *journey*. Yeah, he's on a journey, okay — and the only direction for their fucking journey is *down*. At eighty miles an hour.' She sighed. 'Carrie, it's a different world out there — and it has a different sound nowadays. Maybe you haven't noticed, but those kids today don't sound like Ella Fitzgerald or Barbra Streisand or Sinatra or any of those real singers.'

'Yeah, well, that's for sure.' Carrie reached out for Rosemary's cup. 'You want more coffee?'

'No, thanks.'

As Carrie gathered together the coffee things and arranged them on the tray, Rosemary watched her, taking in the lines of her slim, trimly dressed figure, the soft waves of her honey-blonde hair. The picture was such a familiar one, an image engraved there, immovable, and Rosemary couldn't imagine it any other way. It was as if Carrie had always been there. And so she had, almost...

The two of them had first met in *Save a Place for Me*, a new musical comedy in which Rosemary had the starring role. That had been over twenty years ago. Rosemary was from England originally, having come to the USA following her marriage to Alan Sanderson, the New York playwright.

Then, after less than five years, Alan had gone to play squash and succumbed to a coronary thrombosis on the court, leaving Rosemary with their small son David, the house on the Hudson, and Alan's literary assets — in particular three or four plays that still enjoyed a certain amount (though lately dwindling) of popularity on the summer and winter stock circuits.

Alan's sudden and unexpected death had shaken Rosemary to her core, and for a while she had been too stunned to do much but go through the motions of living from day to day, while trying to give David the care that he required. For a while she had considered selling up and returning to England, but eventually she had decided against it — after all, what would she be going back to? When she had married Alan and come to New York she had left behind a waning popularity in a changing musical scene, added to which she'd hardly set foot back in the place during the many years since she'd left. So, she had decided, America was her home, and here she would stay.

As the months had passed she had come to the realisation that for much of her married life she had merely been marking time, passing the years as if the social life that she and Alan had enjoyed, plus the demands of parenthood, had been enough. But they had not, and without Alan, and cast only in the role of widow and mother, she had found that her life was greatly lacking. So it was that, after weighing everything up, she had decided to try to build a new career for herself. It wouldn't be easy, but she could do it. She *would* do it. And soon afterwards the wonderful opportunity of *Save a Place for Me* had come along, and with

David safely away in school she had jumped at the chance to prove herself anew.

Unfortunately, though, it hadn't worked. That chance of a new start, a new, bright beginning, had failed. The swift and sudden closing of the show had come as a jolt to her newly burgeoning self-confidence, and she had scooted off to Cape Cod to lick her wounds — at the same time consoling herself with that nice-looking young guy. It was after that, a couple of months later and back in New York, that she and Carrie had run into one another again. Carrie, out of work and unhappy, had readily agreed to move in with Rosemary as personal assistant and sometime help and nursemaid to David.

'Just for as long as it suits,' Rosemary had said. 'Till you get on your feet again, or just for a few weeks. Whatever you want.'

Carrie had settled into her new job with ease. She had taken to David, and he to her, and she had cared for him as if he was her own. Not only that, but when he was away at school — as he was for most of the year — she did everything she could to help Rosemary in her professional work. *Save a Place for Me* might have been a disaster, but Rosemary had determined to put it behind her and start over, and she had gone back to working in cabaret, doing restaurants and nightclubs along the Eastern seaboard. Carrie, for her part, her own career on hold, had remained with her, typing her letters, answering the telephone and making appointments and cancelling them. She learned to handle the fights, too, and the occasional disagreements that arose with the managers, the producers and agents. She was always there, going with Rosemary from one town to another, always handy with a glass of Scotch or a safety pin, and if things went wrong, or too far, ready to deal with the hangovers, the depressions and the tantrums. And eventually their time together had stretched into years, and even though David had long since gone from their lives there was no question of Carrie leaving. Staying with Rosemary had become a career in itself.

Breaking into Rosemary's thoughts and reminiscences, came Carrie's voice.

'What's that?' Rosemary said.

'I said I'll go run your bath.' With her words, Carrie picked up the tray and started across the room.

'Tell me,' Rosemary said, as Carrie reached the door, '– what do you think about it – the letter – the CD?'

Carrie turned in the doorway. 'I told you, I think it's wonderful. Absolutely wonderful.'

'You mean it?'

'Yes, I do. I mean – okay, we might not make any money from it, but on the other hand it could lead to – to other things.'

Rosemary nodded. 'Yes – I guess it could.'

'*Better* things.'

'Yes – maybe you're right.'

'But whatever it is,' Carrie said, '– we'll cope.'

As the sound of Carrie's footsteps faded on the landing, Rosemary lit another cigarette and leaned back against the pillows. Oh, yes, she had no doubt that Carrie would cope. Carrie would cope with just about anything. She always had. So often she had shown that beneath her quiet exterior was a surprising strength. And she had given of that strength for a long time. Through so many years now she had been there for everything, the good times and the bad. She had been there when Rosemary was at her happiest, and when she was at her lowest. And at that very lowest time of all, when David had gone.

David...

David... She didn't want to think about him. But nevertheless the thoughts would come. In some ways, over time, she had learned to face the regret and the grief — though they would never be gone. But the memories, and the guilt — that was different altogether. Suddenly he would be right there, nine years old, perfect, beautiful, complete in every detail, frowning over his toys, or smiling up at her, chattering away.

Unable and unwilling to stop herself, she unveiled the pictures just before the ending. And they were always the same. Concerned with rehearsals and plans for a tour of one-night stands that had come up, she had been too busy and preoccupied to give him her time. Home from school for the summer vacation, he had been in the way, it was as simple as that. But then she had discovered that a neighbour's son was going off to summer camp up in the Catskills. 'Darling, it'll be perfect for you,' she'd said. 'You'll drive up with Wayne and his dad, and then I'll come and pick you up and bring you home when my tour is over.'

But he had pleaded with her. 'Oh, Mom, no — I don't want to go.'

'But darling, it's only for three weeks, then we'll have all the rest of the summer together. We'll do something special.'

'But you said I'd spend the summer here with you.'

'Yes, I know, but that was before my tour came up, and you can't come along on that, can you, now?'

'Why not?'

'Oh, sweetheart, be sensible. It would be impractical. And it wouldn't be any fun for you anyway, would it? – schlepping around with Carrie and me, sleeping in hotel rooms night after night, eating all your meals in restaurants. You'll be much better off at camp.'

'I'd *like* all that, Mom,' he'd said. 'You know I would. And I don't like going away on my own.'

'You won't be on your own. You'll be with Wayne.'

'Wayne gets on at me all the time.'

'Oh, darling – please don't make it difficult for me…'

'Can't I stay here?' He was whining now. 'Mrs Ruth will come over and look after me.' Elda Ruth was the maid-cook-housekeeper, and one of the few constants in his young life. 'She can sleep over. We'll be okay, the two of us.'

But no, Rosemary had said, it wouldn't work: Elda had her own commitments. And so, in spite of his protests he had gone off that Sunday afternoon in July, riding with Wayne and Wayne's father in the blue Chevy, and Rosemary had breathed a sigh of relief and got back to the business in hand.

She had learned of the accident later that same afternoon, from the police officer who came to the house, when she was wondering why David hadn't phoned to tell her of his arrival. On seeing the uniformed stranger's set, pale expression she had known at once that something had happened. A moment later, when he took off his cap, she guessed the worst. Haltingly, he told her that there had been a five-vehicle pile-up on the freeway. Struck from behind by an out-of-control semi, the Chevy had exploded into a fireball. There were no survivors. The officer's words had seemed to ring in the room, and she had cried out, striking him on the chest, 'No! No! You can't say that! You can't!' And even now, through the haze of time she could still see the fabric of the man's uniform, see his face – stolid, inadequate to deal with her despair.

Fortunately Carrie had been there.

......TWO

Sitting before her dressing-table mirror, her hair wrapped in a towel, Rosemary gently smoothed moisturiser into her cheeks and around her mouth and eyes. Carrie stood nearby at the wardrobe, arranging Rosemary's clothes. On the bureau a radio played soft, unidentifiable music, interrupted every few minutes by the self-consciously seductive tones of a disc jockey.

'I hate Fridays,' Rosemary said with a sigh. 'It's such a useless bloody day. Damn all ever happens.'

Her accent was a strange mixture. Her East-End-of-London origins were still sometimes faintly noticeable, as were the traces of her West End success. But there on the top, covering the Cockney and cut-glass were shades of the American accent she had unwittingly adopted over the years.

'Did you make my appointment with Carl for tomorrow?' she asked. Carl was her hairdresser.

Carrie nodded. 'For three o'clock.'

'Good.' Rosemary looked at her nails. 'And I need a manicure, too. Yes, and the next – ' She broke off suddenly, and as Carrie opened her mouth to speak she impatiently flapped a hand at her. '*Listen*!'

From the radio came the familiar words of a song, sung by a voice, mellow, rich, and smooth as velvet.

When all the skies were grey,
And all my songs were blue songs,
You drove the clouds away,
And smiled and sang me new songs...

The women listened as though neither had ever heard the song or the singer before. Yet every phrase, every breath was known to them by heart. Hearing it now, after so long, Rosemary forgot for a moment the crow's feet at her eyes and the greying roots of her hair, and saw herself young again, standing at the mike in front of the band, before a sea of adoring faces, the sound of applause ringing in her ears.

The words of the song echoed softly in the room.

And when other friends denied me,
You were there, my friend, beside me.
That was you. You were always there...

The recording had been one of Rosemary's biggest hits, made when she had been in her early twenties, and although the orchestral arrangement now sounded dated, the intervening span of time had imbued it with a distinct, special charm. They listened, catching every breath, every nuance of Rosemary's soft, lilting tone, listened as she caressed the phrases of the middle eight, and the closing bars of the final chorus:

...But of all the things you brought me,
Above it all, you taught me how to care.
For you were always, always, always there.

As the soaring chords of the accompanying chorus and orchestra died away, the voice of the DJ brought the women abruptly back to the present.

' "You Were Always There", sung by Rosemary Paul,' he said. And with a little sigh of admiration: 'And beautifully done too. Rosemary was one of the most popular singers in her native England when that record was made. Which of course was before she came over to this side of the pond. Okay – her star has faded somewhat over the years, but we've just learned that a record company in Britain is issuing an album of some of her best stuff. Let's hope it'll be available soon.' A pause and he added, 'Of course, she was a little before my time, but with a voice like that she shouldn't be forgotten.' There came the blast from a trumpet as the next record began. The sound, though, was drowned by Rosemary's angry voice.

'Turn that fucking thing off!' she yelled, then growled, 'A little before his time? I wish he was here right now. I'd have his balls.'

Carrie switched off the radio. As she turned back to Rosemary she was suddenly struck by how vulnerable she looked with her face devoid of make-up. And how different it was, she thought, from the impression that Rosemary had usually managed to give over the years – that of brittle career woman. Though how much of it was sham and how much the real thing was now academic. There had been many times when Rosemary's tough exterior had proved to be her downfall; other times when it had been her salvation. Whatever it was, though, it was there, and one either coped with it or got out.

Those who coped with Rosemary, Carrie knew, were generally those who saw another side to her. Carrie herself, of course, had seen it over the years, and at no time more clearly than when David had died. David's death had left Rosemary completely shattered, and more and more, in attempts to block out her pain, she had turned to alcohol, until in the end there had come a complete breakdown, and she had been carried, hysterical and screaming obscenities, to Belle Vue mental hospital. Later, when Carrie had brought her back home, under the part-time care and supervision of a nurse, Rosemary had retreated from the world. Moving about the house like a zombie, she had appeared totally withdrawn, hardly speaking, and showing interest in nothing and no one.

After a while Carrie had dismissed the nurse, taking complete charge herself, at the same time doing all she could to give the impression that all was operating as usual. In Rosemary's name she wrote letters, and even signed cheques in a facsimile of Rosemary's signature to pay the bills.

Later, when Rosemary was stronger, the two women had taken a trip together. With no plans or itinerary to adhere to, they wandered from place to place, as the mood took them. There were days in the country, afternoons on sunlit beaches and quiet evenings with other friendly sojourners. And gradually some of the light had returned to Rosemary's eyes and they had begun to shine again with something of their old spirit.

The experience, though, had taken its toll, and Rosemary found that her voice had been affected. The hoarseness when she spoke did not go, and as the weeks passed it was feared that her voice might be permanently impaired. A specialist was consulted and, after a lengthy examination, he confronted her across his office desk. 'The right vocal cord appears to be paralysed,' he said. 'It might be the result of a growth of some kind, or it may have arisen as the result of emotional stress. We shall need more tests.'

When the required tests revealed no malign condition she was given exercises to perform night and morning. And gradually, over the weeks, her voice became stronger, and Carrie began to hear once more the familiar tones ringing through the house. Often strident, laced with impatience and invective, they brought relief and pleasure to her ears.

But Rosemary's singing voice did not come back as it had once been. The soft, mellow tones that she had once produced with ease now seemed beyond her. One evening with Carrie beside her, she sat at the piano and tentatively went over one of her old songs. It was not a success. Her voice cracked and broke on notes that she had once reached with no difficulty. Eventually, stopping in the middle of a phrase, she lowered the piano lid and sat staring ahead.

'It's been a long time, Rosie,' Carrie said. 'You can't expect miracles.'

Rosemary made no reply, but from that day her records were consigned to the basement. On one occasion, much later, Carrie suggested that they fetch them up and play them. Rosemary's reaction was so furious that Carrie knew she must not bring up the subject again.

.....THREE

The house was a large, wood-frame affair situated on the northern edge of Nyack, in Rockland County, upstate New York. Perched on the western bank of the Hudson, it was reached from the road by a long, curving drive that wound through a couple of acres of grounds, a small part of which was formally kept with lawns, while the rest had been left more or less to itself. The land was separated from that of its neighbours by patches of woodland, which had once thickly forested the river's banks. Now thin and straggling, the trees still served their present purpose — that of preserving, to a degree, the house's seclusion.

For Carrie, it was the only home she had known since leaving Fort Worth all those years ago. She treasured her time there, and did all she could to help with the smooth running of the place.

Today, Wednesday, was one of the days she set aside for household chores. There had been a time, years ago, when most of the housework had been done by Elda, but that had been when Carrie had other things to do, helping with Rosemary's career and caring for David. When David had died and Rosemary's career had faltered, she had been needed in a different way. Then, later, when things were on a more even keel again, she had asked Rosemary what the point of paying Elda to come in to keep house was when she, Carrie, was there, and no less capable. So Elda had been let go, and Carrie had taken over her duties. And so it had remained.

Now, after having spent several hours vacuuming and dusting, she had put aside her house-cleaning tools and come out to get some air. She found only a limited comfort, however. The day that had begun so fine had now, by four o'clock, become unbearably humid. She sat for a while with her book in the clammy heat, and then went back into the house and put on her bathing-suit and bathrobe. In the kitchen she poured herself a Coke. She heard no sound as she moved towards the rear door. Rosemary must still be lying down in her room, as she sometimes did on these warm afternoons.

Reaching the pool, Carrie put aside her robe and stepped down into the cool water. A few leaves floated here and there on its surface. It needed a clean, and she made a mental note to mention it to Joe, the young gardener who came to work on the property for one morning each week.

Lunging forward she slowly swam a couple of lengths of the pool, then, returning to the steps, climbed out again. After drying herself off she donned her robe and seated herself on one of the garden chairs. Sheltered from the sun by the leaves of the elms, she sipped her Coke and opened her book again.

It was no good. Her Danielle Steele novel, so promising, could not win against the discomfort of the sweltering heat, and eventually she put it aside, gathered up her things and moved back to the house.

Entering the interior out of the sunlight, she came to a halt, waiting for her eyes to adjust to the gloom. And it was then, to her great surprise, that she heard Rosemary's voice, in song, coming from the music room. Knowing that Rosemary would not welcome any listener, she turned to creep away in silence. However, moving too quickly in the dimness she stumbled against the hall table, knocking over a large brass pot. It fell to the floor with a crash. At once the singing stopped. Then from behind the closed door came Rosemary's voice:

'Carrie?'

Carrie hesitated before she answered. 'Yes...?'

After a moment the door opened and Rosemary stood there. 'What were you doing out here?'

'Nothing.' Carrie picked up the pot and replaced it on the table. 'I just came in from the garden. I couldn't see in the dark.'

'You were snooping.'

'No, Rosie.' Carrie shook her head. 'Of course I wasn't. I told you – I couldn't see, coming out of the sun. I'm sorry I disturbed you.'

'What do you mean – disturbed?'

'Well – your singing.'

At Carrie's words, anger sprang into Rosemary's eyes.

'You *were* snooping!' In sudden fury, Rosemary lashed out, her hand a fist, striking Carrie on the shoulder. There was little pain from the blow, but the shock was enough to cause Carrie to drop the glass, the tumbler shattering on the tiled floor. She stared at Rosemary for a moment, then, covering her face with her hands, she burst into tears.

Still crying, she crouched and began to gather up the fragments. At once Rosemary's hand was on her arm.

'Leave it. I'll do it.'

'It's all right.' Carrie blinked, her vision distorted by her tears.

'Leave it, this instant.' Rosemary's touch, gentle but firm, urged Carrie to her feet. 'I'm sorry,' she said. 'Oh, Carrie, forgive me.'

'I wasn't snooping, Rosie,' Carrie said, sniffing. 'Truly I wasn't.'

'No, I know you weren't.' Rosemary's expression showed her remorse. 'It's just me. I'm so sorry. I just couldn't bear the thought that anyone had heard me — trying to sing. That's why I waited till you were out of the house. I wanted — wanted to see if I could still do it.' She shrugged. 'Well, now I know I can't.'

'Oh, no, don't say that.'

'It's the truth.' Pulling Carrie closer, Rosemary kissed her cheek and gently laid her hand on the spot where she had struck her. 'God, I'm so sorry. I'm just so damned edgy these days. I don't know — getting that letter and then hearing my song on the radio…' She shook her head. 'I don't know what I'm doing.' She noticed that there was blood on Carrie's finger. 'You've cut yourself,' she said.

Carrie sniffed. 'It's just a scratch.'

'Come on.'

An arm around Carrie's shoulders, Rosemary led her to the bathroom where she opened the medicine chest and got out peroxide and cotton wool. When she had cleaned the small cut she covered it with a plaster. 'There.' With a little laugh she lifted Carrie's hand to her mouth. 'Kiss it better,' she said. 'All right now?'

Carrie smiled. 'All right now.'

'You forgive me?'

'Oh, Rosie, of course. You were upset.'

When they had cleaned up the remains of the broken glass, Rosemary led the way into the music room.

The room had rarely been used in recent years. Sometimes, when Rosemary was out of the house, Carrie would venture in and sit at the piano and accompany herself as she sang a few songs. But those times were rare.

Today the piano stood with its lid up and the long-unplayed keys shining in the light from the window.

'You know?' Rosemary said, 'I had a really crazy idea… Hearing my song on the radio and everything, I thought, well, what with my album coming out in England, maybe…' She let her words trail off.

'Go on,' Carrie said.

'Well.' Rosemary shrugged. 'I thought about what you said – that it could be the start of something…'

'Yes…?'

'And I got this crazy idea into my head that – that maybe I could go back.'

'To England?'

'Yes. I thought maybe I could go back and…' She hesitated. 'I mean, this would be the time to do it. Now, when the CD is going into the stores and being played on the radio.' She bent to the piano and struck a note with her forefinger. Straightening again, she shook her head and said, 'I even found myself starting to make plans. Would you believe it? Even thinking about what I'd *wear*. Isn't that ridiculous? The only thing I was forgetting was that I don't have a voice any more.'

She gazed off for a moment, then turning to Carrie, she said, 'Wait here,' and went from the room. A few minutes later she was back, carrying over her arm a cream lace dress.

'Here.' She held it out to Carrie.

'Huh?'

'It's for you. Take it.'

'But – but what for?'

'For my being such a bitch to you just now.'

'Oh, but Rosie…'

'Take it. I know you like it – and it'll make me feel a little better.'

'But you only just got it – and you love it so.'

'Yes, I know that. But there's no merit in giving away something you don't want anyway – so they tell me. Take it. You'll look gorgeous.'

The dress was almost new, and there was no question but that Carrie had admired it. Now she took it from Rosemary and held it against her body, one hand caressing the fabric. Rosemary's gesture was typical. On more than one occasion in the past a flare of anger had been followed by an action equally strong in its generosity. Carrie's wardrobe boasted a number of garments that had come as a result of Rosemary's quick temper.

'I don't know what to say,' Carrie said. 'It's just beautiful.' She started away. 'I'll go hang it up right now.'

Carrying the dress, she went from the room. When she returned a few minutes later she found Rosemary standing at the window, looking out over the yard.

'Rosie,' Carrie said, 'I don't think that's such a crazy idea.'

Rosemary turned to face her. 'What isn't?'

'What you said – about going back to England.'

'Really?'

'Yes, I mean it. You could do it. I'm sure you could.'

'Are you saying this seriously?'

'Of course I am. Why shouldn't you? You *do* have a voice, Rosie. You *do*. You're just a little out of practice, that's all. Maybe that's all you need – a little practice and some confidence in yourself.'

Rosemary sighed. 'Oh, if I thought there was a chance. But I need more than confidence. My voice – it's gone. Shot. You heard me, didn't you?'

'Not really. I didn't get a chance.'

'Well, take my word for it.'

'Okay,' Carrie said, 'but if you're a little rusty it's to be expected. After all, you haven't tried to sing in years. It'll be like learning to walk again. Take it a step at a time.'

A smile twitched at the corners of Rosemary's mouth. 'Take it a step at a time. One thing to be said for you, Carrie, you can always be depended on to say something original.'

Carrie looked crestfallen. 'You're making fun of me.'

'Only in the nicest way, darling.'

After a moment, Rosemary moved to a small table by the piano on which lay several pieces of sheet music. She sorted through them, picked one out and placed it on the stand. 'Okay, let's try a bit of Noël Coward,' she said. 'Let's see what we can do.'

She waited as Carrie seated herself at the piano and played the opening chords of the song. Then, taking a breath, she began to sing.

Mad about the boy,
I know it's stupid to be mad about the boy.
I'm so ashamed of it, but must admit
In some strange way I'm glad about the boy...

She continued through the song. Her voice sounded a little shaky and uncertain, the tone a little rough, and on reaching for one of the higher notes, it cracked. She came to a stop. 'There,' she said, 'what did I tell you?'

Carrie nodded, 'One step at a time, Rosie.' She turned back to the piano. 'Okay. Let's do a little vocalising. We can come back to the song later.'

With this they began work on Rosemary's voice, repeating exercises over and over, with Rosemary running from one note to another on different vowel sounds; exercises that gradually began to loosen her vocal cords. After half an hour her rough, strained tones were sounding clearer, the notes beginning to emerge with a roundness that earlier she would not have dreamed possible.

When Rosemary had completed an exercise that had taken her up to A flat, Carrie said with a nod of approval, 'You can do it. You're getting better all the time. And we'll do more tomorrow. You wait and see. You're going to be okay, Rosie, I know you are.'

'Oh, Carrie,' Rosemary said, 'what the hell would I do without you?'

*

Over the following days they continued to work on Rosemary's vocal exercises, and slowly she began to find a little of her old confidence returning, and although her voice was still at times a little raw and hoarse, with some of the high notes sounding forced, they began to feel that all the effort was paying off.

After a week of work there was a buoyancy and sparkle about Rosemary that Carrie had not witnessed for years. And it was contagious. At dinner one particular evening they both drank a little too much, but it was not just the liquor that brightened their mood. It came also from a glimpse of hope for the future. That morning a package had arrived from Amberlight Records containing a copy of the album. The little booklet that came with it gave information on the songs featured, and on Rosemary's career in its earlier days in England. It was illustrated with two or three photographs, and seeing them Rosemary hooted. 'My God, where do they get those old pictures! They must have raided the ark!'

Then the CD was played, and over their drinks the two sat listening intently while Rosemary's voice, young and smooth and mellow, caressed the familiar songs.

When the last note of the last number had died away, they remained in silence for some moments, then Rosemary put down her glass and said: 'I'm going to do it, Carrie.'

'Go back – to England, you mean?'

'Yes.' Rosemary nodded. 'If I can. It's a chance I can't pass up. And there'll never be another.' She paused. 'Will you help me? You will, won't you?'

'Of course. You don't need to ask.'

'Okay,' Rosemary said with a nod. 'I know my voice isn't what it was, but I think I can do it. I'll work on it.' Her tone grew more intense. 'All these little dreams I've had are going to be real. I'm going to do it.' She pressed Carrie's hand. 'No, *we* are going to do it. You and me. We'll do it *together*. You wait and see. They've got a surprise coming. Like the song says — we ain't down yet.'

......FOUR

In her room, Carrie stood before the long mirror, gazing at
her reflection. She was wearing the cream lace dress that
Rosemary had given her. It fitted perfectly. She coaxed a
lock of hair into a becoming curl over her cheekbone, then
smoothed the fabric of the bodice with gentle hands. The
dress looked good. How kind Rosie could be at times.
Turning, she glanced at the bedside clock. It was just over
two hours since Rosemary had left to drive into Manhattan. She had gone to see her old manager, and it was
certain they'd have a lot to talk about.

Life had been fairly hectic since the Great Decision of
a week ago; at least it had for Rosemary, and Carrie had
watched a change take place in her, seeing a new vitality
there, a new enthusiasm, and a capacity for work she
thought had long since died. Now Rosemary always seemed
to be busy with something or other. If she wasn't driving off
on some errand in connection with her project she would
be in the music room, vocalising at the piano. Carrie, passing the door, would hear the repetition of the scales and
exercises, or the words of familiar songs. It was getting to be
almost like old times.

Sighing, she looked again at the clock. The afternoon was
crawling by, and there was still twenty minutes to go before
the movie started on TV. It was *Up in Arms*. Danny Kaye and
Dinah Shore. It was one of her favourites. Rosemary made

fun of her for watching all the old movies, but Carrie didn't care. 'For God's sake,' Rosemary had said, only yesterday, 'can't you watch anything other than those ancient old pictures, with those clapped out old stars! Joan Crawford, Doris Day, Clark Gable. For Christ's sake, most of them are dead. Haven't you heard of George Clooney and Meryl Streep? Somebody who's actually breathing?'

It made no difference to Carrie; it was water off a duck's back. Watching herself in the mirror, she gave a little shake of her head and launched into 'Tessie's Torch Song', the way Dinah Shore did it in the movie.

> *Here is a story, 'bout a gal.*
> *Folks called her Torchy Tess.*
> *Because she trusted, her heart got busted.*
> *Love made her life a mess…*

After singing the verse she went into the refrain, all the while eyeing her reflection. She did it well. She moved her hands, her fingers, just the way Dinah did, used her voice in just the same way, perfectly copying Dinah's mellow tone, singing the words in the same gentle bluesy way. Then, as suddenly as she had begun, she stopped, letting her arms fall to her sides. She stood there for a few seconds and then slowly took off the dress.

The walls of her room were hung with prints and photographs. Standing with the white dress over her arm, she gazed at a photograph of herself taken not long after she had started out in her career. She had been pretty then, there was no denying it, and she had envisaged a great future. And certainly for the limited time she had spent in the business she had done well. Her reviews had all, without exception, been excellent. And she kept them still, all the newspaper clippings. A couple of times she had been tempted to throw them out – all useless relics of a time gone by – but always, at the last minute, she had held back. And so still they nestled in a drawer, held between the covers of a large album, along with the photographs and the theatre playbills.

Putting down the dress, she opened the bureau drawer and took out the album. Then, sitting on the bed, she began to turn the pages. She knew the words and the phrases of some of the reviews almost by heart. *'The standout was a newcomer to the company,'* she read. And another: *'The scene owed its success to the finely tuned performance of Carrie Markham...'* *'Carrie Markham is pretty and talented, and we'll be seeing a lot more of her in the future...'* So they went on. And there were the photographs as well. There she was as Sarah Brown in the Maine summer stock production of *Guys and Dolls*; there as the cheerleader in *Call a Halt!* And there in her beautiful costume as the professor's daughter in *The Charm-Spinner*.

And there she was with Michael.

The photograph showed them at rehearsals for *Save a Place for Me*, going through their duet, 'You Could Be Good for Me', the song and dance number they had so enjoyed doing together. The words went through her brain.

You like your steak rare with a Waldorf salad,
A gentle song from Peggy Lee,
Maybe a soft and sentimental ballad,
You could be good for me...

In the photograph they were wearing their rehearsal clothes, jeans and shirts, their legs kicking out in the well-remembered strut, faces bright and happy.

Michael.

In the photograph his eyes shone and his smile was white against his suntanned skin. He looked so young. They both did. Young, vibrant, good-looking – and happy. Handsome Michael with his dark hair, and pretty Carrie with her pale blonde. They looked the perfect couple.

And there was Rosemary, too. Out of focus in the picture, she stood, a shadowy figure in the background and partly out of the frame, waiting for her cue to come in.

After the photograph the album was empty, the blank pages showing only too clearly the abrupt end to Carrie's brief career.

Save a Place for Me should have been her beginning, not her end, she said to herself. After all the footslogging, the rounds of agents' offices, the seasons in summer- and winter-stock, she had been given a chance to show what she could do, and in something that really mattered. A great part in a major new production, a real chance to sing, to dance, to act; a chance to show herself, to say to the world: *Here comes Carrie Markham.*

How could it have all gone so wrong? How, when it had all started out so well? And with Michael, too. How had that happened? They had discovered an immediate rapport, both offstage and on – and then – then it was all over. Looking again at the photograph, she took in their bright smiles. When the picture was taken she had never dreamed just how soon her reason for smiling would be gone.

It was all down to Brewster, of course. Ian Brewster, the show's director. And she would never forgive him for the way he had turned against her.

At first he had liked what she did. He had told her so, and he had shown his approval. Over the first days of rehearsal he'd been so nice, so pleasant, and complimentary about her work, remarking on the way she approached a particular scene, or the way she delivered a certain line. And it wasn't only him; there had been expressions of approval from the other members of the company, Rosemary as well.

And then it had all changed. Brewster had begun to criticise her for things — things with which he had previously appeared quite satisfied.

And of course she knew why.

She had been alone in the green room one day, during a break in rehearsals. And Brewster had walked in. He smiled at her as he came across the carpeted floor, and she put aside her script and smiled back at him. He was a tall, wiry man, late thirties, good-looking.

'So,' he said as he took one of the easy chairs across from her, 'our Carrie's taking a well-earned break. Good for you.'

Carrie smiled back, gave a little shrug. She would always be a little in awe of him. 'I'm just looking over my scene with Rosemary in act two,' she said.

'Oh, your big scene,' he said. 'Absolutely, and we have to get *that* right. Though I reckon you're just about there. It's going well, very well.'

Carrie nodded, happy. 'Well, thanks, Ian. Thank you very much.'

'Oh, I mean it,' he said. 'It's gonna be great. It's a vital piece, as you know, but I think you've about nailed it.'

'Thank you...'

'I was looking over your CV,' he said. 'You've done some interesting things.'

'Well, a *few*,' she said.

'That's okay. You have time in front of you. How old are you?'

'Twenty-three.'

'Like I said, you have time. You have an agent?'

'No, I was really lucky with this job. I got the audition from an open call.'

'Well, good for you — there's a lot of competition out there. But you'll get an agent from this production, no question about it.' He paused. 'You've got talent, Carrie. I know it when I see it, and I saw it at once when you did your audition — doing that number from *South Pacific*. And if this show does well, I'm sure it'll open up all kinds of opportunities for you. You'll be doing it all — TV and movies too. It'll all come. And you deserve it.'

'Thank you.' She smiled, glowing.

Smiling back, he rose from his chair and came towards her. Standing before her, he bent slightly, put a fingertip under her chin, and lifted her face. 'Look at me.'

She raised her head a little, self-conscious, half-smiling into his face. Gently he placed his hands on either side of her cheeks. 'Oh, yes,' he said, 'you play your cards right and you'll be off to Hollywood before you know it.' He gave a nod. 'I can see that face on the big screen.' Then, bending lower, he kissed her lightly on the lips.

The action was swift, and for Carrie quite unexpected. In the second that his lips touched hers, she jerked back her head, while at the same time raising her hands to cover her mouth.

Brewster straightened, his smile fading. 'Oh, well, excuse *me*,' he said. 'Was I being a little forward there? Oh, dear, we can't have that, can we?' He gave a cold little laugh. 'Look at you, sitting there so demure. Don't worry, I'm not going to do anything like it again. You don't need to carry on like you're Mother Teresa.'

Her newfound joy vanished, Carrie was aware of him turning, starting across the room. In the doorway he turned to face her. 'It was a friendly gesture, Carrie,' he said. 'That's all.'

*

She didn't tell Michael what had happened. She wouldn't tell him, she decided. The less said about it the better. She must let it go, let it pass.

But it didn't pass. From that minute, it seemed, Ian Brewster changed towards her.

The first signs came that same afternoon, when she went to rehearse her scene with Rosemary. Whereas before he had given her little words of praise and encouragement, now he seemed intent on finding fault — and about the most trivial things.

Back at the hotel that evening she tried to hide her misery from Michael, but he was aware of it, of course. Like everyone else he had seen her humiliation. All he could do was sympathise, try to comfort her. 'He'll get over it,' he said. 'Don't worry about it.' She said nothing to him of the kiss.

But it was the same the next day, and the day after that. And it just seemed to grow worse. No matter what she did, Brewster would be ready with some caustic, barbed little comment, so that she began to dread her turn on stage, knowing that however hard she tried he would bring her to a stop with some biting word that would leave her crushed and humiliated. More than once she retreated into the shadows with tears in her eyes, avoiding the sympathetic but embarrassed glances of her fellow actors. It must stop soon, she told herself. The way he was going on, he would destroy her.

That evening, in Michael's room, she lay sobbing in his arms while he smoothed her hair and whispered that everything would be all right.

'But it's so unfair,' she said. 'My part in the show — it's such a great part for me, and I'm *good* in it. I *know* I am.' She sniffed, wiping the tears from her cheek. 'Oh, Mikey, I just don't know what to do any more.'

'You want me to have a word with him?' Michael said. 'I will if you want me to.'

'Oh, no,' she said. 'That would make it worse — and he'd have it in for you too, then.'

'Okay.' He nodded. 'But somebody should say something.' He was silent, thoughtful for a moment, then he said, 'Maybe you should ask Rosemary.'

'Rosemary?'

'Well, she's the leading lady, I mean. The star's gotta

have some clout. Maybe she'd have a quiet word with him. Ask her.'

'Oh, no. No, I couldn't do that.'

'Why not? They get on well. I've seen them together. They're like real buddies.'

Carrie shook her head. 'Oh, I don't know.'

'He'd listen to her, I'm sure.'

'No. No.'

'Well, he can't go on like this — making you so damn miserable. Somebody should have a word with him.'

And somebody did.

And as it turned out, that somebody was Rosemary.

The following afternoon, after working on some individual scenes, the cast were called together to go over one of the big musical numbers, 'Never Trust a Man', a rousing little song involving most of the company. In Carrie's part, as Ella, she had one chorus in a duet with Rosemary. It took up just thirty seconds of the whole number, but it was an effective little moment, and Carrie loved it. She and Rosemary sounded great together, she thought, their voices so in tune, with their sweet harmonies right on the button.

With the MD, Glenn Thomas, at the piano and Brewster watching from his seat, the company went into the number. It started well. Halfway through, the moment for Carrie's duet with Rosemary arrived. On cue, Carrie stepped up to the front, coming to a stop at Rosemary's side. Then, together, while the rest of the cast continued their slow, rhythmic dance moves behind them, they took up the song:

Trust a man to be the smartest mathematician,
Trust a man in any way you can.
Trust a man to be the dumbest politician,
But never trust a man to be a man.

They got no further. Abruptly Brewster rose and
stepped forward, holding up his hand. 'Okay, enough! I'm
afraid this isn't working — not like it should.' He lifted a
forefinger in Rosemary's direction. 'Rosemary, I think you
could come in a fraction stronger, okay? Just step it up a
little, okay?'

Rosemary nodded. 'Fine, Ian. I'll do that.'

He smiled at her, then turned his attention to Carrie,
his smile fading as he looked at her. Shaking his head, he
said, 'I don't know, Carrie. I just don't know.' He paused.
'Do you like the number? You happy with it?'

'Oh, yes, yes,' she said. 'I love it. I —'

She got no further. 'You *love* it?' He was frowning. 'Well,
you'd never know it. Not the way you're doing it here,
that's for sure.' He jerked a thumb over his shoulder. 'I
don't know whether you're aware of it, but there's gonna
be an audience out there. And they've got to be *lifted* by this
number. Absolutely lifted by it. And they're not gonna get
it the way you're doing it.' He shook his head again. 'I don't
know — maybe you're just not cut out for it. Maybe it'd
work better with Belle doing it.' He turned to Rosemary.
'How'd you feel about that, Rosemary? Belle's familiar with
it.' His glance moved to Belle Samuels, a young actress
standing nearby. 'Would you like to try it with her, Rosemary? It's only one little chorus. You want to give it a try?'

While Carrie, red-faced, stood trying to keep back the threatening tears of hurt and humiliation, Rosemary took a step forward.

'Just a minute, Ian,' she said, raising a hand. 'I'm sure Belle could do it perfectly well. But, come on, now — it's Carrie's bit. I know we might have a little way to go to get it polished, but we'll get there soon, I promise you. So just give us a break, okay? I mean — we have a little time left, and going by what I've heard, Rome wasn't built in a fucking day.'

She ended her words with a little laugh, and it was the only sound in the room. Brewster was not laughing, not smiling. After a moment he gave a little nod. 'Fine,' he said. 'Have you finished?'

Rosemary had not. 'Just let me say one more thing, Ian,' she said. She half turned towards Carrie, reached out and touched her arm, a brief little gesture of support, of friendship. 'This girl,' she said, 'this pretty, talented girl is working her goddamn ass off for you here. Maybe you're not aware of it, but *I am*. I don't know why you keep knocking her, but I reckon it's about time you cut her a little bit of slack.' She paused, as if waiting for a response, but none came. 'Fine — okay.' She nodded. 'There's a lot riding on this show, we all know that, and we've got to please the investors, but we're not goddamn machines, Ian. So, please, if you don't mind me saying so, let's just — just calm down a little, all right?'

The silence was like a fog. There was hardly the sound of a breath. When Brewster spoke again his voice was cold, the faint smile that touched his mouth without a hint of warmth.

'So, Rosemary,' he said, 'you think I need to calm down a little, is that right?' He gave a little nod. 'Well, let me say something, and I'll be as calm as I can while I say it. To please *you*, you understand? After all, you're the star of this show, right?' He waited. 'Is that right?'

'Ian, listen — ' Quickly Rosemary took a step towards him, hands lifting, palms out. 'Wait a minute. I didn't mean it like that — I just — '

'*No*.' Brewster's voice was sharp, his nostrils flaring as he looked directly into her face. 'I won't wait a minute, and I won't listen. I've heard enough. Let's get something straight here — you might be the star of this show, Rosemary, but you were engaged as a *performer*. You were engaged by our producers, those wonderful men, Charles and Irvin, in the hope of getting this show to Broadway. And there is no doubt that with your very considerable talent we've got a chance of getting there. But let me tell you something else, remind you of something else: I am the director of this show, and our wonderful producers didn't hire me for my looks, or my singing voice, or in the hope that I can dance like Fred fucking Astaire. No. They hired me to direct.' He leaned in towards her. 'You get that? To *direct*. Because that is what I do, Rosemary. Did you know that? Or maybe you'd like to check my CV? I'm a director, and I know what I'm doing — okay? — and *they* know that too, our producers.' Slowly he drew back, his eyes still fixed on hers. 'Let's not forget what our roles are in this business, okay?' Then, raising his voice a little, taking in the others in the room: 'And that goes for everybody here. We do what we're hired to do. But while I'm the director of this show,

I am *just* that — the *director*. And if I want anybody's advice, you can be sure I'll ask for it.' He glanced at his watch. 'Okay, everybody, that's it. Be back tomorrow morning, 9.30 — sharp. Glenn will be working on your numbers.'

Without another word, he turned and went from the room.

*

That night, lying beside Michael, sleepless in the bed, Carrie went over the events of the afternoon. As if watching some terrible accident filmed on a loop, the whole thing was repeated over and over in her head. She couldn't stop it. She kept hearing Brewster's damning words, his cruel suggestion, in front of everybody, that Belle take over her duet with Rosemary. And she thought too of Rosemary, of her brave words as she had stood up to him, speaking up for her. She had seen humiliation there, too, in Rosemary's pale face.

And now she had to face tomorrow. Tomorrow morning she was due to go through her solo number. She had worked on it with Glenn, the MD, and with Clarke, the choreographer. In the morning, Glenn had said, they'd be polishing it up, getting it more or less finished. So she had to be ready.

Sighing, she turned, trying to find comfort. Beside her, Michael slept soundly, his breathing deep, even. Slowly the wakeful hours crept by.

*

Sitting at the piano, Glenn limbered up with a few chords, then looked over at Carrie where she sat waiting at the side of the rehearsal area. 'Okay, Carrie — we all set?' Yes, she was ready, she said, getting up from her seat. Deep breaths, she told herself. Everything would be fine. There was no sign of Ian Brewster, she was relieved to see. He didn't always show in the mornings when they were rehearsing the numbers, so with luck she'd have it wrapped by the time he came in. Just keep calm, she urged herself. After all, she knew the number like the back of her hand. The song, 'Stick Around With Me', was a bright piece with a strong, rhythmic beat. It suited her well, and she had worked hard to get it right.

'Okay, Carrie?' Glenn said as she took the centre, and she nodded back, 'Yes, ready.' He played her intro, and over the last bar she took a breath and then began to sing.

> *You want to get your peppermint some pep,*
> *Well, you're barkin' up the right old tree.*
> *Want to feel that special spring in your step,*
> *Well, honey, stick around with me.*

After a slightly faltering start, she found her voice and her rhythm, and with them, her confidence. With renewed heart she started into the dance move, first left then right, striding out, then to the centre again for the second chorus:

> *You want to find you're at the head of the line,*
> *For affection to the nth degree,*
> *That'll give your eye that shimmering shine,*
> *Well, honey, stick around with me.*

A turn, a kick, another turn, then into the middle eight:

You think I'm teasin', I'm just crowd-pleasin',
I'm only setting out to play.
I tell you, I'm not jokin', when I have spoken,
I mean every word, every single word I say.

Her smile bright, her voice ringing out, she went into the final chorus:

If you're looking for a heart that's true,
And you're...

And suddenly she saw Ian Brewster there, at the back, standing in the shadows, notebook in hand. How long had he been there? As she looked at him, their glances met and he started forward, coming down to the front. He took a seat before her, all the well-rehearsed lines of the song flew from her mind. She came to a halt. Forcing a smile, she turned to look over at Glenn at the piano. 'I'm sorry, Glenn,' she said. 'I lost my way there. Could we – could we take it again? From the middle eight?'

'Sure thing.' Glenn said, but before he could play a note, Brewster's voice came in: 'No, take it from the top.'

Glenn nodded, played the intro, and Carrie came in, a little tentative now:

You want to get your peppermint some pep,
Well, you're barkin' up the right old tree.
You want to feel that —

She got no further. Breaking in, his voice sharp over the music, Brewster said, looking over at Glenn, 'Hang on there, Glenn. Hold on a minute.'

He turned his attention then to Carrie. 'Carrie, sweetheart,' he said, 'have you looked at this song?'

'Well — yes,' she said, puzzled at the question.

'Okay, so tell me, what do you think about it?'

'Well, I — I like it, and I — '

'Whether you like it is immaterial,' he cut in. 'I don't care whether you like it or whether you think it's a bunch of crap. Tell me what you think it's *about*.'

She stood silent.

'The song,' he said, 'talks about getting pep in your peppermint, a spring in your step — right?'

'Yes.' She saw that the rest of the company had come in, were standing watching, listening.

'It's about energy,' Brewster said. 'You know what I'm talking about?'

'Yes.'

'Right, let's try it again.' He turned to Glenn, 'From the top, Glenn, okay?'

The intro came, and with it Carrie's cue. Aware that every eye was upon her, she summoned all her energy, fixed her smile and began to sing.

And it seemed to be working. After the chorus, she went into the dance. Stepping out in the well-rehearsed routine, she reached the side at stage-left, turned with a swirl and began the strut back to centre. But any feeling of confidence she felt was soon gone. As she took a breath to take up the reprise she dared to steal a glance at Brewster.

And in that moment she saw him close his eyes as if in despair and shake his head. Then, raising his notebook in his hand, he slammed it down heavily on the floor.

Thrown, Carrie faltered and came to a stop, while Glenn, finding himself playing solo at the piano, came to a halt behind her.

In the silence, Brewster got to his feet. 'What happened?' he said, frowning, eyes fixed on Carrie. 'You stopped. Why did you stop? Did I tell you to stop?'

She cleared her throat. 'I – I thought – I thought you didn't – didn't want me to go on. I thought …' With a shake of her head, her stumbling words came to a halt.

For a second or two Brewster just glared at her. Then, taking a few steps forward, he crooked his finger and beckoned. Heart thumping, Carrie went to him. As she came to a stop before him he said, his voice low and clipped: 'Maybe you missed what I said yesterday. I said I'm the director of this show – do you remember?'

She gave a nod.

'And it's not for you to question whether I want you to stop or to go on. Do you understand that?'

She didn't speak.

'Do you understand that?' he repeated.

'Yes.' The faintest whisper.

'Good.' He turned from her, speaking to the pianist and the stage manager. 'Glenn, Rich, it's not working. The number's cut.' He looked back at Carrie. 'You hear that? And your duet with Michael, that's out too.' He turned and called across the room to where Michael stood nursing a cup of coffee: 'Sorry about that, Mike, but that's the

way it goes at times. That, as they say, is life. Better get used
to it.'

Turning back to Carrie again, he fixed her with his cold
gaze. 'I'm afraid it just isn't happening for you, baby. It just
isn't working. Okay?'

With his words, he turned away, looking over at the
pianist. 'Hey, Glenn,' he said, 'why don't we go over Rosemary's number with the boys. Let's try to get something
done, for God's sake.'

For a moment Carrie remained fixed to the spot, burning with shame and humiliation. Then, tears welling in
her eyes, she turned and fled from the scene.

Michael, entering her dressing room some minutes
later, found her hunched before the mirror, head in her
hands, weeping.

She would have to go, she told him between sobs,
she couldn't stay any longer. She had no choice but to
quit and leave the company. He pleaded with her. Give
it time, he said; it was just a bad patch; Brewster would
get over it. It'd all be okay in a while. But Carrie knew
differently. She couldn't stay now. It would never be right.
Brewster had slashed her part to nothing, and so humiliated her that she could never face anyone again. All
she could do was ask that she be released from her contract. '*He* won't care,' she said. 'He'll be *glad*. He'll give my
part to Belle. She's been covering it. She'll jump at the
chance.'

'But where will you go?' Michael asked.

Where indeed? Home to Fort Worth? No, she couldn't
face that either. 'I don't know,' she said. 'Back to New York,

I guess. The only thing I'm sure of right now is that I don't ever want to set foot on a stage again.'

'Oh, don't say that,' Michael said.

'I mean it.'

She took off her dance shoes, and he watched as she put them into a bag. 'Carrie,' he said, pleading, 'you don't have to go. Please don't go.'

'I have to.' She began to cry again. 'It's not only having to leave the show,' she said. 'It's you as well.'

He nodded. 'I know. That's how I feel too. I can't bear for you to go.'

'I thought we'd be together. But you'll be staying on with the show and – I'm afraid that'll just mean – mean the end for us.'

'No, don't talk that way,' he said quickly. 'It won't be the end – of course it won't.' He drew her to him, holding her close. 'We'll be together in a few weeks, just as soon as the show gets to New York for the opening. Only a few weeks.' He touched her wet cheek. 'I love you, Carrie. You just remember that.'

*

Sitting in her small motel room alone that evening, after sporadic attempts to pack, Carrie heard a knock at the door. Opening the door, she found Rosemary standing there.

'Can I come in for a minute?' Rosemary asked.

'Yes – yes, of course.'

Rosemary entered, closing the door behind her. 'I just came to see how you are,' she said. 'I've been told you're leaving the show.'

'Yes. First thing in the morning.'

'Belle will take over your part, Ian says.'

'I guess so. I don't know.'

'Where will you go?'

Carrie shrugged. 'Back to New York, I guess.'

'You have family there?'

'No, they're in Texas. Fort Worth. My mother and my sister.'

Rosemary nodded. 'Well, it might be a good idea to go back there for a while. Home, I mean. Take a little break — go spend some time with your folks.'

Carrie shook her head. 'I don't know. We never really got on.'

'Okay. I guess you know best. But are you sure you're doing the right thing here, going off like this?'

'It — it's the only thing I can do.' She was near to tears now.

'Oh, but —'

'You were there, Rosemary,' Carrie said. 'You saw it all happening, every day. It's like Ian set out to destroy me, and I just can't take any more.'

Rosemary stepped forward and put her hands on Carrie's shoulders. 'Listen,' she said, 'I know how you must be feeling. But you'll have to put this behind you, okay?'

'How can I? I can't. I just can't.'

'Yes, you can,' Rosemary said. 'And you *will*. You mustn't allow yourself to be beaten by this. You'll go on to bigger and better things. It's only a matter of time. And you're young. The only thing I wonder about is whether you're cut out for all this rough stuff. You've got to be so bloody tough in this business.' She sighed. 'But whatever you do, you look after yourself, okay?'

She turned and moved away. In the open doorway she reached into her pocket and took out an envelope. Setting it down on a small side table, she said, 'A little good luck card.' Another moment and she was gone.

When Carrie opened the envelope she found inside not only a card wishing her good luck, but also a cheque for five hundred dollars. She stood staring at it. The gesture was so generous, so kind, but she couldn't possibly accept it.

Next morning, along with a carefully worded letter expressing her sincere gratitude, she replaced the cheque in the envelope and slipped it under the door of Rosemary's room.

*

Rosemary had been wrong when she said Carrie would forget. Even now, after all these years, the memories were as clear as ever. They had merely been stored away, like the photographs in the album that lay before her.

The melancholy mood still upon her, she closed the album and moved idly to the window. There, glancing out, she saw the cat.

It was the third time this week she had seen it in the garden. She watched the small, thin creature as it crept into the shade of a hedge and lay down. She stood there for a moment longer then went from the room and down to the kitchen. There she got a few small pieces of chicken, scraps left over from yesterday's dinner, and poured some water into a dish. Going outside a minute later she saw the cat was still there. Moving cautiously so as not to frighten him, she placed the dishes on the ground.

'Here, kitty. Here, kitty, kitty, kitty…'

She backed away a few feet, watching as the cat got up on his thin legs. The poor little thing certainly looked hungry. And nervous. Black with white paws, he had a white patch over one eye which gave him an odd expression of surprise. For a moment she thought he might turn and run, but he had found the food. Seconds later he had eaten the chicken and was lapping up the water.

She watched as he wiped a paw fastidiously over his mouth and looked up at her. 'Was that good?' she said. 'There'll be more tomorrow if you want. I'll get you something nice from the store.'

The cat remained a moment longer looking up at her, then, turning, moved off into the shrubbery.

In the shade of the elm leaves Carrie sank down, stretching full-length on the dry lawn. The grass pricked through her slip, and she scratched languidly at the itch. A fly hummed drowsily around her head, and she flapped at it a couple of times then closed her eyes, her head cushioned on her arm. There was something on her mind, and like a child who feels compelled to pick at a scabbed knee, she couldn't leave it alone.

'Michael…' Her lips moved in a soundless murmur.

Once again her thoughts went back to their last meeting, when he had gone with her to the bus station, to see her off on her return to Manhattan. From the bus window she had gazed back at him as he stood watching the bus pull out, until he was no longer in sight.

And that was the last she had seen of him.

A few weeks later she had read how dramatically and completely *Save a Place for Me* had flopped, closing out of town, the hoped-for Broadway opening gone for ever. And she was glad. Glad. For Rosemary's sake there were real feelings of regret, but mainly her feelings were of satisfaction. She was glad that it had happened to Ian Brewster. It served him right.

Apart from Brewster getting his comeuppance, though, the show's failure had promised another positive outcome; it meant that Michael would be free to come to her sooner than she had anticipated. She couldn't wait for their meeting.

But that meeting had never taken place.

He had called her several times over the last weeks of the show's brief life, but to her great surprise and dismay, after the show's closing she heard nothing more from him.

And then it was that she learned that her mother was sick. Her sister Janice telephoned with the news. 'Carrie,' she said, 'Mom's in a bad way, and she's asking for you.'

'She's sick?' Carrie said. 'Why didn't somebody tell me?'

'I'm telling you now.' There was no warmth in Janice's voice.

'Is it — is it serious?'

'She's had a stroke. And things don't look good. I think you should come home as soon as you can.'

Yes, Carrie had said, she would be there just as soon as she could get away. But she didn't go. She stayed where she was, waiting for the mail, listening for the sound of the telephone or the doorbell; some word, some sign from Michael. She had no choice, she felt, for she knew that the very moment she set off for Texas, he would be there, looking for her. And so she had gone on waiting. One day more; just one day more. And those single days had become many, and in the end it was too late. When she at last got back to the family home it was to find her mother lying in her coffin.

Returning to New York after the funeral, Carrie had hoped, desperately, that she would find some word from Michael waiting for her. There was nothing.

Along with her distress at Michael's silence, there was also the matter of earning a living to take care of. Her mother had left her money in her will, but it would be some time before that could be touched. She had to find work. For the time being she was not particular what it was, but she had to find a job of some kind.

It was while she was on her way to one of the larger department stores one afternoon, in the hope of finding something, that she and Rosemary met again.

*

They came together on the corner of Broadway and 54th Street.

'Rosemary?' Carrie came to a stop, her face lighting up as Rosemary suddenly came into view.

In the same moment Rosemary halted in her tracks, eyes wide in surprise. 'Carrie! Hello!' Stepping forward, she put her arms around Carrie and briefly held her close.

'Oh, Rosemary,' Carrie said as they drew apart, 'it's so good to see you.'

'And *you*,' Rosemary replied. 'And what a surprise.'

Carrie was all smiles. 'I've thought of you often – so often,' she said. Which was true; of all her memories from the fiasco of *Save a Place for Me*, her only fond memories were of Rosemary.

Looking tanned and well, Rosemary said that she had just returned from a trip to Cape Cod – 'God, I had to get away, take a break somewhere,' – and had come into the city that day on business.

'Are you in a hurry?' Carrie asked. 'Could we – could we go someplace and have a cup of coffee or something? It's just so lovely to see you again.'

'Sure, why not,' Rosemary said. 'I'm running ragged here, and I could do with a rest for a half hour.'

A short walk down 54th Street and they came to a small coffee shop. Going inside, they were shown to a table where they sat and ordered coffees. Over their cups they talked of this and that, and then, in a lull in the conversation, Rosemary reached across the table and pressed Carrie's hand.

'I was so sorry at the way things turned out for you,' she said.

'Thank you.' Carrie nodded, memories of the show flooding back afresh. 'I appreciate that.'

'How have you been managing since you got back?'

'It could be better.' A pause. 'My mother died.'

'Oh, my dear, I'm so sorry.'

'It's okay, thanks. I stayed for a while there, in Texas, after the funeral. I haven't been back that long. Now I'm looking for a job. I need to earn some money.'

'You auditioning for anything?'

'No. Oh, no – I think I'm finished with all that.'

'What? With the theatre, you mean – your acting?'

'Yes.' Carrie nodded. 'Like you said to me, you have to be tough in the business, and I guess – well, I think maybe I'm just not cut out for it.'

Rosemary sighed. 'Well, it can be a bitch, there's no two ways about that.'

Carrie nodded. 'Anyway,' she said, 'how about you? How's your little boy – David? He away at school?'

'Yes, he is.' Rosemary's smile was warm, full of tenderness. 'And he's wonderful. And coming home in a week. My God, it's going to be frantic. I've got so much to do, and now I only have Elda, my helper, to lend a hand. But I can't wait to have him back.'

A moment or two went by, then Carrie said, 'I read about the show closing, of course. I'm sorry it didn't work out for you.'

'Oh, *that*.' Rosemary shook her head. 'Darling, it didn't work out for *anybody* – the writers, the company, the producers – *nobody* – and least of all the critics. They hated it. But it taught me something – stay away from the theatre.'

'Really?'

'You bet. The only time you'll ever get me in a theatre again is in the audience, with a seat in the stalls. From now on I'll stick to cabaret. I should never have got into it in the first place. I didn't really want to, but when the offer came up my agent persuaded me.' She shrugged. 'So there you are – the mistakes we make. And let me tell you, Carrie, you were well out of it. I know you won't see it like that, but it wasn't a good show. I know we all had great hopes for it, but it wasn't. And look at some of those songs. That one of yours. Those lyrics — *You want to give your peppermint some pep* — Jesus Christ. I ask you. It's no wonder the critics let us have it. Not a good word for anybody.'

A moment's hesitation, then Carrie said: 'How was Michael in it? Did he do okay?'

Rosemary looked up over her coffee cup. 'Michael?'

'Michael — he played Christopher.'

'Oh, yes — Michael.' Rosemary shrugged. 'Search me, darling. I don't know. I think it was every man for himself.' She was silent for a moment in the hum and chatter of the place, then she said, 'He — Michael — was he a bit — special for you? I mean, I know you used to hang out together, but —'

'I loved him,' Carrie said.

Rosemary gave a slow nod. 'Oh, I didn't know it was that serious.'

'No,' Carrie said with a sigh, 'I don't think Michael knew it either. I never heard another word from him afterwards, not after the show closed. Not a word.'

Rosemary reached out and briefly pressed Carrie's hand. 'My dear, you've had a hard time lately. But things'll get better, you wait and see. And as for your Michael — well, maybe you're better off without him. Like they say, there are plenty more fish in the sea. A pretty girl like you — you shouldn't have any trouble. There'll be somebody else — you wait.' She paused for a moment, then, her tone brightening, she said, 'Listen, I'll tell you something that'll cheer you up a bit.'

'Oh?'

'Belle – remember her?'

'Belle?'

'Belle whatever her name was – who took over your part.'

'Oh, her – yes.'

Rosemary nodded. 'The critics – they shredded her.'

A little touch of pleasure brushed Carrie's heart. 'They did?'

'They sure did.'

Carrie took this in. 'And Ian?' she said. 'Ian Brewster?'

'Oh, he didn't come out of it well either. But I doubt you'll lose any sleep over that. I can't forget the way he was with you. It was unforgiveable. And for no reason at all.'

'Oh, yes,' Carrie said. 'There was a reason. I know why he was like that.'

'Oh?' Rosemary leant forward a little. 'Tell me.'

'I don't like to think about it,' Carrie said, 'but, well, he – he made a pass at me.'

Rosemary's eyes widened. 'He did what?'

Carrie nodded. 'It was nothing too terrible – just a little kiss. But I overreacted, I guess – and it upset him. He changed towards me from that moment.'

Rosemary gave a nod. 'So that's how it was. The bastard. That explains it. Oh, darling, I wish I could have done something.'

'Oh, you already did so much. The way you took my side that day.'

'Oh, *that*.' Rosemary waved a hand, dismissing it. 'Forget it. I got pissed off. It was nothing.'

'No,' Carrie said quickly, 'it was *not* nothing. You stuck up for me, in front of everybody, and I'll never forget that. And you got it in the neck too, from Brewster, for trying to help me out.'

'That man,' Rosemary said, ' – that son-of-a-bitch took no prisoners, that's for sure. He's somebody I won't miss, I tell you.' She lifted a hand, palm out. 'Anyway, let's forget him. It's all in the past.' She looked at her watch. 'I shall have to go soon. I've got so much to do – and now that Debbie, my assistant, has gone, it's leaving me with so – ' She came to an abrupt halt. She remained silent for a moment, frowning slightly, considering, then she said, 'You said just now you're looking for work.'

'Oh, yes, I am. And I need to find something soon.'

Rosemary nodded. 'Can you type?'

'Pretty well. And I have a clean driver's licence. Non-smoker, social drinker only.'

'Good with children?'

'I know I would be, oh yes.'

'And with grouchy, demanding women?'

Carrie's smile was wide. 'I can learn.'

Rosemary smiled. 'Okay. Let's talk.' She turned to the waitress who was just coming by. 'May we have two more coffees, please?'

Ten minutes later Rosemary's offer of a job had been made, and Carrie had moved in with her later that week.

*

'Carrie, what in God's name are you doing out here in your underwear?'

Rosemary's voice cut across the warm afternoon as she stood jangling her car keys from pink-tipped fingers. 'Who are you trying to turn on? There's nobody can see you, sweetie. You're wasting your time.'

Carrie got to her feet, picking at the bits of grass that clung to her damp legs and arms. 'There was this cat...' she said.

Rosemary, not listening, said, 'Well — I think I got myself a manager.'

Carrie frowned. 'I thought you already had one. Arthur Hampshire. Isn't that who you went to see?'

Rosemary shook her head. 'Oh, darling, he's past it. He's ready for the bone yard now. He's giving up the business, he told me.'

'So — what's happening?'

'He got this other guy on the phone. Rosti his name is. Douglas Rosti. A really good guy, so Arthur tells me.' She hitched up the waistband of her slacks. 'I had a few words with him and he sounds pretty keen. I'm meeting him tomorrow for lunch.'

Carrie stooped and picked up the empty dish. Rosemary saw it and frowned. 'What's that doing there?'

'I started to tell you,' Carrie said, 'there was this cat.'

'A cat? What are you talking about? What cat?'

'I gave him some water and a few scraps. Poor thing's so thin. I don't think he belongs to anybody.' A wistful note crept into her voice. 'I wish we could have a pet, Rosie. It would be so nice.'

'A *pet?*' Rosemary said. 'What in God's name do we want with a pet? Darling, if everything works out we shall be moving around a good deal. You won't be in any position to look after any dumb pet. Christ, that's all we need — some flea-bitten, mangy moggy around the place.'

......FIVE

Rosemary sat facing Douglas Rosti across a table in a small French restaurant on West 63rd Street. They had finished their lunch, and coffee had just been served. She studied him as he sat before her. He was about forty years old, she reckoned. He had sandy hair, short-cropped, which also showed bristly on the backs of his small hands. He was of less than medium height, with a slight frame, his head small and narrow, with rather pinched features. But his lack of looks was unimportant, she reminded herself; if he was good at his job, that was all that mattered.

'I've been in touch with Amberlight Records in the UK,' he was saying. 'And it was a very encouraging chat.'

'Go on,' Rosemary said.

'Though your sales of this particular album are never gonna be big, you understand.'

'Oh, I know that,' Rosemary said. 'I know we're not talking hit parade here.' She smiled. 'I'd reckon half the people who buy it will be on crutches by now.'

Douglas laughed. 'Well, maybe it's not that bad, but they're certainly not the younger crowd – not generally, anyway.'

'Who exactly is buying it?' she said. 'I mean, I know who *used* to buy my records – the young people of the time. But it's a different scene today. You see them on TV – all those wailing singers with their interminable songs without hooks or shape. And then there's that grotesque thing they call twerking – what the hell is *that* all about?'

Douglas nodded, laughing again. 'Yeah, you're right,' he said, 'but I don't think they'll be expecting that from you. But seriously – not everybody wants the latest thing. Granted, the kids want what's new – that's what they're all about, but they don't represent the total record-buying public. People don't really change their musical tastes, you know that as well as I do. They tend to cling to the music they grew up with. Apart from which, there are some artists who never go out of fashion. So even today you're still going to have people buying Glenn Miller and Benny Goodman and singers like Sinatra and Ella Fitzgerald.' He smiled. 'And why not Rosemary Paul too, now that they've got the chance?'

He moved his gaze to the small notepad at his side and touched at the page with a fingertip. 'These figures from Amberlight ... Although the sales are small so far, they're nevertheless very encouraging. Evan Blanchard, the guy I talked to there, he says the digital downloads are going up all the time. And some of the tracks are getting good air time too – on the BBC and other radio stations.'

'That's good to hear,' Rosemary said.

'It is indeed. And it's bringing a lot of your old fans out of the woodwork. As well as a few of the younger ones who are discovering you. And let me tell you something else. I made another call to London. An old buddy who's got his fat fingers in all the pies. He was telling me how at the height of your career you were one of the hottest properties around. Of course that was before you quit the UK and came over here.'

'I got married,' she said with a shrug. 'My life changed.'

'I know.' Douglas nodded. 'Anyway, he said that no one over there seems quite sure what happened to you since that time. There have been rumours, naturally – mixed up with the more factual reports, I guess.' He paused. 'People knew about your husband's death, of course, and then what – what happened with your little boy.' He ended the sentence with a brief, sad shake of his head.

'Yes, well,' Rosemary said, lowering her glance, 'that's all in the past.'

Douglas nodded. 'Apparently,' he said, 'the new interest in you started with a series of articles in one of the Sunday tabloids. A series on the whatever-became-of-so-and-so theme. One of the articles was about you, telling about how you'd lost your voice following your – your son's accident, and that you were now living quietly just outside of Manhattan. But there were a lot of unanswered questions, I guess, and it looks as if you became something of a mystery woman.'

'A mystery woman, eh?' Rosemary gave a wry smile. 'That's a new one.'

Douglas smiled with her. 'Anyway, I guess the time was right, and now Amberlight has cashed in on the memories and the nostalgia and put out the album. And what it boils down to is that you're in demand. It won't last indefinitely, of course, but right now there is great interest in you. So if you really want to, I think you could do it – go back and cash in on that demand, that interest.'

'Well, that's what I want to do,' Rosemary said.

'Good.' He nodded, clearly pleased. 'But it's going

to need a lot of work to make it pay off. And there's no time to hang around. You've got to strike while the iron's hot.'

'I realise that.'

'Good. Great. So, if you want me to work with you we'll plan it together. Every step. And in the meantime you must start working on your material.'

'Yes. Yes, of course.'

'Right, and one of the first things we've got to do is get you a good arranger and MD. Have you anyone in mind?'

She shook her head. 'No, I haven't. I don't know anyone today. I've been so out of touch, for so long.'

'Well, I know somebody. His name's Hellman, Kurt Hellman. His name mean anything to you?'

'I just told you, I've been out of touch.'

'Right – well, he's a good guy, take my word. Very talented – and getting to be pretty much in demand.'

She nodded. 'Sounds promising.'

'Oh, he's really good. He's just had a notable success with that Off-Broadway show, *Second Chances*. He's young, but he has a great future ahead, believe me. If you like I'll talk to him, see if he's interested.'

'See if he's interested?' She raised an eyebrow. 'You sure he isn't too exclusive for me?'

Ignoring the note of sarcasm in her tone, he said, 'Rosemary, you want the best, don't you?'

'Of course I want the best.'

He nodded. 'Fine. So I suggest that if Kurt's available you can get together and talk things over, see if you like each other.'

'*You* like him, obviously,' she said. 'You know him pretty well, do you?'

'Pretty well.' He chuckled. 'Yes, indeed. He's my cousin, as a matter of fact.'

'Your cousin?' Rosemary said. 'What is this – jobs for the boys?'

He hesitated a moment, then said evenly, 'No, Rosemary, it's not jobs for the boys. I'm simply trying to suggest the right man for the job for you. And I mean the *right* man. But if you'd rather find someone yourself, that's okay with me too. You just let me know.'

This was going off in the wrong direction, she thought. 'No,' she said quickly, 'he sounds fine. Just fine. You talk to him. And then call me.'

'I will.' He took a drink from his coffee cup. 'And if this all goes ahead you'll need some good new material – though of course your fans will expect you to do a lot of your old stuff.'

'Oh, they're sure to.'

'Absolutely. You don't want to change your image. All those people who come to see you will want to see *you* – the Rosemary Paul they remember.' He smiled. 'And there are a lot of them. Though as you said, they're not all young any more. But they'll be there. And the usual gay crowd, I guess.'

'Oh, yes. I always had that special little gay following. They were wonderful.' She gave a broad smile. 'And they always bought my records.'

She picked up her cup and finished the last of her coffee. Then, putting down the cup, she opened her bag, took out a compact and touched up her make-up. Douglas watched her for a second then turned and signalled to the waiter for the check. Turning back to her, he said:

'So? What do you think, Rosemary? You want to take a chance? And it *is* a chance. I mean, there are no guarantees in this business.'

'I know that,' she said. 'But yes, I'm ready for it. Are you?'

'Oh, yes, indeed.'

'Good.' Now she smiled at him.

He smiled back. 'I'll get in touch with Kurt,' he said. 'You'll hear from me again very soon.'

*

'How did you make out?' Carrie asked when Rosemary got back to the house. 'Was it okay?'

Rosemary nodded. 'Yes, it was okay.'

'What did you say his name is?'

'Rosti. Douglas Rosti.' Rosemary kicked off her shoes and flopped down on the sofa.

'You think you'll get on with him?'

'Yes...I think so.'

Carrie heard the qualification, and frowned. 'You *think* so? What's he like?'

'To look at?' Rosemary shrugged. 'Well, let's be kind and just say that Brad Pitt's not going to lose any sleep.'

Carrie laughed. 'That bad?'

Rosemary shook her head. 'God, I hate having ugly people around me. I can forgive anything but that. But he'll be okay. He's going to fix up a meeting with this guy. He's his cousin. A guy named Kurt Hellman. Apparently a very talented musician. And if he looks anything like Mr

Rosti I'm going to find it very easy to keep my mind on my work,'

Carrie laughed. 'Oh, Rosie…'

Rosemary lit a cigarette, blew out smoke in a stream and said: 'Anyway, never mind all that. We shall manage. All those people who took it for granted that I was finished. I even got to believing it myself. I got to thinking it was all over, that my life was fading out.' She gave an emphatic shake of her head. 'Well, that's not the way it's going to be.'

Carrie was watching *The Wild Heart*. Watching as Hazel — that was Jennifer Jones — her pet fox in her arms, ran across the horizon, her slim figure silhouetted against a wide, dramatic sky. From behind the running girl came the baying of hounds and a huntsman's horn. The sounds were still some way off, but they were steadily getting louder.

Leaning forward in her chair, rapt, Carrie's eyes were wide with expectation. The ice that floated in her glass of Coke melted unnoticed.

Jennifer Jones ran on, while the cries of the hounds came closer. Could she save Foxie? Carrie leaned closer to the flickering television screen, willing the girl to succeed. The hounds were drawing nearer. Nearer still. And then, coming riding, thundering ahead of the hounds, one of the huntsmen caught up with the running girl.

'Oh, help her!' Carrie whispered. 'Do something!'

Pounding along at the girl's side, the rider shouted to Hazel/Jennifer to drop her little fox. 'Drop it! Drop it, you little fool! They'll pull you down!' The girl took no notice and ran on. And suddenly another huntsman, the squire (that was David Farrar), was there, emerging from the trees. He had loved Hazel/Jennifer, had been captivated by her free, untamed spirit. And now, seeing her running before the pack, he galloped across the field towards her.

Oh, yes, he would be the one to help her, Carrie said to herself. Oh, yes, *please*, she prayed. *Please, help her.*

The horse's hooves thudded on the grass as the squire spurred his horse on, striving to overtake the hounds. And eventually he did, and caught up with the running girl. 'Give her to me,' he yelled, riding beside her, leaning down to her out of the saddle. 'Give her to me.'

'Oh, yes!' Carrie breathed. 'Give Foxie to him!'

But Hazel/Jennifer took no heed and dashed on, plunging down the hill, making for the parsonage and safety.

Ah, yes, but in her path lay the old mineshaft.

'Oh, my God!' Carrie cried, putting a hand to her mouth, 'She's heading straight for the mineshaft.'

'Okay, honey, snap, snap.'

Rosemary's voice cut sharply into the drama as she picked up the TV remote and clicked off the picture. Carrie hadn't even heard her come in.

'Oh, *Rosie*,' Carrie wailed, 'I was enjoying that movie. It was right at the end. It was so beautiful, and now I won't know what happened.'

'Who cares,' Rosemary said. 'Come on, we've got to get busy.'

Carrie got up and followed her into the kitchen. 'How did you get on?' she asked. 'Did you meet the new guy, Kurt Hellman?'

'Yes, in Douglas' office. And I've invited him for dinner this evening.'

'This evening?'

'At 6.30, to be precise.' Rosemary turned, looking around her, thinking out loud. 'Now, what shall we have?'

*

Wearing an ankle-length gown of deep blue silk, Rosemary moved to the window and peered down the drive. It was 6.50 and there was still no sign of Kurt Hellman. She began to fret, thinking about the duck in the oven. She should have left the dinner to Carrie; the last thing she wanted was for Kurt to arrive and find her in an apron, with grease on her fingers. Turning from the window, she crossed the room and flung open the door. 'Carrie…!'

From Carrie's room came the sound of Carrie's voice in song, and Rosemary recognised the familiar words of 'Ten Cents a Dance.'

'Ten fucking cents!' Rosemary muttered as she strode along the landing. Wrenching open Carrie's door, she walked in. Carrie, standing before the mirror, broke off singing. 'Sorry, Rosie, she said, 'I didn't hear you knock.'

'I didn't knock.'

'Is he here?'

'No, he's not. And when you've finished with your Doris Day impersonations I'd like you to go down and look at the bird. And be ready to let Kurt in when he rings. Okay?'

'Okay, of course.'

*

When Kurt Hellman arrived a few minutes later, Carrie showed him into the living room. He was not what she had expected. She had guessed from Rosemary's behaviour that he must have more attractions than Douglas, but she had not been prepared for him to look quite like this. In his late thirties, he was tall, over six feet. His hair was almost black, his eyes a deep blue. He had a straight nose and firm, strong jaw. The smile he gave showed white, even teeth. He wore a light-weight grey suit and his pale-lemon shirt made a striking contrast with his tan.

At the bar Carrie poured him a Scotch and soda. As she handed him his drink, Rosemary came into the room. Smiling, she moved to Kurt, hand outstretched.

'Welcome,' she smiled. 'Glad you could get here.'

'My apologies,' he said. 'I'm afraid I got held up in traffic.'

'It doesn't matter,' said Rosemary. 'Anyway, we're eating very simply.' She gestured to the sofa. 'Take a seat while I get myself a drink.'

As Kurt sat down she poured herself a vodka-tonic then moved to sit at the other end of the sofa. While she and Kurt chatted, Carrie sat for the most part silent, listening to their conversation. After a few minutes Rosemary put down her drink and got up.

'Carrie, darling,' she said, 'give me a hand in the kitchen, will you?'

'Yes, of course.' Avoiding Kurt's gaze, Carrie murmured, 'Excuse me,' and followed Rosemary out of the room.

In the kitchen, Rosemary reached for her apron, saying as she did so, 'If you can tear your eyes away from his crotch for five minutes maybe we can finish preparing dinner.' Then, seeing the expression of outraged horror that swept over Carrie's face, she added quickly with a laugh, 'Only joking, for Christ's sake.' She patted Carrie lightly on the cheek. 'Little Miss Goody Goody.'

*

Dinner was a success, and when it was over, Rosemary

went back out to the kitchen to make coffee. A minute later Carrie was at her side.

'I'll give you a hand.'

'Thanks,' Rosemary said. 'After coffee we're going to go through a couple of numbers. See how it shapes up.'

'You're gonna sing? Great.'

'Well, we'll do our best.'

Half an hour later Rosemary led Kurt into the music room. Carrie watched them go, then let herself out of the house.

The humidity of the day had gone, and the evening was cool and clear. A light wind was gentle on her bare arms, and she stood breathing in the sweet night air. From inside the house came the sound of the piano as Kurt played a few chords and arpeggios. Then, after a little introduction came Rosemary's voice as she began to sing. It was an old Rodgers and Hart song:

> Once I laughed when I heard you saying
> That I'd be playing solitaire, uneasy in my easy chair.
> It never entered my mind...

The familiar song was too melancholy for Carrie's mood, and she moved away from the sound. Near the lawn she saw, glowing dimly in the grass, the cat's dishes, both now empty. She took up the water dish, refilled it at the garden tap and placed it on the grass again. 'Sorry about that, Kitty,' she murmured. 'I'm afraid you slipped my mind. But I won't forget you tomorrow.'

Moving past the pool to the end of the garden, she

stood looking down to where the dark, wide expanse of the Hudson flowed by. She felt very much alone tonight. Somehow the completeness of the duo in the house made her feel superfluous and slightly resentful, like a third child when only two can play.

She moved to the bench and sat down. She had never realised, until this moment, just how insulated their lives — hers and Rosemary's — had become over the years. Rosemary's absence from the world of entertainment had brought them a new way of living — detached and separate from the world they had known. Away from the shows, the glare, they had, over time, found a simpler life. And now it looked as if that simpler life was going. Changes were taking place. She had encouraged Rosemary, but now she wasn't sure how she felt about it. She wanted Rosemary to be happy, of course she did, but even so...

As she shifted restlessly on the bench something soft and warm moved against her foot. She started slightly and, looking down, saw the cat.

'Hello, Kitty.' Her voice was a murmur. 'I didn't see you there.'

She stooped and gently lifted the animal onto her lap. For a few moments he remained tense, ready to spring away, but she soothed him, stroking his soft fur. 'It's okay,' she said. 'There's nothing to worry about.' Her voice was low and crooning. 'How come you hang around here?' she said. 'Don't you have any home of your own, a pretty little kitty-cat like you?'

As she held the cat in her arms she felt the tension drain from his body, and after a while he began to purr.

.....SEVEN

Two weeks had passed since their first meeting, and Rosemary and Kurt sat on the porch, sipping their drinks while the shadows lengthened on the lawn and the smoke from their cigarettes drifted on the late afternoon air.

They were alone at the house now, Carrie having driven into Manhattan to see a show. With several hours' work behind them on various songs and arrangements, the subject had turned to other matters concerning the forthcoming concert.

'I guess you haven't heard anything from Douglas,' Rosemary said, 'about finding a producer for the show?'

Kurt shook his head. 'No, he's said nothing to me. But it's early days yet.'

'Yes, I know, but the time will go so fast, I just know it.' She stubbed out her cigarette. 'We're meeting tomorrow. Maybe he'll have some news for me then. We've got to find the right venue, too.'

'Oh, Doug'll deliver the goods, Rosemary, you can depend on it.'

She nodded. 'You have a lot of faith in him, haven't you?'

'Yes, I have.'

'It's hard to believe you're first cousins. You're not at all alike.'

'No, we're not. Not in looks, anyway.'

'But you're close, right?

He nodded. 'I guess we are. We grew up together.'

'So he told me.'

'His mother raised me after my own mother died.' He took a drink from his glass. 'And Doug always looked out for me. Being those few years older he was always pretty much like a big brother.'

Rosemary watched him as he put down his glass. During their hours of working together she had learned a little of his history. He had been married, but was now divorced. Added to that, he appeared to be presently unattached – romantically, at any rate.

'What time's Carrie due back?' he asked.

'Not till pretty late, I'd guess.'

He nodded. 'I have the feeling she doesn't exactly approve of me.'

'What? Why? What makes you say that? What has she said?'

'Oh, it isn't anything she's said.'

'What, then?'

He shrugged. 'It's just a feeling I have.'

'No, you're imagining it.'

'I don't think so.'

'Well,' she shrugged, 'I wouldn't worry about it. I don't think she exactly approves of *any* man.'

'You mean she likes girls?' He looked both amused and surprised.

'Oh, no!' Rosemary laughed. 'Don't get that idea. It's just that – well, once she was let down pretty badly by a guy, and she took it hard. You think people get over things like that — but maybe not everybody does. I don't think Carrie has. And I think she now mistrusts men — generally. A little scared of them too, I guess. You mustn't take it personally.'

'Oh, I'm not bothered by it.' He took a drag on his cigarette, stubbed it out. 'I'd better think about starting back,' he said.

'You have to go?' Rosemary said. 'Why don't you stay on for dinner?' She spoke as if the idea had just occurred to her.

'Thanks — I'd like to,' Kurt said, giving a rueful smile, 'but I can't, I'm sorry. I have a date.'

Rosemary shrugged. 'Oh, well, it was just a thought.' All at once she felt a little defeated and frustrated. And in the absence of his interest she became suddenly aware of her ageing neck and thickening waist. She sat there for a moment, then got up from her chair. 'Excuse me,' she said. 'I have to make a telephone call. I'll be right back.'

*

At 8.30, with Kurt long since gone, Rosemary stood alone on the porch, looking down to where the winding drive got lost in the shrubbery. At any moment Brett Martin's Buick would turn the corner. She looked at her watch. He was three minutes late. The tall jug of water and full ice-bucket stood ready along with the bottle of Chivas Regal and the highball glass. Her own glass she held in her hand. The house was very still. Silently she blessed Carrie's absence. She needed these times now and again. The chilled glass against her cheek, she leaned against the doorpost, her eyes on the drive. She thought once more of Kurt as he had appeared that afternoon, suntanned, handsome — and unavailable. And she thought of Brett Martin. Well, at least there was no pretence with Brett. No formalities to be endured — at least not in the social sense. He knew what she wanted, and he supplied it, readily.

From the drive came the distant crunch of tyres on gravel, and a moment later the car was coming towards her, then moving on past, round to the side of the house. She heard the slam of the car door, footsteps, then as she opened the screen door he came towards her, shambling slightly, shyly smiling.

'I couldn't get away from the station,' he said as he stepped up onto the porch. 'Urgent repair job came in.'

'Never mind,' she said. 'You're here now. And we've got plenty of time.'

Unmarried, unsophisticated, forty-three years old, Brett Martin had first met Rosemary five years earlier when doing a repair operation on her car. He had been to her house many times since then. It was always tacitly understood that when she wanted him she would call him, and until she did he made no move to get in touch.

Rosemary began to pour him a drink. 'How's your sister?' she asked, not wanting to know, but feeling the need to be polite.

'Fine. She thinks I'm going to the bar.'

They talked desultorily while moths and other flying insects threw themselves at the screen in an effort to get at the light, and then after a few minutes Rosemary got up from her seat. 'Shall we go in?' she said.

He rose and followed her inside and up the stairs and into her bedroom. A big man, he moved almost gingerly, not at home in such surroundings.

In the soft glow of the lamp they undressed, and in the silence he wrapped his arms around her and drew her to his strong, hard nakedness. Under her hands she felt the hair that covered his chest, the curve of his back, his slightly misshapen shoulder. He was taller even than Kurt.

*

She awoke the next morning to find Carrie hovering over her with a tray of coffee. 'Oh, hello, sweetie,' she said. 'Is it late?'

'Just after nine.'

Rosemary sighed, stretched and sat up, took the cup and murmured her thanks. 'So, how was it, the show? Did you enjoy it?'

'Oh, yes.' Carrie's nod was enthusiastic. 'But I always love Andrew Lloyd Webber.' A pause. 'I hope I didn't wake you when I got in.'

'No way, darling. I was dead to the world.'

'That's okay, then.' Carrie smiled. 'I had a really nice time. I ate Chinese.'

'Good. As long as you enjoyed yourself.'

'Oh, I did. You should have come with me. You missed a really nice time.'

Rosemary smiled into her coffee cup. 'Maybe I did, darling. Maybe I did.'

*

After breakfast Carrie went upstairs to help Rosemary get dressed and found her sitting at her dressing table, chin in hand.

'Come on, Rosie,' Carrie said. 'You'll be late for your appointment with Douglas.'

Rosemary gave a groan. 'What the hell does it matter?'

'What's wrong?' Carrie said. 'What's brought this on?'

Rosemary turned to her with a pained expression. 'I just got this terrible shock,' she said.

'A shock? What are you talking about?'

'I was sitting here, minding my own business — about to do my make-up, when I look up and see this terrible, godawful sight.'

'What?'

'I caught sight of this raddled old bag staring out at me from the mirror.' She patted her breast. 'Jesus Christ. Gave me quite a turn, I can tell you. But the biggest shock came when I realised it was me.'

Carrie laughed softly. 'Oh, Rosie…'

'I'll tell you something,' Rosemary said. 'When I arrive back in London nobody — but *nobody* — is going to recognise me.'

'Oh, come on, now…'

'Well, just look at me! And there's Douglas talking about me having photographs taken!'

'Well, of course.' Carrie was taking Rosemary's dress from its hanger. 'You haven't had any pictures taken in years.'

'I know that, but — well, how can I? I mean, look at me! Take a look.'

Carrie peered at her. 'Okay, I'm looking. So what's new?'

'*Nothing's* new, you idiot! That's the trouble! It's all so fucking *old*!' She turned back to her reflection. 'Look at me.

I look like some pox-ridden old hag who's been pensioned off from the red-light district.' She nodded. 'Well, there's only one thing for it — I'll have to go under the knife.'

'You mean — surgery?'

'Well, yes, if you must be so crude. But we don't call it that.'

'We don't?'

'Of course not. Look at all those gals on TV and those movie stars who've had all the works. You don't think they ever admit to going under the knife, do you?' She put on a nasal, Hollywood drawl: 'Cosmetic surgery, sir? How dare you suggest such thing!' She laughed. 'And ask them how come their skin looks so smooth, they tell you they owe it all to good diet, soaking in olive oil and keeping out of the sun.'

Carrie laughed along with her, then said, 'D'you mean that — about having something done?'

Rosemary nodded. 'Yes, I do. I should have done it years ago. But there just didn't seem much point in it. After all, people weren't exactly queuing up to look at me. But things are different now. And as I've never had it done before it'll probably be all the more successful.'

'Is that the way it works?'

'I don't know. But there must be a limit to the number of times you can yank all the flesh around.' Carefully she applied lipstick, blotted her mouth with a tissue. 'You see some of these women and *nothing's* in the place where it started off,' she said. 'And look at the way they get those huge cheek implants. So puffed up they look like fucking chipmunks storing up for the winter. And then they get all the fillers in the lips, and the big silicone tits, and so much botox they can't even frown any more.' She sighed and gave a laugh. 'Yep. Sounds like just what I need.'

The two of them laughed together, and then Rosemary said: 'No, but seriously, I could sure do with a little help from a good surgeon. Not too much — though. I don't want to end up with my navel round my neck.'

'Oh, stop it, Rosie,' Carrie said, chuckling.

'You think I'm joking,' Rosemary said. 'I'm not.' She soothed a brush over her cheeks then touched at her hair. 'Now — I must get on or I shall be late.'

*

When Rosemary had gone from the house, driving off to Manhattan, Carrie finished loading the dishwasher, then went out into the backyard.

'Kitty… Here, Kitty…'

The cat came at her call. They were good friends now. He wove about her ankles for a moment, then followed her when she started back into the house. She allowed it happily — and with a slight feeling of daring; encouraging his presence indoors wasn't something she'd do when Rosemary was around.

In the kitchen she got a dish of French vanilla ice cream from the freezer and added some strawberry syrup. Then, with the cat still following, she went into the den and settled herself in front of the television. She watched the screen for a few moments, then, turning, called to the cat, patting her lap. 'Here, Kitty — come on.'

Lightly he sprang up onto her knee, padded softly for a moment and then settled. Carrie smiled down at him, adjusted the cushion at her elbow and took a spoonful of ice cream. Focusing on the screen again, she sighed, content. One of the afternoon movies was about to begin. *Smilin' Through*, she read to the accompaniment of the violins. She gave a quick, fond glance down at the cat asleep in her lap.

'Oh, you're going to love this, puss,' she said. 'It's Jeanette MacDonald.'

*

At the same time that Jeanette MacDonald lay dying at the altar, held in the loving arms of Brian Aherne, her wedding dress stained with her life's blood, Rosemary was sitting in Douglas's office drinking coffee.

The concert, it had been decided, would take place in early spring, in March, and from the vantage point of September, Rosemary felt the time would never come. Don't worry, Douglas said, the time would pass all too quickly. There would be so much to do. And one of the first things they must arrange was to get some new photographs.

Rosemary shook her head. 'No photographs,' she said firmly. 'Definitely no photographs.'

Douglas spread his hands. 'But, Rosemary, we talked about this. You know damn well we've *got* to have pictures if there's gonna be any kind of publicity drive. We must have them.'

'You heard me, Douglas,' she said. 'No photographs. When I get in shape again, okay, but not before.'

'But Rosemary—'

'No. I said no.' Somehow he had a talent for irritating her, for rubbing her up the wrong way. Thrusting her present irritation aside, she forced herself to smile. 'Come on, Douglas. Stop looking so bloody miserable. When I get myself fixed up you can have all the pictures you want.'

'Fixed up?'

She nodded. 'I've decided to go to a health farm for a couple of weeks. It'll probably kill me, but at least I might be fit to be seen in public again.'

'Fine, and what do we do for pictures in the meantime?'

She shrugged. 'Use some of my *old* pictures.'

'What? You're joking.'

'I'm not joking.'

'Rosemary, listen to me,' he said, 'you look just fine. I don't know what you're worrying about. You look great. And I can get a really good photographer — a genius at lighting who —'

'Stop while you're ahead,' she cut in. 'Douglas, I'm a mess. And no one's going to see me like this. When I left England all those years ago I was young and in shape. But since then I've been round the block a few times, and it shows. And I don't want to go back looking like some withered old has-been.'

'But the publicity —'

'Let people remember me the way I was — until I'm ready.' She forced a smile. 'Believe me, when the time comes there'll be a bunch of photographers waiting to get that first shot of me. I can hear them now, can't you? "Let's see how the old bag's held up." Well, they're going to get a surprise.'

Douglas sighed. 'Okay — if that's your decision…'

'It is, Douglas. Trust me on this one.' She put down her cup and got up. 'Trust me. I know I'm right.'

......EIGHT

'Carrie, for Christ's sake, how many times do I have to tell you? Don't put that fucking sugar in my coffee.'

'I'm sorry, Rosie,' Carrie murmured. 'I forgot. Habit, I guess.'

'Well, stop guessing, will you? I'm on *Sweet and Low*. You know that.'

'Shall I get you some more?'

'Forget it.'

As Carrie left the room, Rosemary turned to Kurt and took in his expression. 'What's the matter?' she said.

'Nothing.'

'Don't worry about Carrie,' she said. 'She knows it's only me.' She turned back to the piano. 'Come on – let's go over the song again.'

Kurt played the opening bars of the song and Rosemary began to sing.

Look at my heart, broken in two.
How could you cause me such pain?
Tell me you love me, kiss the hurt better. . . .

When the song was finished she gave a little sigh, half relief and half anxiety. She was pleased with the results of Kurt's work. Over the weeks he had taken some of her old successes and brought their musical arrangements up to date, while at the same time retaining the elements that had helped make them so popular all those years ago. But while she was delighted with his superb input she was also well aware of her own shortcomings. She sighed again and shook her head. 'Oh, God,' she said, 'will I ever sound right?'

'Rosemary, stop worrying,' he said. 'You're getting better all the time. When the time comes we'll be ready – *both* of us. And you'll be great.'

'I hope to God you're right,' she said.

He nodded. 'You wait – when the time comes.'

'Yes,' she said, 'when the time comes.'

Picking up his cup, Kurt drank the rest of his coffee. 'It's getting late,' he said. 'Time for me to get back.'

When he had gathered up his music, she followed him onto the porch and watched as he got into his car. As the vehicle rolled down the drive she closed the latch and briefly leaned back against the door. God, but she was tired.

Entering the kitchen a moment later she found Carrie seated on a stool. Her eyes were red-rimmed.

'Carrie – what the hell's up with you?'

The note of exasperation in Rosemary's voice was all Carrie needed, and she put her hands to her face and began to sob.

Rosemary raised her eyes to the ceiling. 'Oh, for God's sake, Carrie, what on earth's wrong?'

'Nothing. It's nothing.' Carrie continued to cry.

'Well, if it's nothing you're making a hell of a lot of fuss about it.'

'Forget it.' Carrie took a handkerchief from the sleeve of her sweater, and blew her nose. 'It's just – the way you talk to me sometimes. In there.' She nodded in the direction of the music room. 'When I took in your coffee.'

'What? All this because of some dumb cup of coffee. All I said was that I don't take sugar in it any more.'

'It's the *way* you told me. In front of *him*, too.'

For a few moments Rosemary stood there, then she put her arms around Carrie and pulled her close. At the display of sympathy and affection, Carrie's sobbing burst out anew.

'Oh, sweetheart,' Rosemary said, 'you mustn't take any notice. You know me by now, don't you? And if *you* don't, then who *does*, for God's sake?' She drew back and gently lifted Carrie's chin, looking into her eyes. 'I don't mean it when I get mad. You know that, don't you?'

'I guess so.' Carrie sighed, then said, 'Everything's changing, Rosie.'

'Changing? What do you mean?'

'It – it's all different – from the way it used to be.'

Rosemary frowned. 'But don't you *want* it to change?'

Carrie gave a little shrug. 'I – I guess so. Oh, I don't know.'

'Oh, honey,' Rosemary said, 'don't you see what all this means to me? We *want* it to change. That's what we've been working for, the two of us. I thought it was what you wanted – as much as *I* do.'

'Oh, I do!' Carrie said passionately. 'I *do* want it. It's just that – I sometimes feel lately that I'm not – not needed. And I get to be afraid that – that once you're on top again

you won't want me around any more.' She took Rosemary's hand, gripping it. 'I couldn't stand that, Rosie.
You're all I've got in the world. You have been ever since
that day we met again — in Manhattan, after the show
closed. I was so lost and so low and, and — Oh, I'll never
forget what you did for me then.' She held Rosemary's
hand more tightly still. 'Rosie, you're all I've got. Being
here with you — helping you — that's all there is for me.'

'Hey, come on now.' Rosemary put an arm around her
shoulders. 'What absurd idea is that — that I could get to
the point where I wouldn't need you any more? God — I
need you more than ever now. You think I could manage
without you? You must be mad. I couldn't even *begin* without *you*. And if I *am* a success I shall need you as never
before.' She smiled down into Carrie's tear-stained face.
'Besides, I can't think of anybody else who'd put up with
me, can you?'

Carrie smiled now. 'Oh, Rosie...' She let out her breath
on a deep sigh. 'I'm just so silly. I really am.'

'Look,' Rosemary said, 'don't take any notice of me. I'm
bound to get a bit edgy these days, and I don't mean to take
it out on you.' She waved a derisive hand. 'Those other
idiots — they're expendable. But not you, sweetie, not you.'

Carrie smiled, nodded.

'Okay?' Rosemary said.

'Okay.'

'Good. Everything's going to be fine. Remember that.'

'Yes.'

'So no more tears, okay?'

'No more tears.'

'Good.' Rosemary gave a little laugh. 'Stick with me, kid, and like the saying goes, you'll be up to your ass in buttercups.'

*

Carrie, working in the hall, glanced around to see the cat slip by and into the study, and noticed at once that he was carrying something in his mouth. Setting down her duster, she followed him into the room.

'What have you got there, Kitty?' she said, standing in the doorway.

The cat crouched low on the carpet, eyes riveted on something before it. And as Carrie watched she saw movement, a tiny shape that crept away. It was a mouse.

'Oh, Kitty,' Carrie cried, 'how *could* you?'

The cat appeared to be quite unconcerned as the mouse scurried away across the carpet. But then suddenly it leapt, caught the mouse in its claws and almost in a continuation of the same movement, tossed it up into the air.

'Oh, Kitty, shame on you!' Carrie shook her head. 'How can you be so *cruel*?'

But Kitty could, and clearly enjoyed it, and Carrie watched as the whole procedure was repeated. At this point she decided to intervene, but the moment she stepped forward the cat snatched the mouse up into its jaws; it wasn't going to be deprived of its prey. Carrie stood back. After a while the cat relaxed a little and dropped the mouse back on the carpet. At once the mouse made another attempt to escape—only to be caught once more. Carrie felt helpless. The poor little creature must be in torment. Every time it seemed to be on the point of escaping, the cat captured it again.

But the end was in sight. Yet again the cat released the mouse and then crouched, watching as it made another attempt to get away, at the same time tensing, ready to spring. And then, but too late, it saw the partly open door of a cupboard. Just an inch ajar, it yawned before the desperate little creature's eyes. Quickly the cat sprang. But not soon enough. With one last, desperate scrabble, the mouse slipped through the gap. A second later Carrie, leaping forward, slammed shut the cupboard door.

'*There!*'

The cat clawed futilely at the wood for a second, then looked up at Carrie entreatingly. But not to be entreated, she picked him up and carried him out onto the porch. Shooing him gently, firmly out into the garden, she closed the screen door. Returning to the study, she knelt and carefully opened the cupboard door.

The mouse lay in the furthest corner, between Carrie's sewing-basket and some old movie magazines. Drawing up her courage, she reached in. Her hand trembling slightly, she gingerly touched the mouse's soft fur. It didn't move.

There was a film of sweat on her palm as her fingers closed tenderly around the soft, warm little body and drew it out. The mouse lay still in her open palm.

'Oh, Kitty,' she murmured, 'you've killed him.'

But then she discerned the faint movement of its breathing, and seeing the tiny round eyes regarding her, her heart gave a little leap of joy.

'Oh,' she breathed, 'you're all right. You're *alive!*' Gently she touched the mouse's soft back with her fingertip. 'And you're not to worry any more. Auntie Carrie'll take care of everything.'

Some minutes later she had brought a small wooden box up from the basement, and after furnishing it with bits of newspaper and odd scraps of fabric, she placed the mouse inside. Over the top of the box she laid a piece of wood, leaving a very narrow gap, just wide enough to allow the creature to breathe.

She placed the box in the safety of her room. She was glad Rosemary was out of the house right now. Rosemary didn't take kindly to mice, and there was no sense in upsetting her.

*

'I think we should give a party,' Rosemary said when she returned from the market a little while later.

'What for?' Carrie asked. 'What's the occasion?'

'Well – it'll be a good way of saying goodbye to everyone.'

Carrie hesitated. 'Can we – can you afford it, Rosie?'

'To hell with affording it. It'll be fun. We'll just ask a few people.'

'Okay,' Carrie sighed. Rather than talk of giving parties, she thought, they should be trying to economise. Still, once Rosemary's mind was made up there was nothing to do but go along with it.

*

Later that evening, in her room, Carrie lifted the cover from the little crate and looked in. At the disturbance, the mouse scuttled into a corner, vainly trying to hide. 'Don't worry,' she whispered, 'I won't hurt you. I'm the one who saved your life.' She was pleased to notice that the creature had eaten more of the bread and drunk some of the milk she had provided. Gently, she lowered the cover again. It was nice to have a pet. And now she had two.

The fact that she was the mouse's saviour instilled in her heart a warm, motherly possessiveness. The cat was adorable, but he came and went at will, showing no real love for her, only a love of his own comfort. He took everything, and any warmth that came from him had to be taken; it was never given. Maybe the mouse would be different. And perhaps when it was fully recovered it wouldn't want to leave. It needed only to get used to her, to learn that it could trust her. Perhaps, in its tiny mouse's heart, it could show her the love and gratitude that it so surely owed.

*

An hour later, after a trip to the pet department of a local store, Carrie unwrapped the little mouse cage she had bought. Now it stood before her on the chest of drawers, resplendent in its newness, and unutterably cute. 'Oh, Mousie,' she breathed excitedly, 'you're going to love this.'

Lifting the wooden cover from the box, she smiled down at her pet. The sudden invasion of light startled it, and for a few seconds it scurried about, stopping to rear up on its hind feet, tiny pink nose sniffing at the air. Carrie giggled. He really was the cutest thing, and so adorable.

'You, you little sweetheart,' she cooed, 'are going to your new home today.' She cocked her head, smiling down. 'What do you think of that, huh?' Forefinger extended, she put her hand into the box. The mouse reacted by scurrying into a corner. 'Come on, now,' she cooed. 'I'm not going to hurt you. I'm the one who saved your life. I only want to help you. You and me — we're gonna be friends.'

And now she had both hands inside, fingers outspread, but the mouse only ran from her. He couldn't escape, however. In another moment he was in her grasp, his fur warm and silky-smooth. She lifted him, fingers close around him, so that only his nose was visible in the cradle of her hand.

'Oh, God, but you're sweet.'

She lightly touched the soft fur of his ears while he gazed at her, deathly afraid.

'There...there now... You see, little mousie? There's nothing to be afraid of.' She went on stroking. 'Isn't that nice?'

Mousie didn't think so. Inside her fist he struggled. 'Hold still now,' Carrie chided him. 'You've got to get used to me. You've got to learn to trust me.'

And slowly she felt a stillness creeping into the little creature's body. His panic was easing a little, she thought, and she allowed her fingers to relax their pressure. He was going to be good. But then all at once, feeling her fingers slacken about him, the mouse pushed violently upwards, body squirming, feet scrabbling as they searched for purchase. He was about to escape, but quick as a flash her other hand was there, catching him as he emerged. Giggling breathlessly, she found herself rotating her hands while the mouse, running furiously, moved from one hand onto the other. She laughed with delight. It was like a game.

And then Mousie tired of the sport. Tired of the torment, and, desperate to escape, he bit, hard, his needle-sharp incisors cutting deep into Carrie's forefinger. She gave a piercing squeal of pain and shock. Her hands jerked, and the mouse fell back into the box.

'Oh, you—you *thing!*' she cried, her voice breaking. '*Oh…*'

For a moment she gazed at her damaged fingertip and then, with one quick, angry movement, she snatched up the wooden cover and slammed it in place.

She was bleeding, blood welling from the little punctures in her flesh. She put her finger to her mouth and sucked on it. The wound hurt, too. Apart from the pain, though, she felt anger. How could he do such a thing? She had rescued him, literally from the jaws of death. She had given him milk, bread, love and kindness and he had reacted by biting her.

Pushing back the wooden cover a little, she glared down into the shadowed interior of the box. 'After all I did for you,' she said.

For another moment she glared down at the tiny Judas, then, sucking on her injured finger, she turned and went from the room.

She came back carrying a pair of thick leather gloves. She put them on and reached down into the box. As before, the mouse scrabbled to get away from her, but this time she did not hesitate as she pursued him.

'Got you!'

There was a note of triumph in her voice as she felt his futile struggling in the grip of her gloved hand. 'Bite me now,' she muttered. 'Just try to bite me now.'

*

Rosemary, at work in the music room, looked up as Carrie went past the window towards the garden. She saw that she was wearing gloves and carrying something in her cupped hands. Going after that dumb cat, she guessed. She really shouldn't encourage it to hang around the place, feeding it all the time. Then she shrugged. What the hell – if it made her happy. She turned back to her music while lightly on the afternoon air came Carrie's voice, sweet, musical, as she called up the path:

'Kitty…Kitty. Here, Kitty. Come and get lunchies.'

*

'What happened to your finger?'

Rosemary asked the question as she and Carrie sat at dinner that evening. Carrie gave a casual glance at the Band-aid that covered the bite, and brushed the question aside.

'Oh, that. It's nothing.' She shifted slightly on her chair. Her left buttock ached dully as a result of the tetanus shot the doctor had given her. 'It's just a little scratch,' she said.

*

The next day she went back to the store, taking with her the mouse cage, quite unused. She got a credit note in exchange and with it bought a couple of DVDs of old MGM musicals. She got *Seven Brides for Seven Brothers* and *Singin' in the Rain.* She had always adored Jane Powell and Gene Kelly.

......NINE

'Well, look at you!' Carrie said admiringly.

It was the evening of the party. The hired bartender and maid were in place and busy, and now Rosemary emerged from her room, finally dressed to meet her guests. She was wearing a new gown of deep blue satin, around her shoulders a long, lavender silk stole.

'I look okay, you think?' Rosemary said.

Carrie nodded enthusiastically. 'You look wonderful — and that stole — it looks so beautiful. But I always loved it.'

Rosemary caressed the silk. 'Yes, my lucky little wrap,' she said. 'My God, but it's old now.' Smiling with the memory, she said, 'I bought it all those years ago, when the band played at the Royal Variety Performance.' She gave a little sigh of pleasure. 'Imagine that — me singing for royalty.'

'I wish I'd been there,' Carrie said.

Rosemary nodded. 'It's nice to have some good memories. And they don't come much better. Anyway,' she waved a hand at Carrie, shooing her off, ' — you go and get ready now, or you'll be late. They'll be arriving any minute.'

As Carrie went off to her room, Rosemary started downstairs to check that all was going well. The guest list had risen to fifty-two, and it promised to be a busy evening. When she had first said that they must hire a maid and bartender, Carrie had protested: 'Rosie, we can't afford them. We can manage without them.' 'Listen,' Rosemary had said, 'I want to enjoy this too. I'm not going to spend hours cooking in the kitchen and the rest of the time dishing it out.'

And now the frantic work was behind them, and at last, it seemed, everything was ready.

Twenty minutes later, the first of the guests appeared.

Kurt was one of the last to arrive. Rosemary answered the door to his ring and greeted him warmly, kissing him on the cheek. 'Come on in,' she said, 'and get a drink. Douglas arrived a few minutes back.'

As Kurt followed her into the living room he surveyed the throng of guests. 'You told me just a few people,' he said. 'This is your idea of a few?'

She laughed, took his hand and led him towards the bar, where the bartender set about pouring him a drink. Looking over her shoulder at the assembly, she said, 'There are people here that even *I* don't know. Still, it makes a change not to see the same tired old faces.' Kurt's drink poured, she handed it to him. 'Talking of tired old faces,' she said, 'how do I look?'

'You look great, Rosemary. Just great.'

'Why Cap'n Butler, you say the most lovely things.' She narrowed her eyes. 'But next time don't wait to be asked.'

She stayed talking to him for a few more minutes then went to give her expansive welcome to two more guests who had arrived. She was in her element. There were few things she enjoyed more than being surrounded by people who were all — at least outwardly — affectionately disposed towards her.

Standing near the bar, Carrie watched Rosemary's progress, wishing that she herself could give an impression of such relaxed confidence. But it was no good wishing. She felt uncomfortable in the turquoise dress that Rosemary had persuaded her to buy (*and* it had cost a fortune!) and was all too conscious of her slightly exposed cleavage. 'Darling, it looks *marvellous*,' Rosemary had told her, but Carrie remained unconvinced.

'Hello, Carrie.'

Carrie turned at the sound of her name, and saw that Douglas had come to the bar to get a fresh drink. They had not met before this evening, but over their brief introduction earlier she had found him pleasant and relatively easy to talk to. Now, smiling, he gestured with a wave of his hand, taking in the many guests. 'You and Rosemary have done wonders,' he said. 'I don't know how you do it.'

'Not I,' she said. 'It's all Rosemary's doing.'

He nodded. 'If you say so.' He looked around. 'Are we allowed to smoke?'

'Oh, sure.'

He took out cigarettes, offering one to her, but she shook her head, 'No thanks. That's one vice I've avoided.'

He nodded approvingly. 'You're a smart lady.'

They began to talk, and she found herself almost relaxing with him. He showed interest in her, and asked her about herself, about her life. He evinced a wide knowledge of the entertainment business, and when he learned that at one time she herself had had something of a career in the theatre, he was keen to know more. Prompted, she named a couple of the productions in which she had appeared, and when she mentioned the Off-Broadway production of *The Charm-Spinner* he said, a smile breaking over his plain features, 'Yes! You were Caroline, the professor's daughter. That was you, wasn't it?'

'Yes.' Her smile lit up her face. 'You saw it?'

'Oh, I did! And you were wonderful.'

'But it was so long ago,' she said. 'That was years ago.'

He shrugged. 'But I remember it. It was one of the first things I saw after arriving in Manhattan.' He gave a little wondering shake of his head. 'Your performance — it stayed with me.'

Carrie began to thank him, but over her words came Rosemary's voice as she approached, expansively gesturing towards the dining room. 'Okay, folks, dinner is served, so do come and eat.' Smiling at Douglas, she added, 'Enough talk for now, Douglas. Come and eat.'

In the dining room the buffet supper had been laid out, resplendent on the wide table. Rosemary stood at Douglas's side while other guests filed by, filling their plates. 'Look at them,' she whispered to him, 'like a pack of vultures.' She shrugged. 'Still, we're none of us any different, I guess.' She urged him towards the table. 'Go eat, while there's something left.'

As Douglas moved away she saw Kurt coming towards her bearing a fork and a loaded plate. He nodded appreciatively as he got to her side.

'Great stroganoff, Rosemary.'

'Thanks. Have you got a drink?'

'I'm taking it easy. Have to drive later.'

'You don't have to go,' she said. 'Why don't you stay over?'

'Thanks,' he said, 'but I'm driving Doug back to the city. And anyway, I have to make an early start tomorrow.'

'Okay, suit yourself.'

When most of the other diners had served themselves Rosemary went to the table and took up a plate. In the course of making her selection – a little rice, stroganoff, a little salad – she glanced up and saw two brown eyes regarding her across the table. She smiled at the young man. 'Everything okay?'

'Oh, sure, thank you. Everything's fine.' He was somewhere in his early thirties, she guessed. He had dark hair and a wide, slightly diffident smile.

'You're Tom Ringler, right?' she said. 'You came with the Davisons.'

'Yes, I'm staying with them.' He helped himself to salad. 'I'm surprised you remembered my name – with all these people here.'

'Oh, I've got a good memory – when it suits me.' She looked directly into his eyes. 'And faces I always remember. Well, *some* faces – the handsome ones.' She took up a napkin and a fork. 'Come on, Tom Ringler-who-came-with-the-Davisons, let's find a place to sit. I've been on my feet all day.'

They sat side by side on the stairs, picking at their plates, sipping at their drinks and chatting casually of this and that. Rosemary found herself warming to him. 'Listen,' she said to him during a lull in the conversation, 'you don't have to sit here talking with me.' She gestured towards the living room where the guests came and went. 'There are three or four very attractive young ladies out there, you know.'

'Yes, I know,' he said, smiling at her. 'But I'm happy where I am.'

She smiled back. 'Well, that's nice to hear.'

When she had finished her plate, he picked it up, rising from his seat. 'Would you like some dessert?'

'No, thanks.' She smiled. 'But get something for yourself and come on back.'

When he had gone, she lit a cigarette and sat looking out over the comings and goings. Then, above the voices and the soft music from the stereo she became aware of the ringing of the doorbell. Who could be arriving this late? And then she recalled that one of her guests had asked if he might bring along an acquaintance who was down for the weekend and had expressed a wish to meet her. This must be the friend, she thought.

The sound of the bell came again, and seeing no sign of the maid, she got up from the stair and made her way down into the hall. Opening the door, she saw a man standing on the threshold. She didn't recognise him.

'Good evening,' she said as she offered her hand. Then added, smiling, 'I think you might be Wes Tarrant's friend, are you?'

'Yes, I am, Rosemary,' he said, smiling. They shook hands. He was tall, slightly running to fat, his thinning hair greying. 'I'm late I'm afraid,' he said. 'Wes left me a note with your address. I hope it's okay, inviting myself like this. I said to Wes I'd really like to see you.'

'Yes, of course. I told Wes you'd be most welcome, so long as you don't mind taking potluck.' She turned, gesturing off. 'Wes is through there in the dining room. Let me have your coat.'

He took off his coat, handed it to her. They were alone, away from the hubbub. She was waiting for him to give his name, but he stood silent, gazing at her. And then after a few moments it came to her that there was something familiar about him. She was about to speak, when he said, not taking his eyes from her face, 'You don't know who I am, do you?'

'I — I think I do,' she said. 'Have I met you with Wes sometime?'

'Oh, no. We met way back. Well over twenty years ago.'

'Over twenty years? Oh, so far back.' She gave a little laugh. 'Of course you realise I'd have been all of twelve or thirteen then.'

Going along with her joke, he said with a chuckle, 'Twelve or thirteen! Oh, if *that*!'

She frowned. 'But I do know your face. Were you on bass for me when I played at the Apollo Gold?'

He shook his head, leaned forward a little. 'D'you remember a show called *Save a Place For Me*?'

And the familiar look, the familiar voice that had hovered in her mind now settled.

'Michael,' she said.

He smiled. 'You got it.'

She stepped back, her eyes suddenly cold. 'What do you want?'

'What?' His smile had vanished.

'I asked you what you wanted.' Her words were measured. 'What are you doing here?'

'What do you mean? I came along to see you, that's all.'

'Okay, so now you've seen me.' She held out his coat. 'Here, take your coat. I'm afraid you can't stay.'

Frowning, he took his coat from her. 'Jesus Christ, some welcome.'

She pointed back towards the living room. 'Listen,' she hissed, 'Carrie is in there.'

'Huh?'

'Carrie. Carrie Markham. You have to go.'

He just stood there.

'What's wrong with you?' she said. 'You fucking deaf?'

'Well, I didn't know she'd be here.'

'Well, you know it now.' She stepped past him and opened the door. 'You have to leave – this minute.'

'How was I to know?' he said.

'Just go.' Her eyes were like ice. 'I want you off my property and out of my sight.' With her words she put her hands on his chest and gave him a shove. He staggered back, and for a moment had to fight to keep his footing. 'Hey – hey,' he said, 'take it easy.'

'Get out!'

Standing on the porch, he faced her, breathing hard, his face pale. 'You need to watch your manners, Rosemary,' he said. 'I came here in good faith and –'

'Get out.'

He raised a hand, forefinger pointing at her. 'Okay – but just remember – two can play at that game.'

'Get out,' she said. 'Get out, you son of a bitch! Get the fuck out and don't ever come back!'

He gazed at her a moment longer, then turned away, stepping down from the porch. As she watched him start off along the drive she heard her name called. Turning, she saw Tom Ringler coming towards her.

'There you are,' he said. His smile was broad. 'I was beginning to think you'd run out on me.'

She closed the door. I was just saying goodbye to one of my guests.'

'He was leaving so early?'

'Yes — something came up.'

'Would you like a drink?' he asked. 'Let me get you one.'

She shook her head. 'No, thanks. Not right now. I — I must circulate.'

He reached out and briefly touched her arm. 'If you like, I can stay around for a bit later on — help you clear up a little.'

Such an invitation from this nice young man was something that, only ten minutes ago, she would have welcomed. Not now. What magic there was had gone out of the evening.

She smiled at him. 'Ah, that's so nice of you, Tom, but I feel I've got a bit of a head coming on. I think when all this is over I shall just go straight to bed.'

......TEN

Sighing loudly, her impatience growing, Rosemary sat facing Douglas across his desk, waiting for him to complete a telephone conversation with one of his clients. But then, at last, with a firm 'G'bye now', he replaced the receiver and turned to her, giving an over-bright, now-you-have-my-undivided-attention smile. Her answering smile was fleeting and lukewarm. She got straight to the point.

'Okay, Douglas, what's happening?' she said. 'What have you done?'

'What have I done?'

'Yes, what have you done? Have you fixed anything yet? Have you found anyone interested in producing my show?'

In response he raised his hands, as if warding off an attack. 'Hey, hey,' he said, his smile uncertain, 'slow down a little, Rosemary. Take it easy.'

'I'm taking it as easy as I can,' she said evenly. 'Just tell me what's happening.' Watching his face as he ducked and groped for answers, she realised, quite suddenly, that in spite of all her efforts to do otherwise, she simply didn't like him.

'Rosemary, I'm working on it,' he said. 'Believe me, I am.'

She nodded. 'You're working on it. What does that mean?'

He sighed. 'Rosemary, these things take time.'

'You're damn right they do — *too much* time. Listen, I want to make sure I get the date I'm after. And the right venue. I don't mind telling you, I'm getting nervous. I can't see what's so difficult.'

When he did not respond, she said sharply, 'Douglas, tell me — what exactly is the problem here? There must be any number of producers who'd be ready to back me.' He remained silent. 'Well, aren't there?' she said. 'You have tried, haven't you?'

He nodded. 'Of course I have.'

'Well, tell me.'

He shrugged. 'Okay, well, I've approached a few of the bigger ones, but sorry to say they all seem fairly — committed — to other projects...'

She frowned. 'Committed? What are you trying to tell me?' She leaned forward in her chair. 'You trying to tell me they don't want to handle the job? Is that what you're saying? I don't believe it. Who did you try?'

'Well — John Balfour first, then Jason Brierly.'

'What? You're telling me Brierly didn't want it? I know him. He would have jumped at it.'

Douglas shrugged, spread his hands. 'Well, I'm sorry, but he didn't. I'm afraid he's already got his commitments.' He could hardly tell her the truth, that Brierly's reaction had been one of amused surprise, followed by a firm, unequivocal statement that he was not in the least interested.

'Well, to hell with him,' she said. 'Try King and Waterman.'

'Well — I don't know...'

'Well, *I do* damn well know,' she said. 'And I'm telling you.'

He wilted slightly under her attack. 'All right – I'll get in touch with them. I'll write them today.'

'You'll *write* them?' she said witheringly.

'Rosemary, listen –'

'No, *you* listen. This isn't some pen-friendship where you drop a line every Christmas and birthday. This is my career. And you're supposed to be looking after it. Don't write to them, Douglas – get on the phone!'

For a moment they glared at one another, then Rosemary, feeling that she had overstepped the mark, shrugged and looked away. 'I'm sorry. Look – do it the way you think best. I guess you know how to handle these matters.'

He didn't look at her. 'Leave it with me,' he said, tight-lipped. 'We'll get you there.'

She sat in silence for a moment, then got up, walked to the window, and stood looking down onto the busy street below. 'This isn't an easy time for me,' she said with a deep sigh. She turned back to face him. 'I know you think I can get pretty impossible – but nothing's come to me on a plate. I've had to hustle all my life.' She sighed again, then added, 'I have to say – Kurt's done wonders with the music.'

'That's good to hear,' Douglas said. 'And we've got some pretty sharp publicity underway. Things are moving. You want to look at these?' He took some newspaper cuttings from a file and laid them on the desk before him, spreading them out. They were from British national newspapers and magazines, all giving reports of Rosemary's impending return to England. Rosemary moved back to the desk, put on her spectacles and began to glance over the clippings. After a minute she gave a little nod of approval.

'Yeah, well, okay,' she said, 'that'll do for a start.'

'Aren't you satisfied?'

'Like I said, it'll do for a start.'

'I worked damn hard to get this stuff out,' Douglas said. 'And I'm no PR man.'

'You did fine,' she said. She took off her spectacles and glanced at her watch. It was nearly time to meet Kurt for their lunch date. 'I must be going.' She turned, heading towards the door. 'I'll hear from you, right?'

'Yes, indeed,' Douglas said, arranging files on his desk. 'I'll be in touch.'

'Yeah, sure. Good.' She nodded to him and left.

*

Later, over the restaurant table, Kurt smiled at her. She smiled back and sipped at her dry martini.

'So how did your meeting go with Doug?' Kurt asked.

She frowned. 'I was afraid you'd ask me that.'

'Hey? Why?'

As she hesitated, searching for words, he said, frowning, 'Tell me, Rosemary. You can tell me.'

'Can I? Your loyalties are with Douglas.'

'Listen, I like to think I can be objective.'

She nodded. 'Okay, well, the truth is, I'm getting concerned.'

'Concerned?'

'Yes. Things aren't going as I'd anticipated. I don't know which end is up. I'm not sure of anything. I'm getting very jumpy. I just hope it's all going to work out okay in the end.'

'I'm sure it will.'

'Yes? I wish I could be as sure.'

'Rosemary,' Kurt said, 'this is not an easy business, you know that. But I trust Doug – implicitly. He's a great guy – and you must remember that his own reputation's on the line here. He's not gonna risk looking like an idiot. He's not in this for fun. He's in this for success, like you. I'm sure you've got no worries, believe me.'

'That's what I hoped you'd say,' she said, then added with a sigh, 'Oh God, Kurt, I'm like a cat on hot bricks these days. I just can't wait to get back to England and get started.'

He nodded. 'I know how you must feel, believe me. But it'll be okay.'

'I hope so.'

'It will be. And it's going to be an exciting time for you.'

'My God, yes!' she said. 'Say, listen – Carrie's found this little country cottage for me as a base. It's a darling place – down in Berkshire.'

'Berkshire?'

'Berkshire, yes. It's not so very far from London. It'll be great. And there'll be plenty of room, so you'll have to come out there for a break.'

'Yeah,' he nodded. 'Sounds great. I'll do that.'

'It's going to cost a bomb,' she said, 'but so what. I need a place where I can take it easy. We're getting a piano installed and everything. If we're doing my show early in March I shall want to go over there right after Christmas.'

'Two months before? How come you need all that time?'

'Believe me, I shall. I'll need time to work and prepare. And anyway, I've got other things to do besides.'

He waited for her to elaborate, but she said nothing. She had no intention of telling him about her date with the cosmetic surgeon. He'd know nothing about that until he saw the results.

Back on the subject of the concert, she asked: 'How long will you need to be in London before the show?'

'Not that long. I'll have to get the musicians together, rehearse with them. Two or three weeks at the most. The less time the better. They don't cost peanuts.'

She nodded. 'I have no doubt of that.'

He took in her frown. 'It'll happen, Rosemary. Don't worry. It's not going to be easy, and it's not going to be cheap, but it's all going to happen.'

.....ELEVEN

The days, the weeks went by, and now here they were, into November, and still no producer had been found. Douglas insisted that he was exploring all possibilities, but the fact remained that, in spite of his efforts, he'd been unable to find anyone willing to put up the financial backing.

'Jesus Christ!' Rosemary said to Carrie, 'how did I manage to get myself landed with that useless bastard! All the hustlers in this town and I have to pick him. Anybody else would have had the whole thing settled by now. If I leave it to him I'm never going to get there, the bloody, fucking useless shit!'

'Oh, Rosie, Rosie...' Carrie winced at the language, briefly closing her eyes.

'I know,' Rosemary said, 'but that man's enough to make God himself curse.'

Minutes later, her anger growing, Rosemary telephoned Douglas and told him they needed to meet. Could he come out to the house? Hearing the edge in her voice, and anxious to appease her, he agreed at once.

He arrived just after three, and Carrie took his coat and showed him into the living room. Rosemary would be down shortly, she said. As she went to hang up his coat, he sat down on the sofa. Seconds later, Rosemary came sweeping into the room.

'Right,' she said at once, directing her words to Douglas as he got up, 'what's happening? Tell me what's happening.'

'Hi, Rosemary —' Douglas tentatively reached out a hand. She ignored it.

'What's happening?' she said. 'Just tell me.'

'You mean —?'

'You know what I mean. I want to know what's happening. This is my career, and I don't have a damn clue what's going on. So tell me, will you? And no crap! Because I'm sick of it. Just tell me straight — have you managed to come up with anything?'

'Rosemary,' he started, 'you know I've been really trying to —'

'So it's nothing,' she cut in. She gave a contemptuous nod. 'What have you come up with? Sweet fuck all — that's what you've come up with.'

'Rosemary — listen —'

'No, *you* listen,' she said. 'And *carefully*.' She went on, pronouncing the words deliberately: 'There isn't much time left — are you aware of that?'

'Yes.'

'Or maybe that hadn't occurred to you?'

'I told you, yes — I am aware of it,' he said. 'I haven't been sleeping all day.'

She shook her head. 'Douglas,' she said, 'let's get this straight. In all these weeks you haven't been able to interest one single producer or entrepreneur. Not one who's willing to promote the show — or even ask for a part of it. And I know London's got to be filled with people who'd jump at the chance You want to get up off your backside and do something for a change.'

Tight-lipped, Douglas took a step away. 'If that's the way you feel about it, Rosemary,' he said, 'there's no point in continuing this conversation.'

'You're damn right there!' she flung at him. 'I should have known from the start that you'd be useless.'

He turned, set-faced, his nostrils flaring. 'Okay, Rose-mary,' he said evenly, 'if truth is the name of the game, then I'll tell *you* a thing or two.'

'Don't bother.' Her voice was withering, but he went on.

'I've spent a great deal of time, energy and money on you,' he said. 'And all that publicity – all those phone calls – and what have I got for it? What will I get for it? Nothing. I did it all on spec. But I'm not complaining. That's one of the hazards of the job. But don't accuse me of not trying.'

She shot him a look of hatred, then, turning in the direction of the hall, yelled out, 'Carrie? Carrie, are you there?'

In moments, Carrie was in the room.

With a brittle smile, Rosemary turned to her. 'Carrie, sweetie, do me a favour, will you?'

'What? Of course.'

'Go and write me out a cheque, will you? Make it out for – for two thousand dollars.' She indicated Douglas with a toss of her head. 'Pay him off.'

Carrie, wide-eyed, stood looking from one to the other, astonishment showing clear on her face.

'*Now*,' Rosemary said. 'Do it *now*. I want him gone.'

'Yes. Yes, of course...' Carrie nodded, and with one more look at their tense faces, turned and hurried away.

As Carrie went from the room Rosemary turned back to Douglas where he stood ashen-faced. 'I think two thousand should more than cover any work you've done for me,' she said, 'and any expenses you might have incurred.'

He shook his head. 'I don't want your money, Rosemary,' he said, then: 'I'd be glad if you'd ask Carrie to get my coat.'

'You'll get your coat. And you'll get your money too.'

'I told you,' he said, 'I don't want your money. And if you want my advice, you'll hang on to it. You might just find you need every cent you can get.'

'Thanks. If I want your advice I'll ask for it.' She turned and called out in the direction of Carrie's departure: 'You got that cheque, Carrie? Sometime this week would be good.' Moving away, she crossed to the window and stood looking out. A minute of silence passed and then Carrie came back into the room.

'Here it is, Rosie.'

Carrie held out a chequebook along with a pen, and Rosemary turned and took them from her. 'Thanks,' she said, 'now go get his coat, will you?'

As Carrie moved away, Rosemary looked at the cheque, scribbled her signature on it and tore it out.

'Here.' She held it out to Douglas.

He made no move to take it. With a faint, humourless smile, he said, 'I told you, Rosemary, I don't want your money. I'm not that desperate, and I hope I never will be.'

Furious, Rosemary tore up the cheque and dropped the pieces on the carpet. 'Well, you had your chance and now you've lost it,' she said. 'You won't get a chance of such easy money again.' She turned as Carrie came into the room, carrying Douglas's coat. 'Give him his coat,' she said, 'then show him out. If you want me I'll be in my room.' Turning, she started towards the hall.

'Just one minute, Rosemary.' Ignoring Carrie who held out his coat, he stepped across the room and came to a stop in Rosemary's way, barring her path.

'Get out of my way,' she said in a low voice. 'There's nothing you can say to me now that I'd care to hear.'

They stood glaring at one another.

'You've just done your very best to insult me,' Douglas said. A nervous tic had appeared in his right eyelid, causing the flesh to jerk in small, spasmodic movements. 'So I'm going to level with you. Tell you the truth.'

'Tell me the truth? What do you mean?'

'I *tried* to get someone to put on your concert,' he said. 'I tried very hard. But in spite of all my efforts I couldn't do it. And do you know why? Because no one in London is prepared to touch you.'

Rosemary's nostrils flared and her mouth opened in astonishment. After a moment she said in a low voice, 'Don't you dare say such a thing to me.'

'I dare because it's true,' he said. 'I tried them all. First I approached two companies who'd handled you years ago. They almost laughed in my face. You see, Rosemary, they can remember very well what the experience was like – and they've got the scars and the ulcers to prove it. To so many people your name spells one word: *trouble*. And they don't need it. They put up with it in the past because you had something of a following and they were willing to give you a chance. They could see your potential. But that was *then*. Now it's a different story.' He gave a sigh, nodded. 'I'll tell you — one of them said to me — and I quote: "I'm an old man, Mr Rosti, and I can't afford to risk shortening the few years I've got left." His blood pressure was already high enough, he said. Another bout with you was something he just didn't care to contemplate.'

Disbelief and hatred were naked in Rosemary's face, but she made no move to stop the flow of his words. Carrie, standing transfixed, clutched his coat in one hand, the other up to her open mouth.

'Mind you,' Douglas went on, 'I didn't give up easily. Oh, no. Like you, I was convinced there must be somebody out there who'd like the chance to make a buck. But no. No one seemed eager to do so. Strange, yes? You see, apart from your reputation for being a difficult lady, there is also the matter of your having been out of the business for so many years.'

Rosemary said quickly, 'Well, what about my album that's just come out over there? And those reports in the newspapers? That must mean something.'

He nodded. 'You're right. I asked the same question. But as they pointed out, the sales are still very small. And it was also pointed out that the original recordings were made long before your voice went — and *that* didn't happen yesterday.' He looked at her pityingly. 'I'm sorry to say it, Rosemary, but you need to face the facts — you're just too big a risk, in every respect — and they're afraid of losing their shirts — apart from everything else.' He shrugged.

'I tried. Don't say I didn't.' A moment of silence, and he added softly: 'I feel sorry for you.' He turned, took his coat from Carrie's hands and moved towards the hall. 'I'll see myself out,' he said.

*

Carrie prepared dinner for them that evening, but Rosemary remained upstairs in her bedroom, declining to eat.

Close on eleven o'clock, Carrie stood outside Rosemary's room and called out a goodnight to her. There was no answer. Later, in her own room she sat in bed watching a late movie on TV. *The Rains Came.* Myrna Loy was so brave, and Tyrone Power so handsome. Beautiful. She couldn't concentrate, however, and in the end she got up, put on her dressing-gown and went to Rosemary's room and gently tapped on the door. When there was no answer she softly opened the door and looked in. The bedside light was on, and in its glow she could see Rosemary, fully dressed, sprawled across the bed.

'Oh, Rosie…'

She hurried in, aware as she did so of the smell of whisky that hung in the air. At the bedside she stood looking down at the unconscious figure. Seeing Rosemary lying there, her makeup scarred by her tears, Carrie felt rising within her a strange little feeling of elation. She was needed. She really was. Here. Now. She didn't have to make excuses for herself, ever.

'Come on, Rosie.' Murmuring softly, she set to work, undoing the buttons, the zippers, getting Rosemary ready for bed.

*

To avoid being disturbed the next morning, Rosemary had disconnected her bedside telephone extension and turned off her cellphone. When Carrie entered to tell her that Kurt was on the line she turned her face away.

'I don't want to talk to anyone,' she said.

'Okay.' Carrie retreated to tell Kurt that Rosemary wasn't feeling too well just now. Going on into the kitchen, she made coffee. When it was ready she carried it on a tray to Rosemary's room and went in. Rosemary gave no acknowledgement of her presence, but lay there, her eyes closed.

'Rosie, I've brought you some coffee and some cookies,' Carrie said. 'Please — you must have something.'

'I don't want anything. Take it away.'

'Rosie, you must eat. It's three o'clock. You haven't eaten anything all day. Come on — it'll make you feel better.'

'Nothing can make me feel better.'

After a pause, Carrie said: 'Kurt wanted to talk to you about one of your songs.'

'I don't care any more.' Rosemary opened her eyes and looked up at Carrie. 'Don't you understand? It's over. You were there yesterday. You heard what Douglas said. I'm through. Everything is.'

'Oh — Rosie, that's not true.'

'For Christ's sake!' Rosemary said. 'D'you need a ton of bricks to fall on you? Get it into your head. It's *over*. Douglas I can fight. But I can't take on every producer in London. Don't talk to me about arrangements and songs. There's not going to be any. There's not going to be any show. Not this year, next year — never!'

'But – but can't you get another manager?' Carrie said. 'Maybe a different guy could do better.'

'No.' Rosemary turned her face away. 'Let's not talk about it any more.'

For a moment Carrie remained there, gazing down at her. Then, with a sigh, she left the room.

In the kitchen, she placed a dish of cat-food on the floor, then opened the door and called, 'Kitty… Here, Kitty.' Seconds later the cat brushed past her legs and began to eat. 'Oh, you Kitty, you,' Carrie murmured. 'I wish it were as easy to give everybody what they wanted.'

*

A light rain had begun to fall. Carrie looked out at the heavy sky. The day was perfectly in keeping with the mood that prevailed in the house. Grey. Everything was grey. It was as if life had come to a standstill; everything that mattered so much had been taken away. All those plans, all those hopes – they counted for nothing.

The rain began to fall more heavily, and she stayed at the window, watching as the raindrops fell with increasing force, bouncing off the flagstones in the yard. The cat had finished his meal and begun to wash himself. He had no inclination to venture out in such weather. Suddenly, Carrie straightened, a gleam in her eye. Turning, she hurried away. In another minute she was leaning over Rosemary's bed.

'Rosie…'

Rosemary opened her eyes, frowning. 'Yes? What is it?'

'How much would it cost to put on your concert?'

'What are you talking about?'

'How much would it cost?'

'How would I know?'

'Can we find out?'

'I don't know. Why are you asking?'

Carrie hesitated for a second. 'I have an idea.'

'Fine. Go tell somebody else.'

'Rosie, listen to me, please.' Carrie sat on the edge of the bed. 'And don't yell at me.'

'Oh, God…' Rosemary dragged herself up against the pillows. 'Okay, I promise not to yell. Now tell me quickly, then leave me alone.'

Carrie took a deep breath. 'Couldn't *we* put your show on?'

'*We*? *Us*?'

'Yes. Why not?'

Rosemary stared into space for a moment then shook her head. 'No, of course not. That's crazy.'

'Is it?'

'To put up the money to hire a theatre? Pay for all the publicity and the hire of an orchestra? It'd cost a fortune. It would break me.'

'Only if you're a flop, and we know you won't be.'

'Do we?'

'Yes, of course we do. *They* don't know it – those producers, those people – because they don't know *you*. But *I* do. *We* do.'

After a moment Rosemary gave the smallest nod.

'Listen,' Carrie said, ' – let me make some enquiries.' She was already up and moving to the door. 'I'll make some calls, see what I can find out.'

She was back in forty-five minutes. In her hand she carried a notepad on which she had jotted down some figures. Rosemary looked at the eagerness in her face and said: 'Yes? Well?'

'Well, I called a few people,' Carrie said, 'and I got something to go on.' She indicated her notes. 'They're only rough figures – but we can get a pretty good idea.'

'Go on,' Rosemary said.

'Wait a minute...' Carrie made last-minute calculations on the pad and passed it over.

Rosemary gazed at the figures, her eyes wide. 'Jesus,' she said, 'I can't come up with that kind of money.' She threw the pad aside. 'Forget it, sweetie.'

'But you'd get it all back,' Carrie said. 'And more besides.'

'Listen,' Rosemary said, 'things are not going so well as it is. I've had to sell a lot of my stocks and bonds even to get this far. D'you realise what Kurt costs? And he's just a part of it.' She shook her head. 'I don't want to have to start looking around for a job. Can you see me working the checkout at Wallmart?'

Carrie looked away to stare at the rain that drummed against the window pane.

'I've got some money, Rosie,' she said.

'What?'

'What my mother left me. I've never touched any of it. I've never needed to. And I reckon it could be enough – for what we want.'

Rosemary frowned. 'What are you telling me, Carrie? You saying you want to stake me?'

'Well – yes.'

'*Really?*'

'Let's say I want to – invest it. And I'm investing it in you.'

'You'd lend me your cash so that I can hire my own theatre or concert hall or whatever?'

Carrie nodded. 'Or whatever.'

'But – suppose it all goes down the drain…? What if I'm a flop?'

'That's a chance I'll take,' Carrie said. 'But I don't think you will be.'

She turned back to the rain-washed window. The thought went through her head: What if the show *did* turn out to be a flop? But so what? They'd be no worse off. She and Rosemary would still be together, and that was really all that mattered.

'Rosie,' she said, turning back to her, 'we have to do it. We have to *try*.'

'Oh, Carrie,' Rosemary said, 'are you sure about this?'

'Yes, I am.'

After a moment Rosemary nodded. 'Yes,' she breathed, a little excitement now coming into her voice. 'Yes, we can do it. We don't have to depend on those others. To hell with them all. Useless bastards. You wait and see, they'll all be clamouring in the end.' Her hand came out, rested on Carrie's shoulder. 'You know what?'

'What?'

'I'm hungry.'

They laughed together for a moment, then Rosemary said: 'I must call Kurt.' She moved to pick up the phone, stopped and gave a groan.

'What's the matter?' Carrie said.

'Douglas will have told Kurt about what happened – about our fight. What if Kurt wants to back out?'

'Why would he want to do that?' Carrie said. 'Kurt's a professional man. His agreement is with you, not with Douglas. I'm certain he won't let your spat with Douglas get in the way. He's too smart for that.'

Rosemary nodded. 'Well – I hope you're right.'

'I'm sure I am.' Carrie turned and started towards the door. 'Listen, you get dressed and call Kurt, and I'll fix us something to eat.' She started away.

'Honey –'

Carrie came to a stop, turned in the doorway. 'Yes?'

'Are you sure about this?' Rosemary said. 'I mean – it's *your money*. It's going to be a risk. A big risk. You might suddenly need it yourself.'

Carrie gave a little shrug. 'Rosie, I was just saving it for a rainy day.' She smiled, indicating the dismal view from the window. 'And let's face it – they don't come much rainier.'

......TWELVE

Rosemary leaned back in the passenger seat, Carrie beside her at the wheel. They were heading for JFK Airport.

It was a cold, crisp day, and the road before them was clear and dry. The sun, hanging low in the sky, brightened their view with its wintry warmth. That sun, Rosemary told herself — it was an omen. She shivered slightly from excitement. She was on her way.

These last weeks had gone by like something in a dream. Looking back now, in retrospect, it all came to her as one seemingly endless jumble — all the telephone calls, letters, emails, the constant stream of people she had had to see. And somewhere, there in the midst of it all, Christmas had come and gone. Now there was nothing to think about but the present — and the future.

She stubbed out the remains of her cigarette in the ashtray and anxiously consulted her watch. 'Don't fret,' Carrie said, 'we're in plenty of time.' She gave an encouraging smile.

'My God,' Rosemary said with a laugh. 'I'm nervous *now*. What am I going to be like on the *night*?'

*

When they reached the airport Rosemary checked in her bags. That done, they sat together over a cup of coffee. In a few minutes Rosemary would have to take her leave of Carrie and go through Passport Control into the Departure Lounge.

'Have you got everything you need?' Carrie asked.

'Yes, yes. Don't fuss.'

'You want a magazine?'

'When did you ever see me read a magazine?'

'You call me, okay? And write me as well.'

Rosemary sighed. 'All right, Mother, I won't forget. Jesus, it looks like I'll have plenty of time for writing too. By what I've heard of those health farms, there's damn all to do between the massages and warm baths and enemas – or whatever it is they do to you there. And I shall need something to take my mind off all that grated carrot and lemon juice. I shall probably take up knitting.' They laughed. Rosemary went on, 'And you just make sure you get the cottage all ready for when I get there, okay? I can't stand the thought of some dreary, dank little hole at the back of beyond in an English winter with no heating. I've been there, and it's no fun.'

'Don't worry. I'll take care of it all.'

'I know you will.'

It was time to go. Once again Rosemary checked that she had her passport safe – she was travelling under her married name, Rosemary Sanderson, so she had no fear that anyone would know of her imminent arrival in London – and then she and Carrie got up and made their way to Passport Control. At the entrance they came to a stop.

'Okay – you go on back now,' Rosemary said.

Carrie put her arms around her and kissed her cheek. 'I'll see you soon.'

Rosemary nodded. 'Yes, and don't be surprised if you don't recognise me. The packet I'm paying that Harley

Street surgeon, I don't want to be able to recognise *myself*. Just bear in mind that next time we meet I shall be only about nineteen years old.'

*

As Carrie drove back along the highway it occurred to her that until next she saw Rosemary she was quite free. Free to do anything she chose. Pressing her foot harder on the accelerator, she sped on homewards. With luck she'd be in time to catch Joan Fontaine and Orson Welles in *Jane Eyre*.

*

Comfortable aboard the plane, Rosemary unbuckled her seat belt. She'd have liked a cigarette, but such civil pleasures when flying were long gone. The woman on her right tried to strike up a conversation, but she wanted nothing of it, and politely discouraged the attempt. As the woman went back to her book, Rosemary turned to gaze from the window. Below, all around, the world was spreading out like a map. She settled back, closed her eyes, and thought of what lay ahead.

Her first engagement was with the surgeon in Harley Street. At the thought of the coming operation she felt a flutter of nervousness. But it was all arranged now, and it had to be done. To hell with it, anyway, it would be worth it. When she stepped out onto the stage of the New Irving she had to look good.

The thought of the theatre brought a glow, dispelling for a moment her lingering apprehension. The booking of the theatre had been done through a London agent. She would have preferred a more capacious venue, and one closer to the heart of the theatre district – ideally the

Palladium or the Dominium – but the New Irving was the best they could afford – and even that single Sunday night booking was costing a small fortune. And it was all thanks to Carrie, of course, that they had got this far. The money that Carrie had produced would also help pay for the orchestra and the rehearsal studio. And it would help pay for Kurt, too. Kurt… At the thought of him, Rosemary gave a little sigh. Perhaps when he saw her again – the new Rosemary – he wouldn't play so damned hard-to-get.

Lying back with her eyes closed, she gave herself up to the thoughts and imaginings that turned over in her brain, images shifting, falling, forming patterns like the coloured pieces in a kaleidoscope. After a time she slept.

*

Carrie didn't get to sleep until the early hours of the morning. After *Jane Eyre* she had got herself a dish of ice cream – butter pecan with maple syrup – and then read for a while. Later on she made a supper of cold chicken and salad and, with Kitty on her knee, relaxed once more before the television. It was a good night for old movies. She saw *Three Came Home*, starring Claudette Colbert (What that poor woman went through!), then Hedy Lamarr in *Strange Woman*, and finally Fred Astaire and Ginger Rogers in *The Gay Divorcee*. She loved that old movie. Particularly the way Betty Grable (so young!) sang and danced *Let's Knock Knees*. It was a number she'd learned herself and had often performed in front of the mirror.

.....THIRTEEN

In the London private hospital Rosemary gazed at herself in the small mirror the surgeon placed in her hand. A week had passed since her surgery and this morning the stitches had been removed.

'What do you think?' the surgeon asked.

'It — it's a bit of a shock.'

He smiled. 'I'm sure it is. It's bound to be.'

'My face — it feels numb — and the skin looks so tight.'

'Well,' he said, 'there's still some swelling, of course, but that will go — and the scars will soon fade. It's all healing extremely well. You wait — give it just a little time, and you're going to be very pleased.'

The next day she checked out of the hotel where she had been staying, and took a cab to Evergreens, the small health farm situated on the northern outskirts of London. Here she would remain for the next three weeks before going to join Carrie at the cottage.

*

Laden with purchases, Carrie emerged from the Fifth Avenue department store and walked to the corner. She still had a couple of items to get, but they could wait till another day. She was cold and tired, and her feet hurt.

When the lights changed she stepped off the pavement, and started towards the opposite side. She stopped so suddenly in the middle of the street that the young man behind her almost fell in his attempt to avoid colliding with her. 'Stupid ass dumb broad!' he muttered angrily, recovering and swinging on by. Carrie took no notice. She was unaware of anyone but the man who had passed by some yards to her right, crossing in the opposite direction. Turning, she hurried after him.

A few minutes later she watched as he entered a small diner. She hesitated for a moment or two, then followed him through the doorway.

She saw that he had seated himself at the rather crowded counter. And then — and it had to be fate — saw that the stool on his left was vacant. Trembling slightly, she moved to it and sat down. He gave no sign of having noticed her, but gave his order to the waitress for a coffee, then opened a paperback and began to read. Carrie ordered coffee too, and sat there sipping it and wishing that he'd look up — she had to be absolutely sure that it was he — but he remained with his head bent, intent on his book. At last, after taking a deep, nervous breath, she softly spoke.

'Michael . . .?'

He looked up, turning to her. 'Yes?' His expression showed puzzlement.

She gave a wan smile. 'Don't you know me?' Her smile grew broader. 'I wasn't absolutely certain that it was you — not at first.'

'*Carrie*,' he said after a moment. 'Carrie. My God, you of all people.'

She nodded, still smiling. 'Yes, it's me all right.'

'Oh, my God,' he said. 'Carrie.' He shook his head in disbelief.

'What a surprise, eh?'

'I'll say.' He gave a little smile. 'It — it's been a hell of a long time.'

'Yes — it certainly has.'

'Imagine it. I can hardly believe it, seeing you here next to me, like this. It's amazing.'

'It *is* amazing, isn't it?' she agreed. He looked slightly uncomfortable, she thought — somewhat nervous, on edge.

A little silence went by, awkward.

'It — it's good to see you again,' he said.

'Yes, you too.' Another brief silence, then she glanced over his shoulder to an empty booth, way in the corner. 'Hey, why don't we go sit over there for a few minutes,' she said. 'We can talk for a bit. Have a bit of privacy.'

'Oh — okay.'

She could hear a note of doubt in his voice. Nevertheless he rose from his seat.

'We'd better order some more coffee,' she said.

'Yes, right.'

He nodded and turned to the waitress across the bar. 'Two more coffees, please.' Then he added, gesturing, 'We're moving into that booth over there.'

'Yeah, sure.' She gave a weary sigh. The world was full of people who made life difficult.

A minute later, in the comparative seclusion of the booth, Carrie asked:

'So, Michael — tell me, how have you been?'

'Oh, pretty good, I guess. And you?'

She nodded. 'Okay, I guess.' She paused. 'Quite a bit has happened, of course. Well — it's been a few years.'

'Yes, it has.' He was silent for a moment, as if searching for words, then he said, 'How's your family?'

'My family?'

'Well – your mom – she okay?'

'My mom died,' she said, looking down at her hands. 'Right after the show closed.'

'Oh, I'm sorry to hear that. And coming at a time like that, too. It must have been just awful for you.'

'Yes,' she said. 'It was tough – I don't mind admitting.'

'And your sister? Janet?'

'Janice,' she corrected him. 'She's gone too, I'm afraid. Cancer.'

'Oh, Carrie, I'm so sorry. You went through a pretty tough time.'

She gave a shrug. 'Things happen. You have to deal with them.'

'I guess so.'

In the little silence that followed she studied him, thinking how much he had altered. It was a wonder she had recognised him. The change in him was quite scary. His once slim figure now looked overweight and flabby. His hair was greying, and thinning alarmingly, and his once brilliant smile had faded along with the loss of a molar from the right side of this mouth. She thought of him as he had looked in *Save a Place for Me*, and tried to reconcile the image with his present one. It wasn't easy.

A waitress, a different one, appeared, sporting a badge saying, *Hi, there! I'm Rachel, your waitress.* Beneath it was a little yellow sun with laughing eyes and a wide, smiling mouth. Unfortunately neither the sun nor the friendly *Hi, there!*

had been designed with Rachel in mind. With a stony face she set down fresh cups of coffee. 'Anything else?' she said.

Michael looked across at Carrie. 'You want anything else?'

A moment's hesitation, then she said, 'You know, I could be really naughty and – hey, yes, why not? I'd like some – some apple pie and ice cream. Vanilla.'

'One apple pie with vanilla.' Rachel made a note on her pad and moved away.

'So,' Carrie said to Michael, 'tell me about yourself. Are you still in the business?'

'In the theatre? Oh, no.' He shook his head. 'I gave that up a long time ago. Or rather, it gave *me* up.'

'What are you doing for a living now?'

'I work for a warehouse downtown.'

'Oh…okay…'

'How about you?'

'What? Oh, I got out of the rat race too. I never did anything after *Save a Place*. That was the end of it for me. I got out of Manhattan, too. I'm living upstate now. Rockland County.' He said nothing to this, but merely nodded. Carrie said after a moment: 'I'm a kind of companion-secretary now. Or PA as the term goes. Have been for years. To Rosemary Paul. Remember her?'

'Rosemary?' His eyes widened. 'You're *working* for her?'

'Yes, I'm living with her out in Nyack. I have been since soon after the show closed.' She raised her eyebrows. 'You look so surprised.'

He nodded, staring at her. 'I – I guess I am. And you get on okay together? Well, obviously you do. You must do.'

She frowned, smiling at the same time. 'What kind of question is that? Of course we do. Why shouldn't we?'

He said nothing.

'It's been over twenty-two years,' she said. 'That speaks for itself.'

'I – I guess so.'

'Rosemary's in England right now,' she said. 'Getting ready to do a big show there – in March. I'm flying out next week to join her. It's very exciting.'

The waitress approached, set down a dish of apple pie and ice cream, then went away. Carrie picked up her fork and ate a little of the pie.

Michael watched her eat for a moment. 'How is it?' he said. 'Is it okay?'

'It's very good.' She ate in silence for some moments, then said: 'Why didn't you get in touch with me, Michael?' It was clear from his silence that her question had taken him by surprise. When he didn't answer, she said: 'I waited and waited, but after the show closed I never heard another word. There was nothing. Nothing at all.' He was silent.

'I didn't know where you were or what had happened,' she said. 'Why didn't you ever call me again?'

He gave a sigh, dropping his eyes from her gaze. 'I – I don't know.'

'You don't know? You *don't know*? There must have been a reason.'

He shrugged. 'I don't know.'

'You told me we'd be together again once you were back in Manhattan. You promised. You made all those promises to me.'

'Oh, Carrie…' He shook his head. 'It's all so long ago now.'

'What difference does that make?' she said. 'You think just because you've put it out of your mind it doesn't matter any more? You think that that excuses the way you behaved?' Now her tone had taken on a hurt, angry note. 'I waited and waited to hear from you. And you know something? There was somebody who needed me at that time. My mother was sick. But did I go to her? No, I didn't. I stayed here in New York, waiting for you to get in touch.'

'I didn't know about your mom,' he said lamely. 'How was I to know?'

'You weren't around to find out,' she said. 'But this isn't about my mom – this is about me and you.' She glared at him. 'You just didn't care, did you?'

He sighed, a little sound of desperation. 'Oh, Carrie, please. What's the point of all this? We were both very young.'

'Yes. And I must have been very green and stupid too.' She shook her head. 'I believed everything you said to me. And you knew what a terrible time I went through – with Ian Brewster being so mean and making me so miserable, and me having to leave the show like that and everything. I was depending on you.' Tears suddenly welled in her eyes and she sniffed and brushed them away. 'I loved you,' she said. 'I really loved you.'

'Carrie –'

She overrode him, her tone full of reproach. 'And *you* said you loved *me*. We made plans together, and to you they meant nothing, did they?'

'Carrie, listen, I —'

'No, *you* listen,' she said. 'I got back to New York — without a job. But at least I had you — so I thought. And having you I could cope with anything. And I waited, and waited, but nothing happened.' She clutched her fork so tightly that her knuckles showed white. 'You should have been there to help me — like you said you would be. But you weren't. It was Rosemary who had to do it.'

'Rosemary?' he said, a note of wonder in his voice. 'Rosemary?'

'Yes, she was the one who helped me. I was in a terrible state. When I ran into her after the show closed she took me in and gave me a job. If it hadn't been for her I don't know what I'd have done. She saved my life — my sanity.'

'She — she did that?' he said. 'Rosemary?'

'Yes, Rosemary. Are you losing your hearing?' After a pause, she said, her tone sharp, bitter, 'There's just one thing I'd like to know from you — and that is why you never got in touch with me again. Didn't it mean anything to you, what we had?' She gazed at him across the table, her pie and ice cream quite forgotten. 'You made me think I was special, and — ' she could hardly bring herself to say the words '— that you loved me.' She shook her head. 'But you didn't, did you?'

She waited for him to answer, watched as he waved his hands — hateful, soft, podgy, weak hands — in a gesture of helplessness. 'You didn't, did you?' she said.

He made no reply.

'Yet you knew how I felt,' she said. 'I really did love you. I really did.'

It was true. She *had* loved him. Now she hated him. Her eyes narrowed with loathing as she took in his thinning hair, the thick folds of flesh beneath his chin, the fine sprinkling of dandruff on his collar. She wondered how she could ever have felt anything for him. Now the sight of him filled her with disgust. 'You made a fool of me,' she said. Her voice was rising now. 'A complete fool.'

Michael glanced briefly about him, anxious in case they were overheard.

Reading the gesture she said, hissing the words, 'Oh, I'm embarrassing you, am I? Well, let me tell you I don't care if anybody hears me! Why should I care if you feel uncomfortable? Why should I stop to consider *your* feelings?'

'Carrie — please!' He breathed the words and reached out across the table to her in a little gesture of pleading. She snatched her hand away.

'Don't touch me.'

He shook his head. 'Oh, what's the use?' He drew back his hand, laying it over his book, shifting in his seat, as if preparing to rise.

'Don't you walk out on me,' she said through gritted teeth.

He stayed where he was. 'Carrie,' he said, 'what do you want from me?'

'Just tell me,' she said, ' — did you love me?'

She watched as he struggled, searching for an answer. 'Well — did you?'

He sighed. 'I — I thought I did.'

'Meaning that you really *didn't*, is that right?'

He said nothing.

'Did you?' she asked. 'Did you love me or not?'

'No,' he said at last. 'I — I guess not.'

Fresh, hot tears sprang to her eyes. 'No?' she said. 'Not at all?'

He looked away from her, shaking his head. 'No,' he said.

'But — but you were the only man I ever — ever slept with. The only man I've slept with in my life. And you *knew* you were the first. You knew that. And now I see it meant nothing to you.'

Over the years she had made excuses for his silence with stories that she had almost come to believe. In her eager daydreams she had seen him searching Manhattan for her, or imagining him involved in some dreadful accident — the way it had happened to Deborah Kerr in *An Affair to Remember*. But he'd had no such noble excuse. His silence, his heartlessness, had stemmed simply from the fact that he didn't love her, had never loved her.

'You were the first, the only one,' she said. 'That's a very special, precious gift that a woman can bestow on a man.'

He gave a little groan. 'Oh, for God's sake, Carrie,' he said, 'I'm sorry. I'm really sorry.'

'He's sorry,' she said. Then in the phony voice of some cod announcer: 'You hear that, folks? He says he's sorry. That's nice to hear, isn't it.'

'I *am*,' he said. 'Believe me, Carrie, I really am. But — but, you know, we were young. I was young. I made mistakes. Stupid mistakes. I didn't mean to hurt you. I'm so sorry I did.'

She looked at him coolly across the table. Silent for a

moment, then she said, 'This snivelling, this whining — it isn't becoming.'

'Oh, for Heaven's sake,' he said, 'I don't know what to say. I told you, I'm sorry. Can't you forgive me?'

She gazed at him a moment longer, then, clutching the fork in her fist, she raised her hand and plunged it down with all her force. He gave an agonised yelp of pain and horror and looked down round-eyed at the fork embedded in the back of his hand, the blood springing, welling up around the tines.

'We don't do forgiveness,' she said.

Picking up her packages, she rose from her seat. 'Don't get up,' she said flatly. 'And next time the coffee's on me.'

Turning, without a backward glance, she walked away.

......FOURTEEN

Still damp from the shower, Carrie padded along the landing to the telephone in her room and lifted the receiver.

'Hello…?'

'Hi. Is that you, Carrie?'

It was Kurt. Immediately becoming aware of her nakedness she clutched her bathrobe closer. 'Yes, it is…'

'Have you heard how Rosemary's getting along?'

'Yes, I heard from her just this morning. She called from London.'

'Good. How is she?'

'Fine. She's very well. She's having a rest at a health farm right now. She'll be joining me once I'm over there in England.'

'When are you going?'

'In two days. Wednesday. I'm all packed. I'm going straight to the cottage we've rented.'

'I must get the address from you. I have a few things to send her. Some new arrangements and a new song I've been working on.'

'I'll send you an email today – all the details.'

'Thanks a lot. That'll be great. Are you looking forward to going?'

'Oh, yes. It'll be so exciting. I've never been to England. And I can't wait to see Rosemary again. I miss her so much.

I'll be so glad when we're together again. I'm not used to being here on my own.'

'You have no family nearby?'

'No. Rosemary's my only family now.'

'Oh, right. Well, you're very lucky – the both of you – with the friendship you have. It must be good to know there's always somebody fighting your corner. I reckon Rosemary's going to need all the support she can get – a time like this.'

'I guess so. Oh, I so want it to go right, Kurt. It's got to work out for her. It's just got to.'

'Well, with you along, I'm sure it will.'

'Well, I do what I can.' She sighed. 'I can't wait for Wednesday to get here.'

*

Standing at the window of her room at Evergreens, Rosemary gazed out over the shrubbery and lawns of the formal gardens. Most of the other residents of the house would be downstairs in the lounge, she supposed. She had no desire to mix with them. If everything went to schedule, Carrie would be flying in and arriving at the cottage today, so there ought to be a phone call from her pretty soon. She sighed with pleasure at the thought, though there was still the sobering knowledge that she had two weeks to go before she'd be out of this place. Two weeks of no smoking, no alcohol, no meat, no sugar – no anything that might possibly make life bearable. And with nothing to do but take walks in the fresh air, watch television, use her iPad, study her songs (in silence, of course), read, or talk to the other residents, she felt sometimes she might just go off her head. If she could only have a cigarette, and a drink . . .

Interrupting her thoughts came the ringing of the telephone. She picked up the receiver and a moment later heard the reassuringly familiar tones of Carrie's voice.

'Hi, Rosie!' Carrie couldn't keep the sound of excitement out of her voice.

'Hello, darling. I was just thinking about you.'

'How are you?'

'Well — apart from going out of my tiny mind with boredom. Other than that I'm okay. Are you calling from the cottage?'

'Yes — on my cellphone. There's no landline telephone connected here yet.'

'That sounds like the England I used to know.'

'But I hope we'll have it installed by the time you get here. I told the phone company it's essential.'

'It certainly is.' Rosemary gave a groan. 'I don't mind telling you this place is purgatory. I don't know how I'm going to stand another two weeks of it.'

'You will,' Carrie said. 'You just hang in there.'

*

After shopping for groceries, Carrie headed back to the cottage in Holly Lane. The hired Corolla moved like a dream, though she wondered whether she'd ever get used to driving on the left side of the road. Still, the traffic around here was light, and, she assured herself, she'd be fine after a little more experience.

Placed conveniently for the M4 motorway, the village of Ashton Heath was situated at the foot of the Chilterns.

On first entering the village after the drive from the airport, Carrie had been captivated by its appearance. Even on a cold, dreary winter's afternoon it had held a charm that surprised her. It owned not only a village green, but a pond with ducks. And there too was a small, quaint village school.

The cottage, Lavender Thatch, had once been two adjoining farm cottages, but with careful development had become a single, more spacious dwelling. Carrie had loved it from the moment she had seen it, and had lost no time in getting to work, cleaning and polishing. The place was fully furnished — even down to the piano that had been brought in and newly tuned. It had only needed a woman's touch, and she was an expert there.

*

At Evergreens, Rosemary stood before the mirror looking at the slim figure reflected there, and in spite of the hell she had suffered at the place, she had to admit that it had been worth it. Her body looked almost youthful again. The flabby roll around her midriff had gone and she stood slim and straight as a girl. In addition, the scars on her face were fading more with every day. No lines, no wrinkles anywhere. And who said botox and collagen weren't blessings from God. The only thing she needed now, she thought as she gazed at the dull roots of her hair, was a visit to a good hairdresser. But she'd get that fixed soon — on her first day out. She'd do some shopping, too. Just four days to go.

*

Wrapped warmly against the February wind, Carrie once again wandered over the wide area of the cottage garden at the rear of the building. It would be beautiful in summer, with the trees in leaf and the flowers making a blaze of colour. Even now delicate snowdrops were nodding their heads alongside the mauve and yellow crocuses. She had the feeling that she belonged. In a warm, sunlit vision she saw herself sitting in the garden, flowers and birdsong all around her. And why not? There was no reason why they shouldn't return here from time to time. She'd have to talk to Rosie about it.

Briefly, she found her thoughts returning to the house on the Hudson, now all locked up and being watched over by a kindly neighbour who would keep an eye on the place and get in touch should the need arise. Carrie realised that she didn't really miss the house. She would be quite happy here, she thought. A memory of the cat came back to her. Poor Kitty – he would be missing her. But the same kindly neighbour had promised to look after him. He wouldn't starve.

*

That evening she made herself comfortable in front of the television. She had been delighted to discover that quite a few old American movies were shown on the English networks – and now, in her comfortable fireside chair with its rose-patterned cover, she sat watching *Leave Her to Heaven*. It was a wonderful film. And that Gene Tierney character was something else. Particularly that scene on the lake when she sat in the dinghy waiting for the boy to drown – and all in silence; not a note of background music to detract from the drama. Oh, but how could anyone be so cruel?

The film was coming to its climax when the knock sounded at the door. Her first reaction was one of annoyance at being disturbed at such a critical moment. Her second was one of fear. Who on earth knew she was here? Memories of New York muggings and burglaries came rushing back. Her hand shaking a little, she took up the poker from the fireplace and moved stealthily out into the narrow hall. The knock came again, followed by a voice.

'Hello? Is there anyone in?'

A look of relief broke across her features as she recognised the voice. In another moment she had the door open.

'Kurt — what are you doing here?'

His smile was laconic. 'I was invited, or have you forgotten?'

'But — we weren't expecting you till next week. Rosemary's still away. I'm on my own. She's not due to get here till tomorrow.'

He smiled. 'Does that mean you're going to send me away?'

'What? No, of course not.' She gave a little laugh. 'Come on in.'

'Okay — just let me go pay off the cab.'

Carrie waited while he paid the cab-driver, and the vehicle set off back down the drive, then she stood aside as Kurt picked up his two bags and stepped into the hall. She indicated a spot for them, then led the way into the living room. A moment later the television was clicked off.

'Aw, I spoiled your movie for you,' Kurt said.

'Oh, no, that doesn't matter,' Carrie said. She felt a little shy in his presence. 'Sit down. You'd probably like a drink, would you?'

'Thanks.' He took a seat on the sofa. 'Could you manage a vodka-tonic maybe?'

'Yes, we can do that.' She went away to the kitchen and returned a couple of minutes later with his drink. He thanked her, took a sip, gave an appreciative nod and looked around him.

'Carrie, this place is really nice.'

'Oh, I think so too,' she said. 'I could stay here for ever.'

'I wanted to call you when I got in, but I didn't have your cellphone number, and the operator told me there was no phone connected here at the house.'

'No, I know,' Carrie said. 'It's darned inconvenient, but they assure me it'll be all done next week.'

He nodded, gave a sigh of pleasure and leaned back, stretching out his long legs. 'God, that's better,' he said. 'I came here straight from the airport, and let me tell you, it's so good to relax after all that travelling.'

*

Rosemary boarded the train, found a suitable compartment, deposited her bags and sat down. She was alone apart from an elderly man who sat in the far corner, absorbed in his newspaper. In her own corner seat she snuggled down. She had left Evergreens a day earlier than scheduled. Faced with breakfast that morning, she had suddenly decided that she couldn't take another day of it. And what the hell, one day wasn't going to make any difference.

The train was moving. Easing off her shoes, she drew her feet up beneath her on the seat. Her shoes were new, as were her dress and coat. All bought that day in one wonderful shopping spree in the West End. She had been to a hairdresser, too. From her purse she took a small mirror and looked into it, admiring the soft, blonde waves and her perfectly made-up face. Silently she urged the train to go faster; she was on her way at last, and impatient for progress.

In the warm glow of her newfound confidence she pictured ahead the comfort of the cottage and Carrie's welcome. Behind her – and growing more distant with every second – lay the clinic and the frustrating boredom of the health farm. Even further away was the house on the Hudson.

For the tenth time she went over her plans for the weeks ahead. As soon as Kurt arrived he would get together the musicians for the orchestra, and she could start rehearsing with them. In the meantime she and Carrie must get on with the publicity, arrange some press interviews and book time with a good photographer. She had no fear of the camera now.

In the window-glass, darkly, she saw a young-looking woman reflected, slim, almost beautiful. She smiled at her, and the woman in the glass smiled back.

*

Michael Mitchell, ignoring the work on his desk, reread the letter he had just written. Then, lips pursed, his eyes moved from the letter to the hand that held it. Although the dressing had been removed, the evidence of Carrie's vengeance – the scars from the fork – was clearly visible.

When he had folded the letter he enclosed inside it a photograph. On an envelope he wrote the address of the house in Nyack, the house where he had visited Rosemary on the evening of her party. Then, with a final glance at the wound on his hand, he licked the envelope's flap and pressed it down. If revenge and humiliation was the name of the game, then two could play as well as one.

......FIFTEEN

A chill wind was blowing from the hills, but inside the cottage it was warm.

The soft glow of the lamps was complemented by the flames of the fire that crackled in the hearth. Standing by the piano, Carrie watched as Kurt added another log to the blaze and pushed it into place with the tip of the coal shovel. Earlier she had prepared dinner for the two of them, after which she had made coffee. They had spoken very little of the forthcoming concert, and as for Rosemary's dismissal of Douglas, no mention of it was made; it was as if the subject was consciously avoided. Their conversation staying on safer ground, they spoke of their journeys from New York, and the general horrors and inconveniences of aircraft travel in the present day. Kurt spoke of London, with which he was familiar, and Carrie of her time so far in the little Berkshire village.

As Kurt replaced the shovel in the hearth, Carrie picked up a file of papers from the top of the piano. 'The new material you sent,' she said, 'it all got here safely, you'll be glad to know.' She opened the file and took out some music manuscript paper. 'And these two songs you've written for Rosie — I've had a look at them. She's going to be crazy about them.' She held out the written score of one of the songs. 'This one — 'Am I Home?', she said, 'you wrote it for Rosemary's opening number, right?'

'That was the idea.'

'It's perfect. Just perfect. I'd love to hear it.'

'What, now?

'Oh, yes. Please.'

He chuckled. 'God, I'm no singer. Besides, I think I've had a bit too much to drink. Why don't *you* have a go at it? You couldn't do any worse.'

'Oh, no...' she demurred, 'I can't, really.'

'Sure you can,' he said. 'Come on.'

She shook her head. 'No, really. I don't sing any more. I used to, but not any more. You sing it – please, Kurt...'

'Okay,' he said with a sigh, 'but don't say you weren't warned.' He drained his glass and moved to the piano. As he sat on the bench, Carrie said, 'Oh, and let me record it, d'you mind?'

'What?'

'You don't mind, do you?' she said. 'I have this little cassette recorder here. It's out of the ark, but it does the job.' As she spoke she placed the recorder on the table beside the piano, checked the tape inside and then pressed the record button. 'There we go.'

Kurt gave a nod. Putting his hands to the keys, he played the opening chords and began to sing.

*

'Here we are, ma'am.' With his words the driver brought the cab to a halt at the entrance to the driveway. 'This be okay?' he said. 'Or I can pull in if you want.'

'No, it's fine. I can manage.' Rosemary opened the door and got out. As the man deposited her bags beside the gatepost she counted out the fare.

'You want some help with your things?' he asked.

'No, I'll be okay.' She had seen that there was a light in the cottage window. After paying him she closed her purse and picked up her bags. Then, while the cab made off into the night, she started up the drive. Everything of the scene about her was strange, and she hurried through the cold wind towards the porch. Reaching it, she put down her bags and tried the door handle. To her relief the door swung open easily and silently.

Stepping gingerly into the gloom of the little hall, she was met by the sound of a piano and a man's voice, singing. It was coming from the room on her right, the door to which was a few inches ajar. She was about to push the door open when the music came to a stop. Then came the voice again, and now it was speaking her name.

'So,' said the voice, 'what time are you expecting Rosemary tomorrow?'

It was Kurt's voice. Her action frozen, hand arrested as it reached out to the door, she stood still, listening. Then came Carrie's voice: 'Sometime in the afternoon, I guess. She'll let me know.'

'You sure it's okay for me to stay over?'

'Oh, of course. She'd want you to.'

Creeping forward a step, Rosemary peered through the gap into the softly-lit room. She could see the two of them, Carrie standing beside the piano, Kurt sitting on the bench. With their backs to the door the two were unaware of her presence.

'Oh, Kurt,' Carrie said, 'Rosemary's going to be so pleased to see you. And now you're here we can really get on with things. And there's no time to lose – as she keeps reminding me.'

'Well, she's right,' Kurt said with an ironic smile. Then he added in a more sombre tone, 'And she did everything without Douglas, is that right?'

'Yes – that's right.'

'Amazing.'

'Just goes to show,' Carrie said, 'what you can do if you put your mind to it.'

'Right,' he said. 'Though I don't mind telling you, it came as a bit of a shock – her showing him the door the way she did. I wasn't prepared for that. And I know damn well Doug wasn't. That showed me a side of Rosemary I didn't know.' He sighed. 'Anyway, it's water under the bridge now, I guess.' He paused. 'Who did she get, by the way, to replace him? Am I allowed to ask?'

'What?'

'To back her. Who did she get to back her?'

'She's never told you?' Carrie sounded surprised.

'Not a word. And Doug sure as hell doesn't know. He couldn't even make a guess. I know he'd pretty well covered the field. But try as he might, he couldn't find anybody to put up the money. So, who's done it? Doug'll be fascinated to know.'

After a moment's hesitation Carrie said: 'We did.'

'What?'

'*We* did. *We've* put up the money.'

'You're telling me *you* did it?' Kurt's tone was incredulous.

'Yes.'

'Rosemary's put up her own money?'

'Well – not exactly,' Carrie said. '*I* did it. It's me.'

'You? Carrie, you're telling me *you're* staking her in this? *You've* put up the money for it all?'

'That's right.'

'Well, what do you know!' He gave a short laugh. 'You're a dark horse, you are. So you're paying for it all – the theatre, me, the publicity, the band – everything. *Everything?*'

'Yes – *everything*. And we're hoping to get the show recorded, too.'

'My God.' He gave a little whistle. 'Well, I just hope you know what you're doing.'

'Yes,' she said quickly, 'of course we do.'

'I'm sorry,' he said, 'no offence. It's just come as a bit of a surprise.'

'Listen,' she said, 'it's not the first time it's been done, you know. There've been those singers who've hired Carnegie Hall. And Rosie was telling me about a British singer who did it here – way back in the early seventies. Apparently she hired the London Palladium, all on her own, and it was packed to the rafters, the seats selling out within hours. It can be done. And we're going to do it too.'

'Well – I wish you luck.' He got up, stepped to the coffee table and poured more brandy. He took a swallow from the glass, then said, 'Yeah, I wish you luck. Truly I do. And you're certainly gonna need it. I just hope to God you're not throwing your money away.'

'No, Kurt,' she said evenly, 'I am not throwing my money away.'

'Good.' He gave a chuckle. 'But what the hell, maybe you've got so much it doesn't matter.'

'I'm not sure what you're saying,' she said, her tone now a little cold. 'What are you afraid of – that you won't get paid? Because I promise you will.'

He nodded. 'Well – thank you. I'm glad to have your reassurance.'

'Fine, so just don't worry about it, okay?'

'I'll try not to,' he said. 'But I do have to wonder if you know what you're getting into here. Do you? Do you have any idea?'

'Of course,' she said at once.

'That's good,' he said. 'Because this is not all about Rosemary's career, you know.'

'What does that mean?'

'I mean that I have a stake in this too. And I'm not just talking about getting paid. I have a career of my own, in case anyone hadn't noticed.'

Carrie frowned. 'I don't know what you're saying.'

'I'm saying that I don't want this to be some goddamn fiasco – some show put together by a bunch of amateurs.'

'Don't worry about it, Kurt.' Carrie's tone was clipped. 'I told you – it's all going to be fine. We're determined to get it right.'

He nodded. 'I just wonder if you know what you're getting into. I mean – Carrie, this is the real world, you know. I'm guessing you've been protected from it for a long time, the two of you hiding away in that house on the Hudson. But things have been happening outside there. The entertainment business isn't the way it was. It's not some goddamn little cottage industry. It's not some deal based on sentimental memories and hearts and flowers. It's about money. *Money*. And that comes from success. There's no room in the business for anyone who can't cut it. The competition is fiercer than it ever was. When people pay top dollar they expect the best.' He spread his hands, sighed. 'Oh, listen, I know how it is – you and Rosemary have been telling yourself that this is the start of something new and wonderful. But let me tell you – I don't think it's the start of *anything*.'

'Well, I've got news for you,' she said. 'We've come this far and nobody's going to spoil it. You understand? *Nobody*.'

'No, right,' he said smoothly, 'Rosemary can do that on her own, without any help.'

A moment of silence, then Carrie said, 'What do you mean by that?'

'What? Never mind. Forget it.' He laughed. 'The wine and the brandy – makes my tongue run away with me.'

'What did you mean?' Carrie insisted. 'Tell me.'

'Aw, come on, Carrie,' he said, 'let's not make a big deal out of it.'

'Tell me,' she said. 'What did you mean, that she'll spoil it on her own?'

'Oh, for Christ's sake,' he said, 'you know damn well what I mean. You don't need me to spell it out.'

'Well,' she said, 'quite obviously I do. So tell me – please. What did you mean? Are – are you saying there's a possibility that she might – might fail?'

'*Might? Might* fail?' He shook his head in a gesture of wonder. 'Carrie – you two – you seem to be living in cloud cuckoo land. You need to wake up and smell the coffee before it's too late. Rosemary hasn't got a chance.'

Carrie looked at him in silence for a moment, then said, 'Do you really mean that, Kurt? Or is it just the brandy talking.' She paused. 'I'd like to think it's the brandy.'

'Well, yeah,' he said, 'I might have had one too many, but that doesn't mean I've lost all my reason.'

She was gazing at him in wonder now. 'But — why shouldn't she succeed? She's got that album of her old songs coming out, and we're starting to get some good publicity.'

'Yeah, but she's got no new record out, has she?' he said. 'There's no real PR. And a few senior citizens turning out for her isn't gonna spell success.'

'But — but she was so well known here.'

'Yeah, right — but she was never the biggest name. She was no Dusty Springfield, was she? And in any case, the success she had was years ago. You have to face it — she's not the same.'

'Not the same?'

'I mean she's not that same young woman who left England for America. Okay, she had a few hit records behind her then, but her career didn't last, did it? She dropped out of the picture. And when did she last do anything — like make a record or do any cabaret dates? Face it, she's been way off the radar for far too long. And she hasn't been back here to England in years. For God's sake, Carrie, times change. Fashions fade. What was she — twenty-something when she left for the States? Well, she's not gonna be twenty-something when she gets up before that orchestra in a few weeks' time.'

'Well, you listen to me,' Carrie said. 'Rosemary's going to look great. She's been to the health farm and stuff, and – and other things, and – she's going to look just wonderful.'

'Oh, Carrie.' He gave a little groan. 'Get wise. It's not just the way she *looks*. It's the way she *sounds*.' Then, seeing Carrie's eyes widen in horror, he said, 'Christ almighty, you've got ears. You know what she sounds like. Oh, I guess she was okay once, but like I said, time marches on. Maybe if she'd looked after her voice better – like some of those other girls – Dionne Warwick, Streisand – people like that – it'd be different. I'm sorry to say it, but her time is past.'

'I don't believe you're saying this,' Carrie said, eyes wide. 'You – you've been working with her all this time. You've been encouraging her, helping her to believe that she's all set for a glorious comeback. How could you do that?'

'Oh, come on, for Christ's sake,' he said, 'I've just been doing a job.'

'Yes – and taking your fee!'

'Damn right, taking my fee. When somebody's paying you well, you don't turn round and tell them they're no damn good. You don't kill the goose that's laying the golden eggs.' Taking in the look on her face, he added quickly, 'Oh, I know how that must sound. But I wasn't taken on to sit in judgment. No way. And at the start I believed in the dream as well. But now? No.' He sighed, gave a weary shake of his head. 'You know what? I've had to get wise over the past couple of months, and I tell you, if I'd been smart enough at the beginning I'd never have come on board. I'll be blunt – I'm not even sure I want to be a part of this any longer. Fee or no fee. I have a reputation to think about – and if this ends up as a fucking joke it's not going to do me any good.'

'A *joke*?' Carrie said. She put a hand to her mouth. 'Do you realise what you're saying?'

'Oh, for Christ's sake, Carrie,' he said, 'it's about time you faced up to reality.'

'What do you mean?'

'You're too close to her,' he said. 'You can't see.'

'I can't see? What can't I see?'

'Listen to you,' he said. 'I'm not getting through to you at all. I'm talking about the truth. And the truth is that I'm scared stiff that we're heading for a total – total catastrophe. And I should never have got into it.'

Carrie was staring at him, her mouth open. He shook his head. 'I'm sorry,' he said, 'I've hurt your feelings. I didn't mean to. You love her, I know.'

'I *do*,' she said. 'And I *know* her – and I know what she's capable of. And she's going to be terrific.'

'Carrie,' he said with a sigh, 'it's like I said, you can't *see*. You're too close to her to be able to judge.' He shrugged. 'But that's love for you, I guess. Like the old saying goes, love is blind.' He gave a humourless little laugh. 'And as I've come to realise now, sometimes it's fucking deaf as well.'

As Carrie gasped in outrage, he added, 'Face it, Carrie, Rosemary's a has-been. A total has-been. And she'll never be anything else.'

In the brief hushed silence that followed, the echo of his words seemed to hang in the air. And then suddenly, shattering the quiet, there came a loud cry, part groan, part scream. In the same moment the door was violently flung wide and Rosemary burst into the room. Startled and amazed at her sudden and unexpected presence, Kurt and Carrie, open-mouthed, remained fixed to the spot. Then Kurt, the shock clear on his face, sprang to his feet.

'Well,' he said, forcing a weak smile, 'the shit's hit the fan this time.'

The smile was all that Rosemary needed. With a cry of rage she dashed forward and, whirling, hands grasping, snatched up the coal shovel from the hearth.

'You son of a bitch,' she screamed, 'I'll fucking kill you.'

With her words she swung at him, and although he raised his hands in a desperate attempt to protect himself, he was too late. In a moment the sharp edge of the shovel had caught him hard across the throat.

Carrie shrieked, blood spattering onto her shoulder, while Kurt gave a moan, his features contorted in shock and sudden pain. He put a hand up to his neck, clawing at the deep wound there, gasping. 'Oh, God!' he cried. 'Oh, my God.' He stood there clutching at his neck, the blood pulsing through his fingers while Rosemary, silent, nostrils flaring, stood facing him, the shovel in her hand. After staggering two or three steps, Kurt fell heavily to his knees. Tears were pouring down his cheeks. 'What have you done?' he cried out, his voice gurgling through the blood. 'What have you done? Jesus, help me! Help me!' Struggling to his feet again, he turned to Rosemary, holding out a red-stained hand in supplication. She flinched, let the shovel fall and backed away.

The blood sprang from Kurt's throat with a pumping action, bubbling out from between his clutching fingers. The two women watched as he spun and lurched across the room, snatching at the air. His mouth opened again, and again, but now no words came. Then, with a strangled, gurgling whimper, he reeled and crashed to the carpet. Neither of the women moved.

He lay there, coughing, choking on his blood. Summoning her courage, Carrie went closer to him. His body twitched, a foot kicked out and fell back, his head jerked, straining back on his bloodied neck. He lay face up, his eyes open and rolled back in his head. In silence Carrie stood gazing down, listening as his faint breathing faltered and eventually shuddered to a halt. The blood was streaming from his neck, but the flow was growing weaker. At last, after long, long minutes, she spoke.

'Rosie,' she murmured, 'he's dead.'

She remained standing there for some moments, then turned away from the terrible sight.

Going up to her bedroom she took a blanket from a cupboard, then, returning to the sitting room, laid it over Kurt's body.

She turned then to Rosemary. 'Rosie…'

Rosemary had not stirred, had not spoken. Now, at Carrie's words she looked at her and said dully, 'I killed him, Carrie. He's dead. I killed him.'

'Don't,' Carrie said gently.

'I killed him.'

'Rosie, stop it. Please.' Carried reached out and touched her shoulder. 'Come on. Come and sit down.'

With Carrie's hand on her arm, Rosemary allowed herself to be led to the sofa where she sat down. Carrie sat beside her, an arm around her shoulder. As they sat, there came into the quiet a sharp click and Carrie realised that it was the cassette player, coming to the end of the tape and switching off.

She didn't move. Neither moved. There they remained, the two women, huddled together while the fire died, and the room grew cold.

At last the long night passed and eventually there came the dawn.

.....SIXTEEN

Within the acre of land belonging to the cottage was a small copse. In the summertime it would be bright with leaves and overgrown with ferns and brambles; now it stood bare and cold, awaiting the first touch of spring. It was to this untrodden area that the women carried Kurt's body, hammocked in the bloodstained blanket. It was no easy task, and they had to stop every few minutes to rest. Eventually they laid the load down on the bare earth beneath a slender silver birch.

Nearby was a shallow ditch where the earth was a little softer. This, Carrie thought, would be the best spot. In an outhouse she had found a spade and a garden fork and, armed with the implements, she and Rosemary got to work. They had stripped Kurt's body of every vestige of clothing, and now, wrapped only in the blanket, it lay on the ground while the women dug at the soil. They worked wordlessly, the only sounds coming from their laboured breathing and the tools as they struck at the earth. When, after a long time, the hollow was deep enough, they dragged Kurt's body to its edge and rolled him into it. With the action his body became partly uncovered and, head and shoulders exposed, he lay staring dully up at the sky. Seeing the dead, sightless eyes, Rosemary gave a little moan and turned away. Carrie gazed down at the sight for a moment longer, then took up the spade again.

When Kurt's body was completely covered with earth, Carrie spread leaves and bits of shrubbery around in an attempt to disguise the signs of their digging.

*

In the kitchen Carrie made tea and toast. Rosemary drank the tea, but she would not eat. Later, Carrie led her up to the main bedroom, and there helped her to undress. After seeing her into bed, she held out to her a glass of water and two tablets. 'Take these,' she said. 'You need to sleep.' She watched while Rosemary swallowed the tablets. 'Good,' she said. 'I'll come back in a little while and see how you are.'

'Please,' Rosemary said, 'don't leave me.'

'All right.' Carrie sat down on the edge of the bed and took Rosemary's cold hand in hers.

She remained there until Rosemary drifted off to sleep. Then, gently, she extricated her hand and stood up. Looking down at Rosemary's face she noted the smooth, unlined brow, the strangely youthful appearance. Turning, she crept away.

Downstairs, she set to work, cleaning up. It was a long job. At one point in her task she came upon the cassette player that she had used to record Kurt's song. She switched it on, rewound the tape to the beginning and set it to play. And there was Kurt at the piano, singing his song, the song he had written for Rosemary. 'Am I home,' he sang. 'Have I come home?' Afterwards came their conversation, his ugly words about Rosemary. And then there came the loud and violent sounds of Rosemary's unexpected entrance, the shrieking, her voice crying out. There too were Kurt's dying moans.

And later, into the quiet was Rosemary's voice: 'I killed him, Carrie. He's dead. I killed him.' At once Carrie jabbed at the off button and cut the horror into silence.

*

When Rosemary came downstairs late the next morning she could see no sign of the catastrophe of the night before. The carpet had been sponged, mopped and sponged again. No visible traces of blood remained.

'Come and sit down,' Carrie said. 'I'll get us something to eat.'

Rosemary shook her head. 'I'm not hungry.'

'You must eat, Rosie. We have to carry on. We've got no choice.'

'I can't.'

'Yes, you can. Of course you can. It's the only way.'

'*How?*' Rosemary's eyes were pleading. 'After what happened in this room?'

'Listen,' Carrie said, 'no one knows Kurt was here. Except the cab driver — and he's not to know that Kurt didn't leave. In any case, no one's going to come here checking up on him. He came direct from the airport. And if someone did trace him here we'd just say that he went away. We'll have to be prepared with a story and stick to it. No one will be able to prove otherwise.'

Rosemary pointed out beyond the window in the direction of the copse. 'But with that out there...'

'Why should anyone start looking for him here?' Carrie said. 'They'd have to be very suspicious, and there's no reason they should be. Don't worry.'

Rosemary was silent. 'Everything's going to be all right,' Carrie said. 'I won't let anything happen to you. No one's going to hurt you, believe me.'

......SEVENTEEN

'Check these,' Carrie said. 'See that everything you need is there.'

Sitting by the fireside, Rosemary eyed the sheaf of papers that Carrie had put into her hands.

'Kurt's orchestral arrangements,' Rosemary observed dully.

'That's right,' Carrie said. 'What we have to do now is find another musical director.'

Rosemary's eyebrows lifted. 'Are you serious? It's finished.'

'Finished?' Carrie shook her head emphatically. 'It is not finished. We've come too far to stop now.'

'But Kurt,' Rosemary said, 'he said I was no good. He spoke as if — as if I was a joke. He called me a has-been.'

'Rosie,' Carrie said, 'the man was only in it for what he could get. But he didn't know you. *I do.* He was no judge of your talent.' She paused, then added in a softer tone, 'Listen, we've got to get over what's happened, and look to the future. We've booked the theatre — and okay, it may not be the best venue in town, but it will do. You just wait — everything's going to be all right. But till then you must — we've got to get through this time. And believe me, we'll do that too.'

*

Later, Carrie gathered together the contents of Kurt's two suitcases, and in the yard made a bonfire of them. Rosemary, seeing the smoke, came out and stood beside her, watching in silence as the fire burned. Earlier, Carrie had gone through Kurt's pockets, stripping them of everything. And now the flames were devouring it all — the plane ticket, the wallet, the passport, the shoes, the socks, the crisp shirts and the Armani suits.

'We'll get a newspaper tomorrow,' Carrie said, her eyes on the dying fire. 'See if those ads are in. Bookings open on Saturday. And we must find a good photographer. There isn't long to go now. Only a month. We've no time to waste.'

'Oh, Carrie,' Rosemary said, 'how can we go on with this?

'We *can*.' Carrie turned to her. 'Listen to me — not long from now there are going to be hundreds of people lining up, booking seats for the chance to see you. You can't let them down. We're not going to give in now, just because of what Kurt said.' She paused. 'Or is that what you want?'

Rosemary didn't answer.

'Is it?' Carrie said.

'No. No, I guess not.'

Carrie gave a nod, then said softly, 'You'll get cold standing out here, Rosie. And you have to look after your voice. You can't afford to get a chill. Why don't you go back in the house?'

After Rosemary had left her side, Carrie remained until the fire had burned out, then poked at the embers with a stick until she was sure there was nothing left that was recognisable. Giving a last prod at the fading ashes, she stepped back. 'And that's the end of you,' she said.

*

That evening, in an effort to take their minds from the atmosphere of horror that hung about the house, Carrie turned on the television. But it was soon apparent that nothing happening on the flickering screen was registering in Rosemary's brain. Her dull, lacklustre eyes fixed on the picture as if she was looking right through it. She needed more time, Carrie said to herself. Unfortunately, time was a commodity in short supply.

*

The next day Carrie suggested to Rosemary that she work at some of her songs. Rosemary shook her head. 'I just — just don't feel like it right now.'

'Why don't you try?'

'I can't.'

'I see,' Carrie said. 'So everything will have been for nothing.'

'Oh, Carrie, please…'

'I let you have all the money I had, Rosie,' Carrie said. 'Every cent. And I don't think for a minute we'll get back our payment on the theatre. We can't change things. I wish we could, but we can't. We can only make the best of what we have.' She paused, watching Rosemary's tortured face. 'You didn't mean to kill him, Rosie.'

'No — but I did.'

'I know. But we've got to go forward. We can't stop now.'

Rosemary said nothing for a moment, then got up and moved to the piano. Lifting the lid she played a few chords, and began to sing, but falteringly, spiritlessly. Breaking off in the middle of a phrase, she looked round at Carrie.

'Keep going,' Carrie insisted.

'They'll throw things,' Rosemary said. 'I just keep thinking of – of what he said.'

'Forget that. Think about those people who've been buying your album. They love you, and they can't all be wrong. You can't take the word of just one man.'

Rosemary remained silent for a moment, then gave a nod. 'I'll try.'

Carrie left her then and, with the sound of the piano fading behind her, went from the house and down the garden path. Making her way to the little copse, she stood in the fading light and looked down at the spot where Kurt lay buried. She could see no obvious signs that the earth had been disturbed.

As she entered the house a moment later there came to her the sound of Rosemary singing. With a little nod of satisfaction and relief, Carrie came to a stop and stood listening. It would all be all right, she said to herself. It would.

*

Rosemary was in the kitchen making coffee, when Carrie, holding a notepad, came in. 'We've got to get busy,' Carrie said. 'Booking for the show opened on Saturday, and I just called the box office to see how tickets have been going.'

'And?'

'Not so good, I'm afraid. We need to get out and do something. We've got to see some people. Get some publicity going. We've got to get up to London.'

'When do you think we should go?' Rosemary said. Although eager to get away from the house, she dreaded the thought of going out in public. For all the horror connected with the cottage, within its walls she felt relatively safe.

'What about today?' Carrie was brisk. 'We haven't got much time left.' Her voice softened. 'I'm sorry, Rosie. I don't mean to be tough on you, but there are things to do, and we can't put them off any longer.'

'No – of course not.'

'And one of the first things,' Carrie went on, 'is to get some pictures done. I've got the numbers of a couple of photographers who are said to be very good, so we need to get that arranged as soon as possible. We've got to get some publicity working for you. Photographs, a few private interviews. If we can get an appointment with a photographer you can sort out some things to wear for the session – and we'll take them along with us. Get your hair done for the session too – you'll look fantastic.' She paused, looking at Rosemary with a judicious gaze. 'You know,' she added in a softer tone, 'I haven't told you how marvellous you look. But you do. You look really great.'

Rosemary gave the hint of a smile. With everything that had happened she had given no thought to her new appearance.

'You'll want to see about your gown for the show too,' Carrie went on. 'And we still have to find a new MD. I've been making a few enquiries there and I'll make a few more calls. We'll get done what we can today, and maybe go up again tomorrow or the next day. Whatever it takes, okay?'

*

Two hours later they left the cottage and climbed into the Corolla that was waiting in the yard. An appointment had been made for Rosemary in London with a hairdresser, and for later in the day with a photographer. Already on the back seat of the car lay the clothes she planned to wear for the photo session.

'I hope we've got everything we need,' Carrie said as she closed the car door. Then, glancing off, she added, 'Oh – here comes the mailman.'

As the village postman came cycling up the drive, Rosemary said, 'Have you been getting the mail okay? Is it all getting directed here?'

'It all seems to be coming through,' Carrie said. 'The bills too, unfortunately.' She lowered the window as the postman came to a halt at her side. 'Good morning,' she greeted him. 'You have something nice for us today?'

He smiled. 'Just two, three things, ma'am. But nice or not, I couldn't say.' He placed some envelopes in her hand and looked up at the sky. 'Will it stay fine, d'you reckon?'

'I hope so,' Carrie said. 'We're off to London.' She thanked him, and he wished them a good day, turned his bicycle and rode back out into the lane.

Carrie glanced through the items of mail. 'A couple for you and one for me,' she said. 'We'll deal with it later.' She put the envelopes in the glove compartment and turned to Rosemary. 'All set?'

Rosemary gave a hesitant nod. 'All set.'

'Good.'

The sun above was bright. Carrie turned on the ignition, and as she did so, Rosemary leaned across and kissed her lightly on the cheek.

Carrie looked at her. 'What was that for?'

'Nothing. Just that you've been so – so wonderful.'

'Oh – Rosie…'

'You have,' Rosemary said. 'And I won't let you down, I promise.'

'That's all I want to hear.' Carrie's voice was husky in reply. She gave Rosemary a smile, put the engine in gear and started the car forward. 'We'll stop somewhere nice for lunch, shall we?'

'That would be nice.'

At the end of the drive. Carrie eased the car out into the lane. 'Okay, London,' she said, 'here we come.'

......EIGHTEEN

Somehow they had missed the road to the motorway. It had been over thirty minutes since they had set out, and they should have been on it by now.

'We didn't get any satellite navigation with this car?' Rosemary asked.

'Oh, it's there somewhere,' Carrie said, 'but I'm no good at all that. I'd rather use a map. Trouble is, I left it in the house.' She shrugged. 'It doesn't matter — we'll pick up another one and we'll get some gas at the same time — or petrol as you English choose to call it over here.' She gestured off the way they had come. 'We passed a gas station a little way back. Let's try that.'

She turned the car and they set off back. Half a mile along they came to the service station and pulled in. As Carrie braked and switched off the engine Rosemary dipped into her purse and brought out her wallet holding her credit cards. 'Use whichever one you like,' she said. 'And maybe get me some aspirin or something, if they have such a thing.'

'Oh, you have a bad head?' Carrie asked.

Rosemary nodded. 'It could be better.'

'I'll see what they have.'

When Carrie had finished at the pump she made her way to the station shop and picked up a map of the local area and some paracetamol for Rosemary. After paying for it along with the fuel she returned to the car and got in.

'Hey, what say we stop off for some coffee?' she said as she handed Rosemary the packet of tablets. 'We passed a pub or inn or restaurant or something just down the road. It'll give me a chance to look at the map as well. Be a good idea to find out where the devil we are.'

'Okay, that sounds good,' Rosemary said. 'I need to go to the bathroom too.'

A couple of hundred yards back along the road they saw the pub, an old building set high above the road, standing solidly against a backdrop of trees and sky. A nearby sign directed them to a steep, narrow road leading to it. Following the sign, Carrie turned off and took the winding way up the hill. At the top she turned into the parking lot, stopped the car and switched off the motor.

'Here we are.' She smiled at Rosemary. 'Now you go on in,' she said. 'You find us a nice table, and I'll follow you in a minute. I just want to check over the map.'

'Okay, fine.'

As Rosemary moved away across the car park towards the entrance to the inn, Carrie leaned back in her seat with a sigh. The demands on her concentration, from the left-hand driving and the navigating, had made her a little tense. But that would pass. Watching as Rosemary's slim figure disappeared into the inn she felt a surge of warm affection for her. She felt truly needed now, and the call upon her reserves of strength had made her feel stronger than she had ever thought possible. Things might never again be as they had been, she was aware of that – but one thing was certain – from this time on they would be closer than ever.

From the glove compartment she took the map that she had just bought and opened it out on the passenger seat. Bending over it, she found the route to the motorway, and saw where they had gone wrong. Satisfied, she refolded the map and moved to put it back in the glove compartment. As she did so she saw the items of mail that she had put there at the start of the journey. She took them out. The one addressed to her had a New York City postmark and had been forwarded from Nyack. The envelope bore no sender's name and address. Tearing open the envelope, she took out a letter and, unfolding it, found a small photograph inside.

She looked at the photograph, puzzled, frowning. Then, after a few moments the puzzlement disappeared and horrified disbelief took its place. Fingers trembling, she smoothed out the pages of the letter.

When she had read it through she went back to the beginning and read it again — as if in some part of her mind there was a desperate hope that the second reading would somehow give the lie to the first, and all would be different. No, every word, every phrase was the same. She read it through again, and now, with their growing familiarity, the words only seemed to strike more violently at her heart.

She didn't know how long she sat there. Beyond the letter nothing moved for her through the blur of her tears; no sound was there but for her quickening breath, increasing until her despair broke through in a choking sob. Clutching the letter, she hugged herself, rocking to and fro like a child, steeped in misery.

'Carrie…?'

At the sound of her name she turned her head and saw Rosemary at the window. The next moment Rosemary was opening the passenger door and leaning in.

'Carrie.' There was concern in her face. 'What's wrong? What's the matter?'

Carrie said nothing, but sat there, tears coursing down her face.

In moments Rosemary was in the car. 'What's the matter?' she said. 'I couldn't think what was keeping you. What's wrong?' Looking at Carrie with increasing alarm and puzzlement she saw the letter clenched in her hand. 'Oh – have you had some bad news? Oh, Carrie – darling, what is it?'

Carrie didn't answer, but turned away and stared from the window.

'Carrie,' Rosemary said, 'please – tell me what's wrong.' Reaching out, she put her hand on Carrie's arm.

Carrie flinched, jerking away. 'Don't touch me,' she said.

Rosemary frowned, taken aback, baffled, her eyes wide. 'Carrie – what's the matter?'

'Just – just don't touch me.'

On the carpet near her feet Rosemary saw a small rectangle of white. She bent and picked it up, turned it over and saw that it was a photograph.

And with a shock she saw herself, so much younger, sitting at a restaurant table. Beside her, his cheek close to her cheek, sat a handsome, smiling young man, his hand clasped over hers on the tablecloth. She stared at it while recollection came flooding back. Turning, the blood colouring her cheeks, she saw that Carrie's eyes were fixed upon her.

'Carrie...' Rosemary stammered. 'Carrie, I can explain.'

'Old Cape Cod,' Carrie said. 'Does it bring back memories?' She reached out, took the photograph from Rosemary's hand and looked closely at it, taking in Michael's smiling, happy face. Her tears were drying now. After a moment she tossed the photograph into the glove compartment. 'You don't need to explain,' she said. 'It doesn't need explaining.'

'I *can* explain it,' Rosemary said. 'Please, Carrie — you must listen to me.'

'I don't think I need to listen,' Carrie said. 'Michael's letter is very explicit. He was there as well. Or have you forgotten?'

'Your letter — it's from him, is it?'

'Yes. And he's told me everything.' She paused. 'Did you have any idea what Michael meant to me? No, I guess not. He didn't mean anything to you, I'm sure. But he was someone I really wanted. And I never dreamed I'd lose him — at least not in the way I did. I wouldn't want him now. But I did then.' Another pause, for a second, then, almost as if to herself, she added, 'Maybe if I'd had him, kept him, he wouldn't have turned out the way he did.' She smiled a sharp, bitter little smile. 'I guess he just couldn't resist you, could he? Once you'd set your sights on him he didn't stand a chance. Is that the way it happened? And after all, I wasn't around to get in your way. And he *was handsome*, there's no doubt. Just perfect for you to amuse yourself with for a few weeks. Until you got tired of him. He must have been so damned weak. An easy mark for you.'

Rosemary had remained silent throughout Carrie's words. Now she gave a little groan and said pleadingly, 'Carrie – darling, all that was so long ago. And at the time I had no idea you felt so strongly about him.'

As if Rosemary hadn't spoken, Carrie said, 'There I was, moping around Manhattan, waiting for some word from him, and there he was with you – relaxing with you up on Cape Cod. Staying with you – sleeping with you. Making love to you. My God.' She shook her head. 'That's why I never saw him again – because you'd got your hooks into him. And all the thoughts I had of you at that time were such – such *warm* thoughts. I really thought you were so wonderful.'

'Carrie,' Rosemary said, 'listen, please –'

'No, *you* listen,' Carrie hissed. 'This –' she jabbed at the letter, 'is not all about Michael, and your little fling.'

'What – what do you mean?'

'What do I mean? I mean that I *know everything*.' Carrie's voice was cold with loathing. 'And I don't just mean your taking him away with you when the show closed – I mean *everything*.'

'Carrie,' Rosemary said, 'let me – let me tell you what–'

'I don't want to hear,' Carrie said. She glared at Rosemary for a second, then went on: 'Oh, when I think of what happened at rehearsal. The way you stuck up for me to Ian Brewster. And then when I decided to leave the company you were so nice to me. You came to my motel room and you comforted me. You even offered me money. D'you remember? I was so miserable and I thought no one had ever been so kind to me before in my whole life. And ever since that time, whenever I've been unhappy, or when you've been cross with me, or impatient, I've just thought about your kindness to me that time. And it always worked. I forgave you everything, always. I loved you for that – for what you did that day.' She gave a slow shake of her head. 'And all along, it was you. It was you who had me kicked out of the show.'

Rosemary sharply drew in her breath.

'Yes,' Carrie said, 'I know that, too.' She held up the letter and thrust it before Rosemary's face. 'I told you – Michael's told me everything. *Everything.*'

'Carrie…'

'You wanted me out of the show, didn't you? And you were determined that I would go.'

'Carrie…'

'It's no good denying it.' Carrie gave a slow nod. 'I didn't know at the time, of course, but Michael tells me you had a lot of money invested in the show. Is that right?'

Rosemary didn't answer.

Carrie nodded again. 'Yes. Right. So now it all makes sense to me. I was a threat to you, wasn't I? I was just too darn good. You didn't get me out because you had your eyes on Michael. Oh, no, he was just a side issue, a little fling to take your mind off things later on. No, you wanted me out because you were afraid of me. Right? My presence in the show threatened you, didn't it? That's why Brewster cut my songs. *At your orders.* You were so afraid the notices would say that the second lead was better than the star. Is that the way it was?'

'Carrie —'

Carrie ignored her, and went on, 'If I'd known at the time that you'd sunk a lot of your own money into the show I might have guessed a few things.' She sighed. 'I doubt it, though; I trusted you so completely. And of course, as you were paying the piper you had so much influence. You fixed it all up with that bastard Brewster, and then watched it all happen. You *made* it happen. You saw me there on stage, day after day, getting humiliated and torn to shreds in front of the whole company — and it was *what you wanted*. It's *exactly* what you wanted. You wanted me gone — but you couldn't take the risk of having me fired. What reason could you give? You knew if you did fire me I could have gone to the union, and you might end up getting sued. Whichever way, you'd look bad, and you didn't want that happening. Oh, no. So you made it impossible for me to stay on. It had to be *my* decision. And you made sure it was — you and Brewster.' She was silent for a moment, then, the thought suddenly coming to her, she said, 'Yes! Brewster making that pass at me, that little kiss. Oh, my God, you put him up to that, didn't you? To make it look as if he had a reason for it — his turning against me that way.' She nodded. 'I see it all.' She paused. 'Tell me — did you pay him well?'

Rosemary sat silent, one hand up to her mouth.

After a moment Carrie went on again: 'Yes, and then when we met up again, in New York, just after you'd got back from Cape Cod, we went and had coffee together. Remember? And you offered me a job.'

Rosemary bowed her head, briefly closed her eyes.

'Why did you do that?' Carrie asked. 'Was it because you felt sorry for me? Sorry, and maybe a little guilty for what you'd done? And after all it hadn't been necessary, had it? I mean, in spite of all your underhand dealings, the show bombed.' She gave a nod. 'Yes – meeting me in Manhattan that day, you felt sorry for me, didn't you? I mean, there I was – I'd lost everything that was important to me. Not only had I lost my part in *Save a Place*, but I'd lost my mother too – and I didn't even get to see her before she died. And, also, I told you I'd been dumped by Michael.'

Rosemary, sitting hunched in the seat, kept silent, her eyes lowered.

'You know,' Carrie said, '*Save a Place* was going to be my big chance. You can't imagine how hard I worked for it, or how hard I rehearsed once I knew the part was mine. I loved the part, and I loved the songs. And I would have been good. But that was the trouble. Like I said – I was *too* good. Dear, sweet Rosemary Paul. Oh, you fixed my wagon all right. I'll say. After I quit I just never – never got my bearings again somehow. It was all spoiled. I had no self-confidence any more. And it was you who did it. You.' She leaned over, her face close to Rosemary's, the tears starting in her eyes again. 'How could you do it, Rosie? How? I'd never done anything to you.' With a deep sigh she leaned back in her seat. 'And how I've worked for you since that time,' she said. 'Never ever dreaming what you'd done to me.'

Silence in the car, and then Rosemary raised her head. 'Carrie,' she said, looking imploringly at her, 'I know what happened. I don't deny it. I can't. But I didn't know you then. Maybe you can't see that as an excuse for me – but I couldn't have done it if I had *known* you. It wasn't *you* I was dealing with. You were just some girl, some actress, who was in my way. Yes – and I had to do something about it. I had so much hanging on that show.' She nodded. 'And you're right, you were too good. My God, you were brilliant. I could see it very quickly. It wasn't long before I was having second thoughts about the show, wondering what I'd got myself into. All that second-rate material. But you – you took those – those mediocre songs and made them *live*. I watched it happen. And – I couldn't take the chance of being eclipsed.'

'So, you admit it all,' Carrie said.

'Yes, but – oh, Carrie, I was sure you'd soon get over it. With all your talent it would be only a matter of time. After all, it was only that one job in your career, and you were young and starting out. I wasn't. I'd already had one career that had nosedived, and it's never easy to get back on top once you've been down. It was only later I really realised how dreadfully I'd behaved, and the harm I'd caused you.'

With tears springing into her eyes she reached out, but Carrie moved back, avoiding the contact. Rosemary's hands fell back into her lap. 'Believe me,' she said, 'if I could undo it, I would. But I can't.' She paused. 'Carrie, you've come to mean so much to me over the years. And you must know that that's true. Oh, we've had our ups and downs, but that's natural. I am aware of all you've done for me and all –'

'Yes,' Carrie broke in, 'and everything I've put up with.'

A moment of silence, then Rosemary said, 'You're all I've got now, Carrie. I've got no one else. I have no family. I have only you. Darling, listen – what's happened is in the past. I can't undo it. I can only ask you to – forgive me, and let me make it up to you. *Please*. Forgive me, Carrie. Don't hate me, please.'

Carrie looked at her with dry eyes. 'Everybody wants to be forgiven.' She glanced down at the letter in her hand, carefully folded it and then placed it in the glove compartment. 'Let's go inside,' she said. 'I'm getting cold sitting here, and I'd like that cup of coffee.'

She got out of the car, stood waiting until Rosemary had emerged, then locked the doors.

'I *will* make it up to you,' Rosemary said, pulling up the collar of her coat. 'If you give me a chance.'

'Let's go inside,' Carrie said. With her words she turned and started away.

*

The place was almost empty – the only other customers a man and woman sitting in a corner. Carrie led the way to a table beside a window. Rosemary took a seat facing her. 'I'm just having coffee,' Carrie said. 'I don't know what you want.'

Rosemary picked up the menu. 'Coffee is fine.' Glancing down the list she added tentatively, 'I see they've got chocolate mousse – one of your favourites.'

Carrie responded with a cold glance. A young waitress came over and Carrie gave their order. When the girl had gone, Rosemary said, 'I was thinking – when my show is over we don't need to rush back home, do we?'

'Don't we?' Carrie gave a measured shake of her head. 'You're unbelievable, you are. Just listen to you. You're going on as if nothing's been said, as if nothing's happened.'

'No, no,' Rosemary said quickly. 'It's not like that at all.'

'Then what are you talking about?'

'I – I was just thinking – well, it's your birthday soon, come April, and – '

'So what?'

'Well, I thought – I thought maybe we could go away some place.'

'We're already away some place. We've come to England.'

'Oh, I know, but – well, this isn't really a vacation, is it? I thought – while we're here in Europe we should take advantage of it. Perhaps take a trip to Paris, or Rome. Just for a week or so. You'd like that, wouldn't you?'

Carrie shrugged. 'Who wouldn't?'

Rosemary forced a smile. 'Shall we, then?' She paused. 'Where shall it be? Where would you like to go?'

Carrie didn't answer, but turned her head and gazed through the window at the cold landscape.

'Shall we?' Rosemary said. 'Shall we go off some place?'

'Sorry,' Carrie said, turning back to her, 'I was thinking about something else. You want to know what I was thinking about? I was thinking about my birthday.'

'What about it?'

'I shall be forty-six. I was just working it out.'

'Working it out? What do you mean?'

'The time.'

'The time?'

'Like I said, I shall be forty-six. And you know how old I was when we met? I was twenty-three. Work it out. I've been with you half my life.'

'My God, yes,' Rosemary said, 'that's true.'

'Half my life,' Carrie said. 'Twenty-three years.' She eyed Rosemary levelly. 'You took away half my life.'

'Oh, Carrie — ' Rosemary looked pleadingly across the table. 'Please — don't say such things.'

'And there's nothing you can do about that,' Carrie said. 'You can't make up for twenty-three years with a chocolate mousse and a week in Paris.'

'Carrie, please don't talk like this. Haven't these years been good years? They have. They haven't been wasted.'

Carrie gave an exaggerated shrug. 'They've been okay, I guess, for somebody who's happy to settle for a humdrum existence. They've been okay if you don't mind being an appendage to somebody else's life.'

'Don't. Oh, don't say that.'

'It's true. I could have led my *own* life. Instead, I've been doing what *you* wanted, behaving the way *you* wanted me to behave.'

'Oh, but — but things will be different from now on, I promise you.'

'If it hadn't been for you,' Carrie said, 'I'd be a successful actress. Maybe happily married. Have children.'

Silence fell between them. Several more customers came in and took seats at tables and at the bar. The waitress came and placed before Rosemary and Carrie a small tray bearing cups of coffee.

When the waitress had gone, Rosemary took a sip from

her cup then said hesitantly: 'You didn't say — whether you'd like to go away somewhere.'

'You really are astonishing,' Carrie said. 'You're still going on as if nothing has happened. As if you haven't heard a word I've said.'

'Oh, of course I have.' Rosemary looked distraught, near to tears again. 'I know I'm clumsy, but I'm just — just trying to — to put things right. To make things better.' She shook her head. 'I want to do something to please you. I just thought that a little trip would make a change — a pleasant little change.'

'A pleasant little change?' Carrie said. 'Wow, that's rich. But I wouldn't worry about that. I think you'll find there's going to be a whole heap of changes made. But I don't know about them being exactly pleasant.' She picked up her cup, took a sip and with a grimace set it back down. 'I can't drink this stuff.' The bill was on the tray, and glancing down at it she took a note from her purse and put it on the tray. Rosemary, pushing her coffee cup aside, picked up her gloves and bag. At once Carrie held out a restraining hand. 'Stay where you are for a minute.

'Oh, I thought you wanted to go.'

'Don't worry, we'll be going.'

Rosemary looked at her watch. 'Well, if we're going to London we —'

'Stay where you are,' Carrie repeated. Then she added coolly, 'We're not going to London.'

Rosemary stared at her, as if trying to read the expression in the cold eyes. 'What do you mean? You want to leave it till tomorrow? I don't mind.'

'You're not going to London today,' Carrie said. 'And you're not going to London tomorrow either. You're not going to London – period.'

'Huh?' Rosemary looked at her in bewilderment. 'Carrie, what are you talking about? Come on now. Don't you think this has gone far enough?'.

'Yes, it has.' Carrie gave a wide, humourless smile. 'You are so right.' She opened her purse again and brought out the car keys, then, closing the bag's clasp with a snap, she got to her feet. 'Okay, now I'm ready. Let's go.'

Rosemary remained in her seat, looking up at her, bewilderment in her face.

'Well?' Carrie said, 'are you coming?'

'Yes...' Rosemary got up and followed as Carrie, with firm, regular steps, started out from the room.

......NINETEEN

Reaching the car, Carrie tossed her coat onto the back seat and got in behind the steering wheel. A moment later Rosemary climbed into the passenger seat and closed the door.

'Where are we going, if we're not going on to London?' Rosemary said. 'You want to go back to the cottage?' She had never known Carrie like this ever before, had never imagined this other side of her. 'I thought you said there was so much to do – there was no time to waste.'

'Yes, I did say that,' Carrie said. 'But things are not the same now.' She made no move to start the car, but sat still, hands on the steering wheel.

'But the photographer, the publicity,' Rosemary said. 'If I'm to get started – I mean...'

'There won't be any photographer, Rosemary,' Carrie said. 'At least, not for the reasons you think.'

'What?'

'And to answer your other question – we're not going back to the cottage. Your show isn't any further concern of mine.' Carrie looked at her steadily for a moment, then said, 'I've been thinking about all those years you took from me, Rosie, and you're going to have to pay. For every one of them.'

'Pay?' There was a note of fear in Rosemary's voice.

'Yes.' A pause. 'I'm going to turn you in.'

'*What*?' Rosemary gasped. 'Carrie – what are you saying?'

'Oh, I think you know very well what I'm saying.' Carrie spoke slowly, evenly. 'You want publicity? Well, believe me, you're gonna get it. I'm going to turn you over to the police. I'm gonna tell them what you did. Where Kurt's body is. The newspapers are gonna have a field day.' She watched as a horrified incredulity leapt into Rosemary's eyes.

'Carrie,' Rosemary said, 'is this – is this some kind of joke?'

'Joke?' Carrie said. 'You think it sounds like a joke?' She shook her head. 'Joke, she says. No, Rosie, it's no joke. There *was* a joke – for years. And the joke was on me. But no more.'

'Carrie,' Rosemary said, her voice breaking, 'you don't mean this.'

'I don't? You'll see. Just let me find the nearest police station.'

'What?'

'Yes. And I'll tell them what happened – and they'll come out to the cottage. I'll tell them what you did.' She nodded. 'Oh, yes, and there's a cassette tape there too – recording it all – a witness to everything.'

'Carrie, stop!' Rosemary cried, her voice shrill. 'Stop it – now! It's gone far enough. For God's sake, this is insane!' She reached out to Carrie, desperate in her terror, but Carrie, contemptuously shaking off the clutching hands, turned on the ignition and gunned the motor. The next moment the car was lurching forward.

'Stop!' Rosemary cried out again, the tears spilling down her cheeks. 'You can't do this! Carrie, you can't. Whatever

I've done to you this is too much! It's too much! Please, stop the car. Let me out.'

Ignoring Rosemary's pleas, Carrie swung the car in a wide arc, and drove out of the car park. As the car moved onto the top of the steep hill Rosemary reached out, clawing at Carrie's hands as they gripped the wheel.

'Stop it, you idiot!' Carrie cried, fighting to retain her grasp. 'You want to get us off the road!'

But Rosemary didn't stop, and Carrie cried out in pain and protest as Rosemary's sharp nails dug into her soft flesh. Half turning, Carrie swung and struck out, her fist catching Rosemary in the face.

For a split second Rosemary's head spun, and then with a scream she launched herself at Carrie. While one furious, desperate hand raked Carrie's cheek, the other gripped tightly in her hair. Savagely she wrenched, and Carrie shrieked in pain, letting go her hold on the steering wheel to fight off the clutching hands. Next moment the car swerved violently across the narrow way, its offside wheels thudding against the high, hard earth verge before it jolted back onto the track. As it plunged on down the hill, the landscape flashing by in a blur of trees and hedgerow, the two women fought, struggling furiously. The pain in Carrie's head was excruciating and she writhed and screamed, but Rosemary's hands would not let up. Relentless, Rosemary pulled and tore as if she would rip Carrie's scalp from her head. 'You bitch!' she cried through clenched teeth, 'I won't let you destroy me. I've come this far. I won't let you stop me now.'

All at once, through the agony of Rosemary's clutching hands, Carrie glimpsed the grey expanse of the highway looming before them, and she tried to snatch at the wheel. It was too late. Out of control, the car hurtled from the hill, bending aside the stop sign at the corner and plunged headlong onto the main road. Missing an oncoming van by inches, it flung itself across the tarmac and ploughed half-way up the opposite bank to collide, broadside on, with a large oak. As the sound of the smash reverberated over the hillside the car's doors, forced to give under the impact, burst open. Carrie, thrown from the wreck, was flung into the air like some savagely discarded doll. With a dull thud she struck the outflung limb of a tree, hung there for a second, and then fell to the ground.

The car, continuing its progress, turned a somersault on the top of the high bank, in the process throwing Rosemary spinning and flailing out onto the grass. For a moment the vehicle seemed to rest, hovering, until, with a groaning of metal, it tipped back and crashed down onto the highway. Following the sound of the impact there was a second of silence, as if the whole scene was gathering breath, and then, with a loud explosion, the mangled wreck burst into flame.

Up on the bank, Rosemary lay still. Dully she took in the unusual angle of her left arm as it lay thrown forward on the grass. 'I've broken my arm,' she said to herself. 'I've broken my arm...' There was a throbbing in her ears, and she became aware of the warm stickiness of blood that covered her face and stuck her torn clothes to her body. Moving her head slightly, she saw the motionless figure of Carrie lying some two or three yards away, on the very edge of the bank. Opening her mouth, she tried to frame

Carrie's name. But no sound came through the blood and the broken teeth.

On the bank, Carrie moved and quietly cried out. Her own fog was drifting, clearing as consciousness returned. Searing pains stabbed at her body, and a low moan escaped her gaping mouth. Fighting the agony, she clutched at the grass, but her fingers would not obey her brain's feeble command. Turning her head, she found herself looking directly into Rosemary's face, and for a moment it seemed to her that it was all part of a dream, and that reality must soon return. Then memory came back, forcing its way through the mist of her discomfort.

'Rosie...' She managed to force the sound out. 'Rosie...'

Rosemary's eyes opened. Carrie was saying something, speaking to her.

'Nothing — nothing has changed,' Carrie said. A sudden pain, sharp as a razor, snatched at her breath, and she closed her eyes, waiting for the moment to pass. 'I meant it all,' she breathed. 'Nothing — has changed.'

Her words trailed off to a faint, broken murmur. The look in her eyes was of pure hatred. Painfully, she raised herself on one elbow, continuing to fix Rosemary with her icy glare. All around, the air became full of sounds. Voices, shrill in panic and shock, were calling out into the horror-filled day. Cars braked, tyres screeching, protesting on the tarmac, gravel spraying from beneath hot rubber; footsteps hurrying, running.

Using all her remaining strength, Carrie raised herself higher. She knelt, her white dress drenched with blood, a terrible, awful spectacle in the noon light. 'Nothing has changed, Rosie,' she hissed. 'You're going to pay. If it's the last thing I do. With my dying breath I'll make sure of that.' She swayed, teetering on the edge of the bank like a grotesque marionette, then with a soft cry she reeled and fell over the brink.

......TWENTY

Reaching out in the darkness, Douglas Rosti switched on the bedside lamp and lifted the telephone receiver.

'Yes?' His voice was dulled with sleep.

'Doug? Douglas?'

'Yeah, who is this?'

'Dave Reynolds.'

Reynolds? It couldn't be, he thought, yawning. Dave had left weeks ago for London, with Turrov's new musical in its transfer to the West End stage. 'Dave,' he said, 'I thought you were in England. You're supposed to be in London.'

'I *am* in London. Did I wake you?'

'It's only six o'clock.'

'Sorry.' Reynolds didn't sound sorry at all. 'I just thought you'd better know.'

'Better know what? What are you talking about?'

'Your client, Rosemary Paul.'

'Rosemary Paul? She's not my client. I don't look after her any more.'

'Oh — I didn't know that.'

'You woke me up to talk about *her*?' Douglas said. 'Give me a break, will you?' Then before the other could say anything further, he added, 'Anyway, what about her?'

'She's been involved in an accident. An automobile accident. It's been on the news and it's in the morning papers.'

Fully awake now, Douglas sat up. 'Tell me.'

Reynolds told him what little he had learned, that Rosemary and her companion, a woman by the name of Carrie Markham, had been in a road traffic accident on the highway some miles west of London.

'And how are they?' Douglas asked.

'Well, according to the reports from the hospital, it's pretty serious. Though you know what hospitals are like — they never give too much away. But it looks like the companion's in a particularly bad way. Critical, but stable — as they say.'

'Jesus.' Douglas shook his head. After a moment he said, 'Hey, Dave, thanks for telling me. I appreciate it. And look, keep me posted, will you? Let me know if you hear anything more, okay?'

'Sure thing.'

Later, sitting over a cup of black coffee, Douglas thought of the last time he and Rosemary had met. It had not been a pleasant meeting, not by any means, but that was all in the past now. He thought about Kurt, too, who had just gone over to England to join Rosemary and start preparing for her concert. He had no doubt that Kurt himself would be on the phone later to tell him more about the accident.

*

'Miss Paul…' The voice, a man's voice, seemed to be coming from a long way off. He waited, then spoke again. 'Miss Paul…?'

Still no response.

'Miss Paul? Rosemary? Rosemary?'

Becoming aware of the sound, she fought against its intrusion, wanting nothing so much but that it should go away. But still it came, soft, insinuating its way through the blanket of fog that enclosed her.

'Rosemary? Miss Paul?'

At last she opened her eyes.

A man, the man who had spoken, stood directly in her line of vision. He had placed himself deliberately before her, so that she would have no reason to try to move her head. He wore a white coat and had a warm, concerned expression. Seeing her eyes flick open, and the look of growing awareness, comprehension, he gave a small smile of satisfaction.

'I'm Dr Bloom,' he said, 'and I just want to tell you that you're going to be all right. You're going to be fine.'

He waited a moment longer and then quietly, on cushioned heels, he moved away.

Left alone again, she closed her eyes, shutting out the peripheral vision of the bags, the tubes, all the trappings that had become extensions of her body. She was hemmed in by them, imprisoned. She could do nothing but lie there while the memories came back. For a few brief, futile moments she attempted to shift her position, and then gave up, exhausted.

Later the doctor, Bloom, came again. He was a middle-aged man, his tone fatherly. He stood by her bed and looked into her eyes. He spoke softly, encouragingly. In her mind questions formed. She tried to speak, but her lips moved soundlessly over rigid jaws. Panic sparked in her eyes.

'You won't be able to talk,' he said in his English accent, 'so, please, don't try.' He bent closer. 'I'm afraid we had to reset your jaw. You've been very poorly, in fact.' He gave a grave smile. 'But I'm pleased to say that you're out of the woods now.' Reaching out, he gently touched the fingertips that protruded from the end of the plaster cast that encased her left arm. 'You're our prize patient, Miss Paul.' He spoke with a kind of affectionate pride. 'We're all very proud of you.'

He turned then, and moved back to the door. And still he had not told her what she so desperately wanted to know. In the doorway he looked back and saw the pleading glance that followed his progress.

'Please – you mustn't fret about your friend,' he said. 'You just try to get well. You concentrate on that.'

After a while she slept again.

*

The days crept by. She was like a chrysalis, cocoon-wrapped, suspended in space, shielded from the outside world by bandages, silence and consideration. There had been long periods of blackness, and other times when she had been aware of nothing but dull aches and pains that she had never known before.

Every day flowers arrived. And with them came notes and letters bearing messages of love and goodwill. They came from the admirers, the loyal fans who daily searched the newspapers for news of her progress. But she knew nothing of this, the flowers or the good wishes, for many, many days.

*

'Any sign? Any progress?'

Dr Bloom spoke softly to the nurse as he entered the room.

'Nothing at all.' The nurse shook her head. 'There's been no change.'

He moved to the bed and looked down. 'Miss Markham...?'

He touched a hand, pressing slightly, all the while observing the closed eyes.

'Miss Markham? Carrie?'

There was no response, not a flicker to give any hint of consciousness.

'It's been too long,' he muttered over his shoulder to the nurse. Bending closer, he studied the battered, distorted features below him. Gently he placed a hand on the white plaster that wrapped her head, and with the thumb of his other hand gently lifted her right eyelid. The white of the eyeball was in evidence, the iris turned upward. He moved his hand from her face, and bent a little closer.

'Miss Markham,' he said. Then again: 'Miss Markham!' more loudly, as if trying to awaken her sleeping brain.

With a sigh he turned away. Glancing about him, he thought how different this room was. Here were no lush bouquets of flowers. No messages of love, no get-well-soon cards. On the uncluttered bedside locker stood a jar holding a single bunch of crocuses, the merest splash of colour against the pristine walls. They had been placed there by one of the nurses, the small gesture born of the sight of the many tokens of affection and adoration that had come in for Rosemary Paul. Inside the locker lay Carrie's few belongings that had survived the crash and the fire: a scorched handbag containing a partially destroyed driver's licence, a few other documents, and some keys, coins and cosmetics. The nurse had placed the forlorn items towards the back of the shelf; the sight of them was too saddening.

'Miss Markham. Carrie...'

The doctor tried again, then, lips compressed, moved away.

*

'It's all over now, Rosemary,' the doctor said. 'And you'll be relieved to know that nothing as bad is to come. Now it's just a matter of time till you're completely recovered.'

They had just returned from yet another visit to the operating theatre. There, the wires that had held her facial bones together had been removed, and she now lay once more in her room, sweating from the ordeal. She nodded vaguely at the man's words, relief in her eyes. After a few moments she drifted off to sleep again.

Later, when he judged that she was well enough, he came to her and told her something of her condition and what had taken place. Two ribs had been broken, plus her left arm and nose. Her jawbone had been broken in three places, her left cheekbone smashed. Since the accident, he said, she had been literally held together with wires.

'You've had a few operations,' he said. 'We've spent a lot of time on you. But you've come out of it wonderfully. We've given you a new nose, and, if I may say so — ' he smiled here — 'it's rather a nice one. I don't think you'll be at all averse to it. Also, we've had to rebuild parts of your jaw — and I'm afraid you lost a few teeth. Still, they'll be replaced without too much difficulty. You'll be amazed at what can be done today.'

She could move only her right hand, and she lifted it now, painfully, slowly, to touch gingerly at the bandages around her head.

'Yes,' the doctor nodded, frowning, 'I'm afraid we also had to shave your head. We had no choice.' He stepped closer. 'I know it will all seem horrific, and very strange to you for a while, but you'll heal; you'll get well again – I promise.'

She gave a small nod. There was a long pause and then at last she spoke, her voice sounding like some old instrument, long unused, rusting.

'Is there – is there any change with – with…?'

He hesitated, then said, 'I'm afraid she's no better. At the same time, though, she's no worse. And that's something to hang on to. Keep that in mind.' He smiled faintly at her. 'You just think about getting better.' He looked around him at the flowers and the cards. 'Look at all this – there are so many people out there who are anxious about your recovery, you know. You can't disappoint them.'

There was silence in the room again, and she became aware of the distant sounds of traffic. The scent of the flowers was sweet. Then the doctor was bending a little closer, trying to make his voice sound casual.

'About Miss Markham,' he said. 'Does she – are there any relatives, any immediate family?'

She didn't answer, merely closed her eyes.

'They – they should be informed,' he said. He waited. 'Is there anyone?'

After a moment she whispered, 'No…'

'There's no one?'

'No…there's no one. She has no family at all now.' After a pause she whispered, 'You – you're saying that she's not going to – to get well, aren't you?'

'No, no, I didn't say that,' he said quickly. 'We're still very – hopeful. Oh, yes. And we shall remain so. We must, and so must you.'

She said nothing at this, though in her mind the thought went round like a cracked record: *She's going to die. She's going to die.* After some moments of silence she asked, 'How long have I been here?'

'Too long,' he said. 'You've been here five weeks. Much too long.'

When he had gone she lay staring ahead. So many days. So many weeks. The date of the concert had come and gone. All those plans, all those dreams. The hopes, the work – all gone for nothing. There was no appointment that couldn't be broken.

*

At her insistence, Dr Bloom eventually allowed her to have a mirror.

He studied her face, watching for her reaction as she took it and looked at her reflection. When she saw the ugly, swollen flesh, the bruising and discolouration, she gave a small squeal of horror.

'Oh, Rosemary, I know, I know,' he said quickly. 'It's a shock to you, I know. But the swelling and discoloration will go, and the scars will fade in time. And your hair will grow back. I promise you it will.'

Her hand holding the mirror fell, and he saw that she was crying. She lay there, propped against the pillows, her face crumpled beneath the all-encasing, unflattering turban that she wore to hide her shaven head. She made no sound, weeping silently, the tears falling over her scarred, ravaged cheeks.

'I — I can't bear it,' she said. 'It's like I've never seen myself before. It's horrible.'

'Give it time,' he said. 'Just — give it time.'

When her tears had subsided and she was calmer, he took the mirror and placed it in the drawer of her bedside locker. 'It'll be there when you need it,' he said. 'Don't be afraid of it. You can only observe an improvement.' He turned back to face her. 'If you think you look bad now, you should have seen yourself when you were brought in.' He paused. 'And just tell yourself how lucky you are. Believe me, you're lucky to be alive.'

*

Nurse Sims saw Nurse Bainbridge coming towards her, arms laden with daffodils.

At Sims's questioning look, Bainbridge said, 'Miss Paul's orders — to take them along to fourteen, Miss Markham's room.'

'They're beautiful.'

'Aren't they? They come in every day, from her fans. There's so much attention from people. Not to mention the reporters. They're always checking up.'

In room fourteen she carefully arranged the flowers. When she had finished, she adjusted the position of the vase on the locker, then stepped back to admire her handiwork.

Turning, she looked down at the unconscious figure on the bed. 'It's a pity you can't see them,' she sighed. 'But I don't think now you ever will.'

*

'Rosemary,' said Dr Bloom, smiling as he approached her bedside, 'I've come to see how you are today.'

'I'm feeling a lot better, thank you,' she said.

He nodded, pleased. 'That's what I wanted to hear. Is there anything you need? Anything we can get you?'

'Well — since you ask,' she said, 'I'd kill for a cigarette.'

He chuckled and held up an admonishing finger. 'Now, Rosemary, you know better than that.'

She gave a resigned nod. 'Such a spoilsport,' she said. 'But there's no harm in asking.'

'Indeed not.' Then, his smile fading after a moment, he said, 'Listen — I came in to say something to you...'

'Oh? What is that?'

He sighed. 'Rosemary,' his tone was grave, 'I've just come from seeing your friend Carrie, and ...' His voice tailed off.

'What is it?' she said. 'Tell me — please.'

He waited a moment then said, hesitantly: 'It's not easy, but I'm afraid I have to tell you there's a possibility that she - might not fully recover.' He paused. 'But at the same time we're still hopeful, and we're doing all we can.'

'I know you are. Thank you.' With a sigh she gave a weary nod and turned away, avoiding his sympathetic gaze. 'Poor Carrie,' she whispered. 'Oh, God. Poor, poor Carrie.' She turned back to him. 'Can I see her?' she said. 'I want to see her. Please.'

He nodded. 'Yes. Yes, all right. If that's what you want.'

*

Later that day in room fourteen Bloom looked sadly at the two women, one lying insensible on her bed, hooked up to the paraphernalia of her life-giving equipment; the other sitting upright in a wheelchair, battered, bruised, but very much alive.

Over the weeks the doctor had learned something of their long and close relationship that had endured for so many years. Now, in deference to that intimacy he turned away, at the same time beckoning to the male nurse who had pushed the chair. He exchanged a quiet word with the young man, who then moved to the door and let himself out.

'Greg'll be back for you in a minute or two, Rosemary,' he said, turning to her again. Then after a moment he added, 'Perhaps — perhaps you'd like to be alone with Carrie for a moment, would you?'

'It's all right,' she said. As well as she could, she leaned closer to the bed, eyes fixed on the still face before her. 'Carrie,' she said. 'Carrie — can you hear me?'

There was no response, nothing, not the slightest flicker of any vitality to show that her words had even been heard. Again she spoke. 'Carrie, can you hear me?' And now a pleading note crept into her voice. 'Carrie, darling, please — please answer me. It's Rosemary. Carrie, it's Rosie. Open your eyes, darling. Please open your eyes.'

Still no response. Only the steady, regular breathing showed that there was life. Watching from his place by the door, Dr Bloom could only silently shake his head.

'Can you hear me?' she said again. She tried to get closer, but the bulky wheelchair would not allow it. 'Oh, Carrie, Carrie,' she breathed, 'open your eyes and look at me.'

In the silence her thoughts went back to when they had lain together on the top of the bank, bleeding, the twisted wreck of the car blazing below. She could smell the burning metal, the burning oil, taste the blood in her mouth, feel the pain in her body. She could hear the sounds, too, the siren, and the voices. 'This way! They're up on the bank!' 'Hurry!' And the other words: 'You're going to pay. If it's the last thing I do.' The sounds, the voices went on, ringing in her brain.

She came out of her thoughts with a start, finding that the doctor had come to her side. As she looked at him he gave a sympathetic shake of his head.

'I'm sorry,' he said.

'I don't think she can even hear me,' she said sadly.

He shook his head again. Then after a moment: 'Come on,' he said, 'let's get you back to your room.'

*

She was spending most of the daylight hours out of bed now, and with each passing day she could feel the positive signs of her progress. And the letters, the cards and the flowers continued to arrive. One letter, headed *Adrimar Productions*, was of particular interest. It said:

> Dear Miss Paul,
> Please forgive me for writing to you at what must surely be a very stressful time, but I want to say how very shocking and

distressing it was to learn of your accident. I do so hope that by now you are well on the road to making a complete recovery.

I would also like to say how very much I was looking forward to your concert, and how disappointed I was — along with so many, many others, I have no doubt — that it could not take place. What a tragedy, and what a great pleasure we were denied.

I do hope you won't regard this as an intrusion at a difficult time, but with regard to your planned concert I am wondering what the situation is now, and whether you have any thoughts or intentions in respect of holding such an event in the future. I realise that such a thing might be the furthest from your thoughts, but if you are at all interested in discussing the possibility of any such event I would be very happy to visit you to discuss it at any time that's convenient.

Whether or not such a suggestion is of interest I send you my most sincere good wishes for your future happiness and success.

Yours sincerely,
Adrian Marlow

She read the letter through several times, then placed it on her locker and sat staring into space. Later, with the aid of a laptop borrowed from one of the nurses, she did a little research. As an entrepreneur, Adrian Marlow, it turned out, was well thought of, and very much up-and-coming. Not that long in the business, he had nevertheless already made his mark with some notable successes to his credit.

But no, she said to herself — she could never perform now. The idea was insane. On the other hand, it would certainly be nice to have a visitor, some bright, intelligent person to talk to for half an hour.

As she sat there, Nurse Bainbridge came into the room in the course of her rounds. 'You're looking well today, Miss Paul,' she said. 'A bit brighter, too. Something happened to buck you up?'

She didn't respond for a few moments, then with a slow nod and a smile she said, 'Well, maybe. I'm not sure. 'But – I think I might be having a visitor.'

'A visitor. Well, that'll be nice for you – see a different face for a change.'

'Yes…it would be nice. And it'll be a change.' She nodded. 'Sharon, darling – would you be kind enough to get me some notepaper? I want to write a letter.'

......TWENTY-ONE

The April sun shone down on the trees, bright in their new leaves, in the hospital grounds, and through the window touched the white collar and cuffs of Adrian Marlow. He had driven from London that afternoon to see Rosemary, and the meeting was now coming to an end.

Earlier, when word had come from reception that he had arrived, there had been a frantic, last-minute flutter in private room number seven, where the young nurse, Greg, had hovered, trying to reassure his patient.

'Stop worrying, Miss Paul,' he said. 'You look fine. You look terrific.'

'Terrific?' she said, holding her little hand mirror out before her. 'More like bloody terrifying.' Then, as the young man moved towards the door she said quickly, 'No, wait — just a second!' Her tone hinted at panic. 'My hair — how does it look?' Her orange-nailed fingers patted frenetically at the loose blonde locks of the newly-fitted wig.

'It looks nice. Believe me, it really does.'

'You wouldn't lie to me, would you?' She frowned at herself in the mirror. 'Oh, God, look at my eyes. And those scars. Will they ever go?' She picked up her dark glasses, slipped them on, adjusted them, then waved a resigned, dismissive hand. 'Ah, what the hell. If I'm not ready now I never will be. I'm Rosemary Paul, and even at my best I'd never have been up for the beauty pageant.' She gave a sigh. 'Okay, Greg, ask him to come up, will you?'

Adrian Marlow was a divorcee in his fifties, a man of medium height and build, with dark hair, now greying, and square-cut, rimless spectacles. His South London accent betrayed his beginnings, and the fact that his considerable success was something that he had worked for. She found him easy to talk to, and after her initial nervousness began to relax a little in his company. A chair had been placed for him a little way from hers, but even from that distance she knew he could see the scars that she had tried so carefully to hide. A tray of tea was brought in from the pantry, and after they had broken the ice with small talk he got to the point. They were on first name terms now.

'Well, Rosemary…' he took a sip of tea and set his teacup down, ' – to business. I think I made it fairly clear in my letter as to why I wanted to see you today.'

'Yes,' she nodded. 'And I have to say that it came as a huge surprise. I wasn't prepared for anything like that.'

'It isn't something you've been considering?'

'In my situation?' she said with eyes wide. 'I mean, look at me. Are you kidding.'

'I know what you mean,' he said. 'But your doctor tells me you've made great strides, and that you'll be fit enough to be discharged in a day or two.'

'That's right – they're throwing me out, the devils. I've been freeloading long enough, they tell me.'

He chuckled. 'Oh, that is wonderful. So you're feeling okay, yes?'

'Oh, indeed, yes. And I can't wait to get out. Everything considered, I'm feeling pretty good.' She gave a nod. 'Yes, I feel well.'

He was silent for a moment, then: 'Well enough to do a show?'

She gave a deep sigh. 'Oh, Adrian, I knew that question was coming up.'

'And?'

'Oh, I don't know. I really don't know. It isn't something I even thought about until I got your letter.'

'But you've thought about it since — a little, I hope?'

'Well, yes, a little.' She paused, then went on, 'But Adrian, it's not just a question of whether I'm fit enough. I mean — what about *you*? Aren't you afraid you might be wasting your time, not to mention a small fortune into the bargain? What if I turned out to be some godawful flop?'

'No,' he said quickly, 'don't talk that way. I don't think for one minute that you'd be some godawful flop. If I thought that, I'd never have written to you.'

She sat silent. His initial letter had raised within her a little spring of hope; but now, faced with the possible reality, fear had taken its place. 'You're willing to take the risk?' she said.

He nodded. 'Oh, yes, I'm willing to take the risk. If you are.'

After a moment she said, 'I have to be honest with you, and tell you that nobody we approached before thought that way. In fact — we put up the money ourselves.'

'*You* did?' he said.

She nodded. 'Well, not me exactly. Carrie did.'

'Carrie – your friend? She put up the money? Well, that's news.' He gave a nod. 'So – there's someone who believes in you.'

'Oh, yes. Yes, indeed. Always.'

'Well, let me tell you that Carrie isn't the only one,' he said. 'Things have changed, Rosemary. I admit that I would have had doubts about backing your venture earlier – after your long absence, I mean. But now,' he leaned forward a little, 'I don't see how it could fail.'

'You don't? Well, you have to know that they weren't exactly fighting each other for tickets at the theatre box office. We checked. The bookings were slow.'

'Yes, well, that doesn't exactly surprise me,' he said. 'After all, you didn't have any publicity out there, did you – not to speak of? No PR at all – no pictures, just a few ads here and there. That's not enough.'

'I know, I know,' she said. 'But it was just Carrie and me, doing the best we could. But, I mean to say – well, what did we know?'

'Of course you didn't know,' he said. 'That side of the business isn't for you. I understand, absolutely. But things are different now – a *lot* different. The picture has changed, totally.'

'Changed?'

A moment of hesitation, then he said, 'Well, I mean – now, with your – your terrible accident ... I don't think you can lose.'

'What?' She gazed at him. 'Are you serious?'

'Never more so.'

'You mean it?' There was a note of wonder in her voice. 'You say you don't think I can lose?'

'No, I don't.' He spread his hands before him. 'Look at the coverage you've had in the papers. It's unbelievable. The columns have been full of you. I mean — here you are, having made the most miraculous recovery after hovering between life and death for days and days. You've been through the most terrible time, both with the accident and then with all your reconstructive surgery. You've been through hell, Rosemary, absolute hell. And everybody knows about it. They're all aware of the hell you've gone through — and they love you for it. They love you for it, Rosemary. You've become a hero — an icon.'

She gave an ironic smile. 'So, it was a smart career move, my accident — is that what you're saying?'

He gave a little chuckle. 'You could say that. But seriously, it has made the most incredible difference. Your songs are being played on the air, your album has sold out a second pressing, and they're rushing to get out more. Like I said, you're a hero. Everybody loves you and wants to be your friend. They all want you to succeed. Everybody's cheering for you.'

'I can hardly believe this,' she said. 'You — you mean it?'

'Every single word.' He smiled. 'You wanted PR — well, my God, you've got it. After what's happened to you, your audience is guaranteed. *And* your success.' He looked at her face, watching the idea, the realisation, settle and take root. 'So,' he said, 'what do you think?'

Moments passed. 'But — but my voice,' she said. 'Let's be honest , it — it's not what it was. We have to face that.'

'Of course not,' he said. 'And nobody will expect it to be. They'd be amazed if it were. You can't go through what you've been through and be untouched by it.' He paused. 'So — what do you think? Just give me the word and I'll have a contract drawn up at once.' He waited for her answer. 'Well?'

'You really think I can?'

'I don't have the slightest doubt.' He watched as the fear and indecision faded from her face. After a moment she gave a little nod.

'Yes?' he said.

'Yes.'

'*Yes!*' His smile was wide. 'Yes!' He gave a little punch into the air. 'Rosemary Paul,' he said, 'you have just made a very wise decision. You are going to take London by storm.'

'I hope you're right.'

'Trust me.' He paused. 'And now — the next big question.'

'Go on.'

'You think you could be ready in a month?'

'A *month*?' She looked at him with mouth open. 'My God, I've only just started walking unaided. I mean, it'll take me at least —'

'I know it's short notice,' he broke in, 'but we have a theatre available. We'd booked Trevor Halliday for a show at the New Century. May, a Sunday. But now he's in trouble and he can't make it. Like I say, the theatre's booked and paid for, so if you can make the date, it's yours.'

'The New Century,' she said. She had read about the theatre in London, a new, spacious venue that was attracting many of the top names. 'That's quite an offer.'

'It's not made lightly.'

'But – in just a month? What about a musical director, the publicity?'

'You leave all that to me. I'll get you a great MD.' He paused. 'You want a day to think about it? But we can't take too long. If we're going to start we've got to start at once.'

After a moment she rose from her chair and reached out her hand. He got up and took the hand she offered. Her touch was firm, warm.

'I don't need to think about it any further,' she said. She gave a nod. 'A month. I shall be ready.'

*

After Marlow had left, Dr Bloom called in to see her. 'Word's getting round that you've had a visitor,' he said. 'An *important* visitor.'

'Yes.' With excitement colouring her voice, she related her news. 'But it's only a month away,' she added, a look of doubt clouding her face. 'What have I done? I must be mad.' She shook her head. 'I must be out of my mind even to think of it.'

'No,' he said quickly. 'You can do it.' He gazed at her steadily. 'I know you can. I've watched you over these weeks, Rosemary – and I'm convinced there's nothing you can't do if you set your mind to it. I've seen your strength, your will. And I have an idea of what you're capable of.' It was true; he had never failed to be impressed by her spirit. It was hard to believe that this was the same woman who, two months earlier, had entered the hospital broken, bleeding and a hair's breadth from death. If she dealt with her concert the way she had dealt with her injuries and her stress, he had no doubt that she would triumph. 'Rosemary,' he said, 'there are thousands out there who believe in you. You can't let them down. You have to believe in yourself. You can't back out now.'

After a moment she gave a nod, her face calmer. 'You're right,' she said. 'I can't. And I *won't*.' She smiled with her last words, then turned her head away. Studying her, Bloom saw sudden doubt in her face again – and something else, some dark shadow behind the new look of hope. 'What's the matter?' he said. 'Rosemary, what is it?'

'I – I want you to tell me something,' she said. 'And, please – I must know the truth.'

'Go on.' He waited.

'Is there,' she said after a long moment, ' – is there any chance *at all* that – that Carrie will get well?'

Ah, so that was it, he said to himself. In her own happiness she was thinking of her friend. He hesitated for a second then said:

'Well, I did tell you there's the possibility that – she mightn't recover, and –'

'Yes, I know,' she cut in, ' – but how strong is that possibility? Tell me.'

He gave a sigh and sadly shook his head. 'I'm sorry, Rosemary, but I don't believe there's any great chance. Not now. There's been no significant change in her condition since the day she was brought in.'

'But – but she breathes unaided, doesn't she?'

'Oh, yes. Yes, she does. Other than that, though…' He sighed. 'Oh, I'd like to hold out some hope for you, but – her situation just doesn't change.'

219

'Is she — ? Oh, God, I don't know how to say it, but is she…?' Her words trailed off.

'Is she in a — a vegetative state? Is that what you're asking? No, she's not. Her brain is responsive. And we know that miracles are said to happen, but I have to be honest with you.' He sighed. 'Rosemary — I'm sorry to say it, but you should — should try to prepare yourself for the worst.'

She turned her face away. 'Thank you.' A little nod. 'I had to know.'

.....TWENTY-TWO

'Hello, Rosemary.'

'Adrian — hello!'

With a warm smile of welcome, she stood in the cottage doorway, hand outstretched as Adrian Marlow stepped across the porch towards her.

'Come on in,' she said. 'I've got some coffee on.'

He followed her into the bright interior and took off his jacket. As he seated himself in the high-backed chair by the fireplace he glanced over at the open piano, saw the sheet music there on the stand. 'You've been working,' he said, with a nod of approval.

'Oh, yes, indeed,' she answered. 'Every day.'

'Good.' He smiled. 'And how's it going? Are you pleased?'

She returned his smile, but faintly. 'It's too early to say.'

She got the coffee and brought it in, setting the tray on the small table between them. As she poured the coffee she felt his eyes on her face. He couldn't miss the scars. Raising her head, she gave a nod. 'They didn't do too bad a job, did they?' she said.

'I beg your pardon?' He pretended not to know what she meant.

'Oh, come on, now,' she said, 'you know what I'm talking about. But you should have seen me before those wonderful fellows got to work on me. I'm glad I wasn't faced with such a task.' She handed him his coffee. 'They showed me photographs later, when I was leaving I must have been one awful mess.' She gave a little laugh. 'Practically nothing's my own any more. New nose. New jawline.' She raised a hand to her hair. 'And this is a wig. Still, at least my own hair is growing back. At least that's not gone for good.'

'Rosemary,' he said warmly, 'I think you look absolutely great.'

'Well, thank you, sir,' she said. 'And with a kind lighting man, and the right make-up, maybe I'll pass. Anyway, I'm not knocking it, believe me. I'm lucky to be here – I know that.'

He nodded. A moment, and then: 'Is – is there any news?' he asked.

'You mean – about Carrie?' She shook her head and turned away. 'No. No, nothing.'

Watching her, he observed her quiet strength. To see her going ahead so bravely with her plans filled him with the greatest respect and admiration. He could only guess at how she must be feeling, knowing that her dearest friend was lying unconscious in a hospital bed, and showing no signs of recovery.

Changing the subject, he looked around him and said, 'You've got a comfortable place here, Rosemary.'

'What? Oh, yes,' she said. 'I love it. It was Carrie who found it. I rush back here after rehearsals. I can't wait to get back. I'm afraid London isn't for me these days – not after all this time. It's not the place I knew. It's changed so much over the years. But I like it here. It's somewhere I can rest.'

'I know what you mean. I can sense the — the peace here.'

She nodded. Yes, she thought, *and if only he knew*. If he only knew that just a few feet from where they sat a man had lain dying, bleeding to death. And even now, out there in the little copse at the foot of the garden ... Earlier that day she had gone out and stood looking down at Kurt's grave. With the coming of spring, new plants had sprung up out of the earth that covered him ... No one would ever guess. Back in the cottage she had opened up the little tape recorder and taken out the cassette. No one else would ever hear it now. Standing in front of the fire she had looked at the damning little item, and then tossed it into the flames. That was finished too.

Into her memories of Kurt, the thought of Douglas Rosti came to her. On her return from the hospital she had found, amongst the mail awaiting her, two airmail letters, both from Douglas. Opening the first, she had read:

Dear Rosemary,

Kurt gave me your address in England before he left to join you. How terribly sorry I was to hear about your accident. And I can only hope that by the time you read this you are well on your way to making a complete recovery. I hope, so much, that the same is true of poor Carrie.

I'm also writing to Kurt — c/o yourself — if you'd be kind enough to pass my letter on to him...

The rest of the letter was taken up with platitudes that she had no wish to read. Tearing open the other envelope she read the words he had written to Kurt. No surprises there; he had asked Kurt how things were going, and for him to make contact as soon as possible. After reading it she had torn it up and burnt the pieces.

'I phoned the box office,' Adrian was saying, breaking into her thoughts. 'They gave me some really good news.'

'Oh?'

'They said the phones haven't stopped ringing.'

'You mean it? Really?'

'That's what they tell me.' He grinned, nodded. 'Well, I told you how it would be.' After a pause he asked: 'So – how are rehearsals going? How's it working out with Kesterson?'

Ray Kesterson was the musical director that Adrian had found for her. 'He's good,' she said. 'He has real talent, and he knows what he's doing.'

'Oh, an excellent guy,' he said. 'With a lot of experience – in the States, too.' Then he added, 'I didn't tell you before, but we've had a couple of calls from Sony, and from Twentieth. There's talk about recording the show, live.'

'Really?'

'Yes, but I'm not surprised, not in the least. And if it's not them it'll be somebody else.' A little silence fell, then he said: 'Do you remember? When I saw you first, that day at the hospital, you had some doubts as to whether you'd be ready in time. Have you any doubts now?'

She nodded. 'Of course I do, Adrian. How could I not?'

.....TWENTY-THREE

'I'm sorry, sir, there's not a seat left.' The girl behind the box office window spoke sympathetically. 'It's been sold out for weeks.'

Douglas frowned. 'Aw, come on. Surely there must be something available.'

'There's nothing at all, sir. I'm sorry.'

He hesitated, then taking a couple of notes from his billfold, he pushed them towards her pearl-pink finger-nails. 'Can't you find anything at all?'

She gave a sniff, looked at the bribe and shook her head. Raising an over-plucked eyebrow she placed a disdainful finger on the notes and, as if they were counterfeit, slid them back towards him. 'I'm sorry, sir, but as I said, there's nothing.' Dismissing him, she looked beyond him to the woman who stood next in the queue. Douglas picked up his money and stepped away.

Over a cup of coffee in a nearby café he wondered what his next step should be. He had arrived just that morning from Manhattan for a series of business meetings, and, hoping to kill a few birds with one stone, also planned to catch Rosemary's show and try to meet up with Kurt again. So far he was having no success where either was concerned.

The inability to get a seat for the concert was of course easily explained by the *Sold Out* notices plastered on the posters, but the matter of Kurt was a different thing. He just seemed to have vanished, and for that there seemed to be no explanation. His absence from the scene was just too strange. He had neither answered Douglas's calls or emails, nor telephoned, or tried in any way to make contact.

An hour earlier Douglas had telephoned the offices of Adrimar Productions, and following a lengthy wait had at last managed to get Adrian on the line. Douglas told him that he had been Rosemary's agent for a brief time in the USA and was right now trying to trace her MD, Kurt Hellman, who had come over from the US to join her and work with her. Adrian responded saying that he had never met Kurt Hellman, and knew nothing of him other than that he had written some of Rosemary's songs and orchestrations. As for Rosemary's present MD, he was a man named Ray Kesterson, and had been contracted by Adrian himself.

'I know him – Kesterson,' Douglas said. Then he added, 'But how come *he's* doing the show? Kurt was coming over from New York especially to do it. What's happened to him?'

'I'm sorry,' Adrian replied, 'but I can't help you. I don't know anything about it. If you want to know more, I suggest you contact Rosemary herself.'

'I'd like to,' Douglas said, 'but I don't know where she is.'

'Well,' said Adrian, 'I'm not happy about giving out her whereabouts over the phone. But – hang on – give me a second…'

Douglas waited, and after a few minutes Adrian came back to him.

'I've checked you out on the web,' he said. 'You can't be too careful, as you appreciate.'

'Absolutely,' Douglas said.

'Anyway,' said Adrian, 'she's rehearsing today at the Premier Hall in the Strand. Her final rehearsals. You won't be allowed to get in to see her, but you can leave a message there for her if you want to.'

*

At the door of the Premier Hall rehearsal rooms half an hour later, Douglas enquired of the doorkeeper whether it was possible to see Rosemary Paul. The man replied that she was rehearsing, and could have no visitors. 'Would you like to leave a message, sir?' he asked.

Douglas thanked him, took a notebook and pen from his pocket, scrawled a note and handed it to the door keeper. 'I'll see she gets it, sir,' the man said, and turned to a young man who sat nearby. 'Luke, be a good lad and see if you can find Miss Paul, will you? And if she's not busy give her this message from the gentleman here.'

As the boy took the note and turned away, Douglas called after him, 'And tell her I'm here now, will you? – waiting at the door.' Nothing ventured, nothing gained.

'Yes, sir.'

Douglas watched his departure. Would she agree to see him? He bore her no enmity. After all she had been through it was impossible to harbour any ill feeling towards her.

*

The boy found her in consultation with the musical director, in a break between numbers. She looked up, smiling as he approached. Handing her the note, he said, 'It's from a man at the stage door, Miss. He's waiting there now…'

Unfolding the paper, she read Douglas's words:

Dear Rosemary,

I flew in this morning in the hope of getting to see your show, but there's not a seat to be had. Is there anything you can do? I am full of admiration for you, and only wish you all that is good. I hope tomorrow night brings you all the success you deserve and that I can be there to cheer you on.

One other thing: can you tell me where Kurt is? He hasn't been in touch, and he doesn't answer his cellphone. He just seems to have vanished. Please say that we can meet. I'm staying at the Connaught.

With very best wishes,

Douglas Rosti

'Is there any answer, Miss…?' The boy was looking in surprise at the sudden pallor of her face. 'Miss?'

'What?' She turned to him, as if just remembering that he was there.

'Is there an answer, Miss?'

'No,' she said abruptly. 'Just — just tell him I'm not available, but that you've left the note for me.' She tried to smile, but her lips felt stiff, her mouth dry. She was aware of Ray Kesterson looking at her in surprise. She turned to the boy, gently dismissing him. 'Thank you.' When the boy had gone she turned back to Kesterson. 'Sorry about that, Ray.' She took a breath, steadying herself. 'Right — where were we? The four bars in after —'

'Are you okay, Rosemary?' Kesterson said, interrupting.

'What?' she said. 'Okay? Of course I'm okay. Why shouldn't I be?

He studied her. 'You — you looked a little pale for a minute there.'

'It's nothing,' she said. 'Let's get on, shall we? We have an opening tomorrow.'

*

When she awoke next morning, after a fitful, restless sleep, the first thought that came to her mind was of Douglas. 'Damn him,' she muttered. What was he doing in England? And why did he have to come snooping around at a time like this? But she couldn't allow herself to think about him. She must not. She needed all her energies for the evening ahead.

*

Long before it was time to leave she packed her suitcase for her overnight stay at the hotel. Her gown for the show, along with the one she would wear at the party afterwards, was already at the theatre. For the journey there, by hired limousine, she dressed in a dark skirt and a simple, pale-green blouse. Her fingers trembled as she dealt with the buttons. She was tense, keyed up. The thought of what lay before her made her heart thud in her breast. But it was hopeless trying to still her fears; she could only pray that once she was out on the stage all the nerves, the terror, would vanish. That was the way it had been in the past. That was the way it was for every performer, and she was no different from the rest.

At last everything was set. She checked her watch. The

car would be here soon. There was just one more thing to do before she could leave. Picking up the telephone receiver she keyed in a number.

'Ashton Green Hospital,' came the familiar male receptionist's voice. 'Good afternoon.'

'Oh, good afternoon. I – I'd like to enquire about one of your patients – Miss Carrie Markham.'

'Just a moment, please.' After a short silence he was back on the line. 'Is that you, Miss Paul?' He had recognised her voice.

'Yes, it is.'

'Will you hold the line a moment, please?'

Why the delay in giving a simple answer, she wondered. She had been making the same routine enquiry almost every day since leaving the hospital. Why was today different?

'Miss Paul?'

'Yes?'

'I'm putting you through to Dr Bloom. He said that if you called he wanted to speak to you.'

'Oh – okay, thank you.' She waited. There was a click and then the doctor's voice was there.

'Ah, Miss Paul. Rosemary. How are you? How's my prize patient?'

'Fine, fine, thank you,' she said. 'I was calling to ask about Carrie. I was told you wanted to speak to me.'

'Yes,' he said, 'that's right.'

There was a gravity in his tone, and in the brief silence that followed his words the thought flashed through her mind: *She's dead. He's going to tell me she's dead.* Forcing herself to remain calm, she said: 'You – you've got some bad news, have you?'

'No,' he said quickly, 'not at all.' His tone was brighter than she had expected.

'No? Then what is it?'

'I wanted to tell you that there's been a slight change in Carrie's condition.'

'A change?' she said a little breathlessly. 'How? In what way a change?'

'Well,' he said carefully, 'Rosemary, listen – I don't want to build your hopes up – and we can't tell how significant it is, but Carrie briefly regained consciousness after you telephoned yesterday. Twice. Just for a very short period on each occasion – but nevertheless...'

After a moment she said, catching her breath, 'Does this mean – is she – going to be all right?'

'Oh – well, we can't say that, I'm afraid. It's much too early to tell.'

'But – but tell me, please, what – what happened?'

'Well, according to the nurse,' he said, 'on two occasions Carrie opened her eyes. And I'm told she actually seemed aware. Mind you, it was only for a few seconds each time.'

A long pause, then: 'Did she – did she say anything?'

'Apparently she did, yes. According to the –'

'What did she say?' she cut in. 'What did she say?'

'I was about to tell you. Apparently it wasn't anything that made any sense to her, the nurse, what she said. It was just five or six words, I understand. The nurse – she didn't catch what it was.' He paused, waiting for a response. 'Are you there, Rosemary?'

'Yes. Yes, I'm here.'

'Look,' he added, and there was a note of entreaty in his tone, 'you mustn't read too much into this. It might not mean anything. I wasn't sure about telling you, because I don't want to raise your hopes – without cause. I can't stress that strongly enough.'

'I – I understand.'

There was a little silence, then he said, his voice taking on a slightly lighter note: 'Well – apart from all that, Rosemary – tell me – how are *you*?'

'Oh – I – I'm well, thank you.'

'And all ready for the concert tonight? Your big night?'

'Let's hope so. We'll soon find out.'

'Thank you so much for the ticket you sent.'

'Oh – it's nothing.' She wanted to end the conversation, to end it now, to get off the phone. She couldn't cope with the pleasantries and platitudes at such a time.

'It was very kind of you,' he said.

'I hope you'll be able to make it, will you?'

'Well, I'm due to be on call, I'm sorry to say, but if I can get away I shall certainly be there to cheer you on. I have no doubt that you're going to be a huge success.'

'Thank you. Let's pray that you're right.'

He wished her good luck, and she thanked him and said goodbye. Her hand shook as she put down the receiver. She couldn't get his words out of her brain. *I don't want to raise your hopes,* he had said.

'No! *No!*'

The words were flung out into the stillness of the room. She wanted to weep. It mustn't happen. Not now. Not when she was so close. Today was *her* day, and nothing must spoil it. Today she would have her chance to really prove herself. It would be the high point of her whole life. She had paid for it, in advance.

Glancing from the window, she saw the limousine turning in at the gate. It was time to go.

*

Sitting aboard the train, Douglas tried to concentrate on his newspaper. But other thoughts kept getting in the way.

On either side, the green banks, dotted with spring flowers, rushed by. Then, gradually, the land fell away, levelling out, and he gazed out over the verdant fields of the English countryside.

*

In the theatre the final rehearsal had just ended.

'All right, Rosemary?' Ray Kesterson said as he put away his baton.

She nodded. 'Oh, yes, Ray. Thank you.'

With the orchestra and technicians she had spent well over an hour going over the programme. Although she had sung hardly at all — she had to save her voice — they had worked their way number by number from beginning to end, tightening the cues, getting the lighting just right until, now, all concerned were sure that they had done as much as they possibly could.

'You going back to your hotel now, Rosemary?' Kesterson asked as the musicians bustled about, preparing to leave.

'You bet,' she said. 'I must go and rest up for a while.' She gave a nervous smile. 'And maybe at the same time try to get up the courage to come back and set foot on this stage again.'

*

Dr Bloom shook Douglas's hand on their introduction and listened to his request to be allowed to pay Carrie a visit. 'You're a friend of Miss Markham's – from New York, you say.'

'Yes. And of Rosemary Paul.'

'Ah, yes, Rosemary.' The doctor gave a little nod of satisfaction. 'She's done so well. We're immensely proud of her, I have to say. And tonight – tonight is her big night.'

'Yes, indeed it is.'

'It's in all the papers. Are you going to her concert? I imagine you will be.'

'I was hoping to,' Douglas said, 'but I'm afraid I haven't been able to get a ticket. None to be had, I'm sorry to say.'

The doctor shook his head sympathetically, then said after a moment: 'Are you a *close* friend of Miss Markham?'

'Well, not a *close* friend – but certainly a friend.'

'It's just that it's against the hospital policy to allow visitors other than family and friends – at such a time.' Then Bloom added, 'But on the other hand, in her present condition it might very well help her. Hearing a voice she knows might possibly be a trigger. It might be what's needed.' He sighed. 'To be honest, we don't hold out too much hope. Although she's briefly regained consciousness a couple of times over the past days, at the same time she's showing certain signs of – of deterioration.' He gave a sigh. 'Anyway – come with me, Mr Rosti.'

With the doctor leading the way, they moved along

the corridor and came to a stop outside the door of room fourteen.

'There's something you must be aware of,' Bloom said.

'Yes? What's that?'

'Well — you'll be remembering Carrie as she was in New York — as she used to be.'

'Well, yes, of course.'

'Quite — but you must bear in mind that her accident was very, very serious. Her injuries were severe. Extremely. I have to warn you — to prepare you. The things that happened to her are — well, they're *very apparent*. We've done what we could for her, but there is a limit — without extensive cosmetic surgery. And in her situation that's not been an option for us to really consider.'

Douglas nodded. 'I understand.'

Opening the door, the doctor led the way into the room. Douglas, following a step behind, saw with something of a shock the scene before him of the bed with all the tubes, lines, drips, monitors and other paraphernalia that made up the life-support system. He came to a halt as the doctor went before him, moving closer to the bed.

'Miss Markham...?' The doctor leaned over the bed. 'Carrie? Carrie, there's someone here to see you. An old friend of yours from back home.'

After a moment he straightened, shaking his head. 'Not a sign.' He beckoned to Douglas. 'Come closer.'

Douglas stepped forward, looked down and saw her lying there, saw her face, the shocking evidence of her terrible injuries. 'Oh, my God,' he breathed, tears springing to his eyes. 'Oh, God...'

Seeing the way Douglas was affected, Bloom turned and moved towards the door. 'Mr Rosti,' he said, 'I'll leave you alone for a few minutes. If you need me I'll be in my office along the corridor.'

'Thank you.'

As the doctor left the room, Douglas drew up the chair beside the bed and sat down. He couldn't keep his eyes from her face, so familiar, and at the same time so terribly disfigured. After sitting there for some moments he leaned forward and whispered her name into the stillness. There was no response. 'Can you hear me?' he said. His voice sounded hollow in the quiet. He whispered her name again, and again, but still there was nothing, no flicker of animation to indicate that she had even heard.

He sighed, straightened, and as he did so her eyes opened, opened wide. Her head turned a little on the pillow, and she was looking straight at him. She stared at him, her eyes locked with his, and her lips began working. 'You,' she said. '*You...you...*' She *knew* him. He could tell. There was a moment of silence, and then she spoke again, muttering disjointed words and phrases which he struggled to comprehend. After a few moments she closed her eyes and fell silent.

'What is it?' he whispered, leaning closer. 'What are you trying to tell me?

And now she opened her eyes again, their gaze boring into his own, and her lips began to move, and then, all at once, as if she had been suddenly freed from some constraint, the words came pouring out of her distorted mouth, gushing out in a torrent, as if they would never cease. He sat spellbound, listening as she spoke, her lips, flecked with saliva, twitching and twisting with the effort. And then, as abruptly as it had begun, the outpouring of words ceased. Her mouth twisted, her body gave a shudder, and she was suddenly still.

He continued to sit there, staring down at her, and then became aware of the door opening behind him, and Dr Bloom coming back into the room.

As the doctor approached the bed, Douglas got up and stood to one side.

'Something — something's happened to her,' he said.

At the bedside the doctor bent over her, felt for a pulse and then, taking from his pocket a small flashlight, shone the fine beam into the half-opened, dulled eyes. With a deep sigh and a shake of his head he straightened, dropped the light back into his pocket and turned to Douglas.

'It's over, Mr Rosti,' he said. 'I'm so sorry.' He touched a hand to Douglas's shoulder. 'I'm afraid she's gone.'

......TWENTY-FOUR

'Miss Paul, this is your fifteen-minute call. Fifteen minutes, please.' The voice of the stage manager came over the speakers in the artists' dressing rooms. The programme's supporting act, rising comic Dennis Haversham, had just finished his routine, and the interval had begun. From the auditorium came the distant hum and buzz of the audience as they waited for the star of the evening to make her appearance.

In the number one dressing room Vera Winfield, forty-seven, ex-chorus girl, stood arranging flowers on a side table. She had been appointed the star's dresser for the evening. Now, as the adjoining bathroom door opened, she looked up.

'How are you feeling, Miss Paul? Better?'

The answer came with a groan. 'Oh, Jesus. Yes. No. God, I feel sick.'

'Can I get you anything?'

'Yes – how about a one-way flight to New York.'

Vera gave a sympathetic chuckle and turned, indicating a large bouquet of roses. 'More flowers have just come. There are so many. It's hard to know where to put them all. More cards too.' Dozens of cards were already on display around the brightly-lit mirrors, while masses of flowers were banked against one wall. 'Oh, and that was your fifteen-minute call.'

'Yes, I heard it, thanks.'

'Is there anything else I can do for you right now?' Vera asked.

A deep sigh, then: 'Well, I – I think I'd like to be on my own for a while, Vera, would you mind? Don't go too far away, please – but give me just a few minutes, okay?'

'Of course.' Vera smiled as she moved away. 'I'll be right outside if you need me.'

Left alone, the only sound in the room was the continuing hum of the audience that came over the tannoy. The sound was terrifying. Then there came a light tap at the door.

'Come in.'

Adrian Marlow entered.

He smiled at her. 'Glad to see you're still here,' he said. 'I was afraid you might have taken fright and decided to make a quick getaway at the eleventh hour.'

She gave a desperate-sounding little chuckle. 'Don't think the thought hasn't occurred to me, because it most certainly has.'

'Well, we're not letting you escape now,' he said with a laugh. 'I just came to wish you luck.' He took her outstretched hands in his, bent and kissed her lightly on the cheek. 'Good luck, Rosemary. Not that you're going to need it – not with all you've got going for you.'

She shook her head. 'Oh, Adrian, I wish I could be that sure.'

'Listen to me,' he said, gesturing off with a wave of his hand, 'there's a whole theatre full of people sitting out there, all of them waiting for you, all of them wild to see

you. Three thousand of them. And all willing you to succeed. Just remember that.'

'I will.' She took his hands again, pressed them. 'And
thank you. Thank you for all you've done.'

He left her then, and when the door had closed behind
him she picked up a glass of water and drank. Her throat,
her lips felt dry. I'm not going to be able to sing a note, she
thought. In spite of the warmth of the room she found
that she was shivering, and she tensed her muscles, trying
to hold her body still. It was the *not knowing*. That was what
was so hard.

She sat there for a moment more, then took her cell
phone from her bag and dialled the number of the hospital. *She had to know*. As the ringing tone sounded, the voice of
the stage manager came over the tannoy:

'Miss Paul, this is your five-minute call. Five minutes,
please.'

Five minutes, only five minutes to go. The seconds were
ticking by. Then came the familiar greeting from one of
the hospital receptionists.

'Ashton Green Hospital. Good evening. Can I help you?'

'Hello, yes.' She must make an effort to control her
breathing. 'This is Rosemary Paul,' she said. 'I'm calling to
ask after Miss Carrie Markham's condition.'

Hearing Rosemary's name, the young woman said at
once, 'Oh, hello, Miss Paul. If you hold on I'll connect you
with Sister Keith. She said if you called she'd like to speak
to you.'

A few moments later there came the voice of the ward
sister. 'Good evening, Miss Paul.'

'Good evening, Sister. I was calling to check on my friend Miss Markham. I'm told you wanted to speak to me.'

There was a pause before the other woman spoke again, and then:

'Yes. Yes, I'm afraid I have some bad news for you.'

'Bad news? *Oh…*'

'Yes. I'm – I'm very sorry to have to tell you that she – Miss Markham – she –'

'She's dead. Carrie's dead.'

'Yes.' A sigh. 'Oh, I'm so sorry to give you such awful news, Miss Paul. She – Miss Markham – she died at five-twenty this afternoon. I'm so sorry.' There was a long pause. 'Are you there? Are you there, Miss Paul?'

'What? Yes,' she said. 'Yes, I'm here.' The walls seemed to be spinning. 'Thank you. Thank you for telling me. Thank you.'

'I'm so sorry I had to. But I'm sure you'll be glad to know that – at the end she was in no pain. None at all.'

'Thank you. Thank you so much for telling me.'

She switched off her cellphone and dropped it back into her bag.

It was over.

*

As Douglas sat in the taxi speeding across London, the questions pounded in his brain: *What should he do? What should he do with his knowledge?*

In his pocket his fingers curled around the theatre ticket that the doctor had given him.

Reaching the theatre, he paid off the driver, then got out of the cab and looked up at the sign.

AN EVENING WITH ROSEMARY PAUL

He was too late to catch the supporting act, but he was
in time for the main event, and that was all that mattered.
He looked up at the sign again and the photographs that
were displayed beneath it. 'Okay, Miss Rosemary Paul,' he
muttered, 'you go ahead and show us. Let's see whether it
was all worth it.'

.....TWENTY-FIVE

'How do I look, Vera?'

'Oh, you look just wonderful, Miss Paul.'

A moment later there came over the tannoy the voice of the stage manager: 'Orchestra and Miss Paul. This is your call, please.' Seconds later there came a knock at the door and the stage manager was there in person. 'Miss Paul,' he said, putting his head around the door, 'I just wanted to wish you luck. Break a leg.'

'Thank you, Brian, darling.' She smiled distractedly as he retreated, then got up and stood before the full-length mirror. Her heart pounding, she studied her reflection. From over the tannoy the distant murmur of the audience took on a new air as the members of the orchestra took their places. Then a few moments later came the sounds of their tuning up, followed by a brief pause and then the opening chords of the old Fain/Kahal classic 'I Can Dream, Can't I?', a part of her overture. Hearing the melody again, she felt her heart give a lurch. She took a deep breath, sucking in the air. With a nervous touch at her hair, she straightened her shoulders, twitched at the neckline of her gown, then turned and moved to the door.

Out in the corridor, with Vera walking loyally in her wake, she moved towards the wings, aware as she did so of the gaze of the backstage staff, while the sounds of the orchestra swelled as if to greet her, almost overwhelming her with the strains of the lovely, familiar melodies, so beautifully arranged by Kurt.

Kurt...

No, don't think about him.

Somehow she found herself in the wings, and there she came to a halt and stood waiting. The music of the overture went on, pulsing towards its end...

And her new beginning.

From where she stood the stage looked vast. At the technical run-through earlier it had not appeared nearly so big, and she had tried to imagine herself standing out there alone. Her imaginings had filled her with terror, and she had thrust the image aside. Now, though, and all too suddenly, it was all real. This was no figment of her imaginings – it was all really happening. Suddenly she became aware that the overture had finished, and the auditorium was ringing with applause. When the music began again it would be for *her*.

And then silence came, and with the silence she knew that Ray Kesterson was raising his baton for her entrance music. And now here it came, filling the quiet with the opening chords of 'Kiss it Better'. All at once the curtain no longer separated the stage from the audience. And the lights were changing, getting ready to illuminate her the second she stepped out. And the music, too – now playing the melody for her entrance.

She couldn't move.

Her hoarse breath loud in her ears, she stood there, rigid, as if her feet were fastened to the floor. Heart pounding, she reached out, her hand groping for support, and felt her fingers touch the wall of the proscenium arch. As best she could she grasped it and remained there, trembling, fixed to the spot.

Just walk out there, she told herself. *Just walk out there. Just do it.*

But still she could not move.

See? — you can't do it, said a voice in her head, the words coming as if from some cruel and mocking entity inside her. *You can't do it. It's too late. You've left it too late.* And at once she answered back: *I can. I can. Oh, I can!* And then another voice came, and this too she answered in her head: *No, Kurt, you can't hurt me now.* Her mouth was dry as chalk. She took a deep breath, let it out on a sigh. *And you too, Carrie — you too. You can't hurt me either. You're gone for ever now.*

Looking to her left, she saw the anxious eyes of the stage manager as he waited for her to make her entrance. She realised suddenly that the orchestra had struck up her entrance music again. She swallowed, took a breath, nodded to the stage manager and whispered: 'Okay. I'm ready.'

Pushing her shoulders back, she tossed her hair, ran her tongue over her dry lips and stepped forward into the light.

*

As she appeared, the spotlight found her, a straight pencil-beam, catching her and bathing her in its brilliance. She stood there, a slim, anxious figure, drenched in the soft amber light. Framed by the massive proscenium arch, she appeared very small, very vulnerable. And very much alone.

For a split second the audience was silent, and then the sound came — a wave of applause, swelling till it drowned the music from the orchestra. Like a wave it swept over her as the people clapped, shouted, whistled and cheered. Dressed in her long, high-necked gown of smoky pink velvet, she gazed out at the shadowed mass. Through the roar she heard their voices calling:

'Rosemary.... Rosie.... Rosie....'

The light that shone down made her hair like pale flame, and caught too on the tear that ran down her cheek. Then the music was ending, and she was moving centre stage and taking up her position at the microphone. She lifted her hands, and the clamour from the auditorium fell away into a hushed silence. Her voice breaking slightly, she whispered, 'Thank you. Thank you.'

She caught at her breath, for a moment fearing that she would be unable to go on. And then from the crowd came a single call: 'Welcome home, Rosemary.' And then another voice: 'Yes, welcome home.' And another: 'We love you, Rosie. We love you.'

The applause, endorsing every syllable of the sentiments expressed, broke out again. Her heart thudding, she fought for control in the face of the overwhelming adoration.

After a few moments she managed to speak. 'Thank you,' she whispered into the mike. She turned her head, and gave Ray a slight, barely perceptible nod. At the signal he raised his baton. The audience at once fell silent, waiting.

Soft, mellow into the hush, came the sound of a clarinet, the first notes of the introduction to Kurt's song, the song he had written just for this night, just for this moment of her homecoming.

And here came her cue. The violins cascaded in, hovering, sweet, like hummingbirds on the air. Then the flute. She took a breath and began to sing.

Am I home? Have I come home?
Once again I can feel my feet
Safe and sound on a well-known street.
And I stand here and keep repeating:
Home. Am I home? Am I home?

When she began, her voice faltered, and her heart sank at the failing. She could hear the weakness and fear in her tone. She tried to breathe more deeply, steadily, and through the insecurity and terror she reached inside herself for the heart and the truth of the song. And finding it, she grasped it and held on. And slowly she felt her voice gaining strength. Slowly she felt the old sureness and confidence coming back, holding her, and she revelled in the touch.

She sang with all the feeling and artistry she possessed, with all her instinctive, God-given knowledge. She sang with warmth and simplicity, believing every word. And the audience believed her too, and after the long, long absence, and the knowledge of her suffering, their love reached out, compassionate and all-embracing.

All those years, the brighter lights,
The lonely towns, the lonely nights.
I was lost. Can it be I'm found?
And the words in my head keep pounding:
Home. Am I home? Am I home?

More than a room, or the dearest place,
Home is a touch, a smile, a special face.

Those who remembered her from all those years ago saw again the old familiar gestures, the old mannerisms. There was the outflung arm, the spread fingers, and in the softer passages the hands limp at her sides or clasped before her. It was as if she had never been away.

Douglas, sitting in the stalls, was astounded. He could not have believed it possible. The thought came to him that she had a truth, a reality that the old Rosemary had never known. It came like a soft glow, totally enveloping, bathing her in its radiance. It had nothing to do with the light; it came from within her. Her voice, too — he had never dreamed she could sing like this. He was surprised to find himself strangely moved. How did she do it? He closed his eyes as the voice poured over him.

All along I have known, I belong here with you,
So if you'll only tell me that you need me too,
Then at last, I shall know, only then shall I know,
Only then shall I know, I've come home.

The last notes of the orchestra echoed and died away. There was a beat — one, two, three — and then, as one man, the audience went wild.

It was as if the cheering would never stop. Visibly affected, tears shining in many eyes, they clapped, whistled and roared. All of them — the elderly couples who had come to relive old memories; the younger ones who were curious to find out for themselves; those who lived vicariously through the dreams and dramas of larger, star-studded careers; the sceptical reporters sent to cover the show; and even the few brittle-hearted cynics who had come hoping for a laugh — all were caught in the aura of her magic, and the spell she wove.

And there she stood, apart but at the centre of it all, a slim figure in dusky pink velvet.

'Thank you. Oh, thank you so much.' And with her spoken words they heard again the familiar tones, sounding a little older now, but nevertheless the voice they knew. More calls came to her from different points in the auditorium, and as there came a new burst of applause she raised a hand in a momentary plea for silence. 'Please — oh, please,' she said with a trembling smile, 'you're making me ruin my make-up, and that's something I can't afford.'

This allusion to the injuries she had suffered brought a fresh burst of applause. It was as if she could do nothing wrong.

Over the next fifty minutes she went through the carefully planned programme. Interspersed with brief comments and the occasional little joke, she sang her songs, giving the adoring audience exactly what they wanted. She caressed them with the wistful 'Kiss it Better', 'The Way You Look Tonight' and 'In a Little Secondhand Store', and on a lighter note with 'Not for All the Rice in China'. Raising the temperature a little there came upbeat renditions of 'Never Quite Enough' and 'Sunny Tuesday'. There too were classic evergreens from the Gershwins, Porter, Kern. And then, finally, came the second song that Kurt had

written – had written for this very moment. It followed the
Rodgers and Hart classic 'Falling in Love With Love', her
mellow voice soft against flutes and a frenetic drum beat.
With the song's last word she stood, arms outstretched,
holding the final note with a power, security and purity of
tone that she herself had not thought possible, then let her
arms fall gently to her sides as the drums came to a halt and
the echo of the flutes and the brass died away.

Timing the moment, she waited till the applause had
reached its peak, then lifted her hands a little before her,
palms open. A solitary saxophone came in, playing the
opening notes of the melody. And then her voice, inten-
tionally a little tentative, a little wondering:

If you ask who am I, take a look and you'll see,
See a lifetime of living, of winning and losing and trying,
And the total is me.
And I cried with the flops, and I laughed with the breaks.
And I somehow got by with the fears and the tears and mistakes.

And you ask, who am I, why I stand here alone.
I soon learned, if there's something you want
You must go out and get it – do it all on your own.
And I aimed for the best. I could show you the scars.
I just hoped I might get me the moon if I reached for the stars.

When a dream went all wrong I just tore it apart,
I took every doubt, turned it clear inside out,
And made a new start.

And you ask, who am I. Well, I learned to survive.
I played all the hunches, I rolled with the punches,
And I knew I was really alive.
So what more can I say, if you turn right away
And tell them I don't give a damn.
Do what you must do, but please grant me it's true
At least I know who I am.

The audience, as one, were spellbound. She stood there as the orchestra took up the melody and, building in power and intensity, played the bars leading to the final verses of the refrain. Hands outstretched to the sea of her adoring admirers, she took up the song again:

Sure you're gonna be hurt if you're not made of wood.
When faced with a test I did what I thought best,
The best way I could.

And if I live this life to a hundred and ten,
And the powers that give it say, 'Take it and live it,'
I'll live it, all over again.
And I'll grab every chance, and I'll lead them a dance.
And get me my share of the jam.
But whatever comes true, all the rage or all through,
At least I'll know who I am.

The song ended, and she stood there, arms outstretched, while the audience rose to its feet, threatening to deafen her with its rapturous applause. Then, arms lowered to her sides again, she remained quite still, her head a little bowed, bathed in the spotlight and the love that poured over her. And the thought went through her head that everything had been worth it — everything — just for this, for these moments. Everything else was behind her now. Nothing of it mattered. Nothing. And this was only the beginning. The past was far away; nothing of it could hurt her now. Goodbye, Kurt Hellman. Goodbye and thank you. Goodbye, Carrie. Poor, poor, sad Carrie Markham — it was you who made it all possible. Thank you, Carrie. Thank you and goodbye.

..... TWENTY-SIX

After the curtain calls, after the champagne in her dressing room, after the breathless change into her other gown, she was escorted, amid cheers, by Adrian Marlow to a waiting Rolls Royce. Turning, she waved to the ecstatic throng, climbed into the car and was driven away.

Douglas was there in the crowd, watching as she bathed in the glory of the moment, while the people clapped and the photographers shot their pictures.

With the star of the show gone, the press and the admirers melted away. Douglas, too, was about to turn and go when the stage door opened again and he saw the familiar figure of Ray Kesterson appear. At once he moved to him.

'Hey, Ray!'

Ray turned and saw him, his face lighting up. 'Douglas! Douglas Rosti!'

'The same.'

'Hey, Dougie.'

Smiling, the men shook hands.

'You just saw the show?' Ray asked.

'Oh, you bet,' Douglas replied. 'And congratulations. I wouldn't have missed it for the world.'

Ray thanked him. It had been quite a night for everyone, he said. 'Did you,' he asked, 'know Rosemary back in the States?'

'I did indeed,' Douglas said. 'We go back a little while. I knew her well.'

'Hey, that's great. And what a performance, eh?'

'Oh, yes.' Douglas nodded. 'What a performance.'

'I think she took just about everyone by surprise.'

Douglas nodded. 'Me for one, that's for sure.'

'Did you get a chance to see her after the show?'

'No – sorry to say I didn't.'

A moment, then Ray said, 'You have anything planned right now? The rest of the evening, I mean.'

'No, nothing. Why?'

'Well, come along with us. We're meeting up at the producer's place. For drinks and stuff. You'll be able to tell Rosemary how much you liked the show.'

*

'Here we go, Rosemary. Now you'll get a chance to relax a bit – and meet a few of your admirers close up.'

Adrian spoke the words as they entered the hall of his penthouse apartment overlooking Sloane Square. As the two of them entered the sitting room a minute later the assembled guests rose to their feet and burst into applause. There they were, the boys in the band, some of the backers, some of the backstage staff, and Adrian's many friends and colleagues. Crowding around her, they offered their congratulations while she thanked them and basked in the adulation. After a few minutes Adrian left her side and reappeared with drinks for them both, then, smiling, he led her away from the clamour. 'Come on outside for a minute now.' he said. 'We can't talk here. Let's get some air, and a bit of peace and quiet. I should think you've earned a break.'

Leaving his guests to be served by the maid and the bartender, he led the way through a rear hallway and out onto the terrace. There, beside the parapet looking over the square, he raised his glass.

'Well, here's to you, Rosemary,' he said, smiling. 'The lady done good tonight, and no mistake.'

'Thank you, so much,' she said, ' — and for believing in me.'

The sounds of the traffic drifted up on the night air, while a gentle breeze touched at the silk stole around her shoulders.

'Are you warm enough?' he asked.

'Yes, I'm fine, thank you.'

He reached out, touched the soft silk. 'That's a very pretty thing — your stole.'

'Thank you. I think so too.' She brushed at its smooth folds. 'My lucky wrap, I call it,' she said.

'Your *lucky* wrap?'

'Yes, it's always brought me luck. I got it way, way back, for a special event when I was singing with the band.' She gestured off into the city. 'At the Palladium here.

'And I bet you put the Palladium in your pocket.'

'I *wish*,' she said with a laugh, ' — but the band was the star, not me. I was just the vocalist.'

'Oh, no, you were never *just the vocalist*,' he said. 'I'll tell you something — you certainly put London in your pocket tonight.'

'Did I do that?' She smiled broadly. 'Well, that can't be bad, can it?'

'It can't be bad at all. And you did it all by yourself.'

She gazed at him for a moment, then said, 'No, Adrian, I didn't do it all by myself.'

He gave a little nod. 'Ah, right — I guess you mean your — your friend, Carrie — yes?'

'Yes.' She sighed. 'None of this could have happened without her.' She turned, looking out over the city.

He observed her for a moment, then said, 'What are you thinking?'

'What? Oh.' She hung her head. 'I was just thinking of her — Carrie.'

'Have you had any further word — as to how she is?'

A little pause, then: 'Yes. I heard earlier this evening. Just before I went on. I called the hospital.'

'And?'

Looking down at her hands she said, her voice husky, 'It — it's over.'

He leaned forward a little. 'You mean…'

'Yes. She — she's gone. Carrie's gone. It — it happened just this afternoon, they told me.'

He reached out and took her hand, gently pressed it. 'Oh, Rosemary, I'm so sorry. I had no idea.' He could see in her eyes the shine of tears. 'I can't imagine how you must be feeling. And you only learned about it tonight — just before you went on?'

She nodded. 'Yes.'

He shook his head in wonder. 'And after getting that news — you went out there and did that. You put on that stunning show. You gave that terrific — absolutely terrific performance. Well, all I can say is that you're an amazing woman. When I think of you, in front of that audience —

after all you've been through — standing up there alone.' He paused, then added with a faint smile, 'But — but maybe you weren't so alone there after all.'

'You mean — Carrie?'

He nodded. 'Maybe she's been with you. There with you tonight.'

'Yes.' And now she smiled. 'I — I'd like to think so.'

'And she'd be so glad for you — seeing your wonderful success.'

'Yes. I — I couldn't have done it without her.'

He nodded his understanding. 'But try not to be too sad,' he said. 'You owe it to her to *enjoy* your success — this great triumph.'

'Yes.' With a little catch of her breath she added, 'Oh, Adrian — I have to tell you that it's better than I ever dreamed it could be. I — I couldn't bear it if everything should come to an end.'

'Come to an end?' he said. 'Good heavens — why should it? It's all yours from now on. This is just the beginning.'

'Just the beginning.' She savoured the words, smiling. 'You promise?'

'I promise.'

He took a drink from his glass, then said, 'Hey, I think I'd better get back to my guests — make sure everyone's getting fed and watered.'

She smiled at him. 'You go on in. I'll join you in a minute. I just want to stay out here a little longer. It's nice to have the quiet.'

'Fine. I'll see you in a minute.' He patted her hand where it lay on the rail, and turned away.

*

Back inside, Adrian went into the dining room where the maids were just putting the finishing touches to a lavish buffet supper. He checked that everything looked right, then moved to the sitting room. As he entered he saw Ray Kesterson coming from the hall. He had a stranger with him.

'Ray,' Adrian said, 'I was wondering where you were. Come on and let's find you a drink. And something for your friend as well.'

'Adrian,' Ray said, 'this is Douglas — Douglas Rosti — from New York.' With the introductions the two men shook hands. 'Douglas is an old friend of Rosemary's,' Ray added. 'I was sure you wouldn't mind if I brought him along.'

'Absolutely not,' Adrian said. 'The more the merrier.' Then to Douglas: 'You're very welcome, Douglas. Take off your coat and get yourself a drink. Rosemary's out on the terrace — getting a little air. Go say hello to her.'

'Thanks very much, I will,' Douglas said. He slipped off his coat and handed it to the maid.

Adrian said, pointing off: 'Go on through the hall there. Rosemary'll be thrilled to see an old friend.'

'Thanks,' Douglas said. 'If you'll excuse me...' Stepping away from the two men he started across the room and into the hall. At the door to the terrace he came to a halt and looked out through the glass. He could see her there, the familiar figure, beside the parapet.

*

Standing alone at the rail, she took another sip from her glass and gazed out over the busy square below. The night was growing cooler, but she didn't care. For the moment she was reluctant to return to the crowd and the babble. There would be time enough. Distantly, from inside, behind her, she could hear a piano being played, a burst of laughter. Then came a sudden, brief swell of noise as the terrace door opened and closed again. She heard the sound of footfalls on the tiled floor, and then a voice.

'Hello.'

Turning, she saw a man standing there. And as recognition came she reeled, clutching at the rail, while the glass she was holding slipped from her fingers and shattered on the tiles. The wind was suddenly chill against her face, while the perspiration broke out, dampening her palms. When he spoke again, his words seemed to echo, coming from a long way off.

'Hello — Carrie,' he said.

TWENTY-SEVEN

For a moment she couldn't move. Then, turning her head away, she gripped the parapet rail. 'Oh, God,' she moaned. 'Oh, God. Oh, God...'

'Don't be afraid, Carrie,' he said quickly. 'Please, don't be afraid.'

She turned back to face him, her eyes darting left and right, as if she was afraid they might be overheard. 'What are you doing here?' she said.

After a moment's hesitation he moved to stand before her. Close up, he could see in her face the subtle changes, the fading scars. 'I saw your show this evening,' he said. 'My God, you were something else.' He shook his head in a gesture of wonder and admiration. 'You were absolutely amazing. Better than Rosemary could ever be.'

Now a little smile touched the corners of her mouth. 'Thank you.'

'Though I still can't take it in,' he said. 'I mean – how did it all happen? What made you do it?'

'What made me do it?' She looked surprised, as if the question was unnecessary. 'I didn't plan it. It just happened. They took me for Rosemary. Her name-tag – it was sewn into the dress I was wearing. It was a dress she'd given me – and her credit cards were in my pocket. Everything else got burned up. They thought I was Rosemary and they *called* me Rosemary, and I – I responded.' A brief shrug, as if it all made sense. 'It just happened – and I went along with it. Anyway,' she added with a note of pride, 'I gave everybody what they wanted, didn't I? They wanted Rosemary – and they got her.'

He nodded. 'They did indeed. But weren't you afraid?'

'Afraid?' She gazed at him, wide-eyed. 'Of course I was afraid! But I'm an actress – as you saw tonight. And I was always terrific at impersonations. Right from when I was a kid. At parties and things I could always be relied on to strut my stuff – taking off all the singers and the old movie stars. And with Rosemary it wasn't difficult. All those years together – let's face it, nobody in the world knew her better than I did.' She gave a nod. 'There were three thousand people in that audience tonight, and I fooled them all. Well, all except you.'

'Oh, you were incredible,' he said. 'But it wasn't only the voice – you had everything about her. Her gestures, the way she walked, her little mannerisms. You had it all.'

She nodded again. 'I'm a perfectionist as well.'

'Oh, yes.' He frowned. 'But what will you do now?'

'What?'

'Well – when they find out that you're not Rosemary.'

'They're not going to find out.'

'Oh, Carrie, they will,' he said. 'Sooner or later you're bound to meet somebody – apart from me – who knew her too well to be fooled.'

She shook her head. 'No, that's not going to happen.' She waved a hand, gesturing back to the apartment. 'Go ask them in there. *They* know who I am.'

'Yes, but they didn't know the *real* Rosemary. There must be lots of people who knew her from way back.'

'Well,' she said, 'maybe you can tell me who these people are. I haven't heard of one person tonight who claims to have known her from her early days.'

'No, maybe not – but they'll be out there. What about all the musicians she worked with? There's bound to be someone who—'

'They're dead,' she broke in. 'The band-leaders, the pianists, the drummers – most of them are dead now. And she had no family. As for the rest, her fans – they didn't *know* her. And how long has it been since any of them actually saw her? I mean, what do they have? A few photographs of her from when she was young, maybe. Some grainy old pictures taken of her on the bandstand, all of forty-odd years ago, when she was pretty and glamorous in her little party dress. That'll be the image they have. They know that people change a lot as they grow older. And after all those years away from the public eye, and people hearing about all the facial reconstruction in the hospital – how could anybody know for sure what she'd look like? Well, look at *me*. If you'd had done to your face what I've had done to mine you wouldn't look quite like you either.'

He nodded. 'It must have been terrible – what you went through.'

'You'd better believe it.' She gave a little smile. 'And shall I tell you something? It was worth it. To be on that stage tonight, and hear that audience clapping and cheering – it made it all worthwhile. Every bit.' Adjusting the stole about her throat and shoulders, she gave a nod. 'And

I'll tell you something else – I *earned* it. It was *mine*, mine by rights.'

He shook his head, looking at her in bewilderment.

'She took my life away from me,' she said. 'Rosemary. She stole *everything*. My career, everything that was important to me. And all this – this success tonight – it was no more than what she owed me.'

'Carrie––'

'I mean it,' she said. 'And you know what? This is only the beginning. I'm only just starting. I've got years to make up.'

'Carrie,' he said, 'you'll never get away with it. You must give it up. You've got to.'

'After tonight?' She shook her head. 'No way. This is all I ever wanted.'

'Carrie––'

'Stop calling me that!' she hissed. 'I'm *Rosemary*. Carrie died in the hospital this afternoon.' Leaning in a little towards him, she added: 'And just get something clear. I didn't do anything to Rosemary. I haven't taken anything away from her. I've *given* to her. *Given*. Without me, she'd be remembered as some pathetic has-been.' She gave a nod. 'Well, you saw for yourself, didn't you? And that must have been some shock, huh? Seeing me up there on stage tonight?'

'I already knew,' he said. 'I knew it wasn't Rosemary I was going to see.'

'You knew? Before you came to the theatre?'

'Yes. I went to the hospital this afternoon.'

'You went to the hospital? In Ashton Green?'

'Yes. I thought I was going to see *you*. And I saw Rosemary lying there. That was some shock, let me tell you.' He paused. 'And I was there when she died,'

She stared at him. 'You were?'

'Yes. I thought she was regaining consciousness. She opened her eyes and looked right at me, and began to speak.'

'What did she say?'

'Nothing that made any sense. Just words. Nothing I could understand. And then – then she died. Right in front of me.' He sighed. 'Poor Rosemary.'

'Yes, poor Rosemary.' Carrie's tone was cold. 'Anyway,' she said, 'that's all over with.' She frowned. 'How did you get in here, anyway?'

'Ray Kesterson brought me along. I know him from way back.'

'Okay.' She nodded. 'And did you come to congratulate me?'

'I told you – you were amazing. It wasn't only that, though. It's Kurt.'

'Kurt?'

'I can't find him,' he said. 'He seems to have just vanished. He told me he was flying out to London, and was—'

'I don't know anything about him,' she broke in. Then, her eyes narrowing: 'What have you come here for? You didn't come here to talk about Kurt.' Her nostrils flared. 'Have you come here to destroy me?'

'*What?*' Douglas's eyes widened in amazement. 'Carrie, what are you saying?' With his words he took a step towards her. At once she stepped back, putting up a shielding hand.

'Keep away from me, you bastard.'

Shocked, he came to a halt, and they stood facing one another while the noise of the traffic drifted up from the square below. He stared at her, now seeing only naked hatred in her eyes. He should never have come, he knew that now. He should never have faced her with his knowledge of the truth. He must go. He would go. Go and leave her to her life.

Lowering his eyes from her piercing glare, he turned and started towards the terrace door.

'Where are you going?' she said sharply.

When he made no answer, her voice came again: 'I said, where are you going?'

Following her words there came the sound of her heels on the terrace floor. He got to the door and reached out for the handle, but she was too quick. In the space of a breath she was there before him, her back against the door, barring the way.

'Have you told anybody else about this – about me?' she said.

'What? No. No, of course I haven't.'

'Yet.'

She took a step towards him, and he drew back, retreating from the fury in her eyes. 'Carrie,' he said, 'take it easy. Calm down.' He raised a hand before him, but she lashed out, striking it aside. 'Calm down?' she said. 'After all these years I've found myself a life – a real life, and you tell me to calm down while you wreck it all! Fuck you, you son of a bitch. That is not gonna happen.'

'Carrie,' he said, 'listen to me. Listen—'

'No, you listen,' she hissed. 'You're not going to spoil

this. You're not going to humiliate me in front of the whole world.' Raising her fist, she struck him a violent blow on the chest, sending him staggering. In the next second she was upon him, her hands thrusting him backwards, and all at once he could feel the parapet rail pressing into his back. 'No!' he cried out in sudden fear. *'No! Carrie, no!'*

But nothing can stop her now. With both hands she pushes, heaving with all her strength. In her passion she is strong, and in a moment he is half over, the yawning acres of the city below him. 'Christ, no!' he screams. Desperately, he snatches at the rail. Her face is right there, close, ugly in her rage and determination. He can feel her breath, burning hot on his cheek. 'Go down, you bastard!' she spits. 'I won't let you destroy me.' He grips the rail tighter with one hand, while his other hand reaches out. Flailing, it touches the fabric of her stole, her lucky wrap. He snatches at it. As the silk yanks at her neck she goes to scream, but the sound is cut off by the tightening noose. Her hands go clawing at her throat, but there is no release, the silk is round her neck like a band of steel. For a few moments she and Douglas form a grotesque tableau as they struggle there above the city's noise and lights. It cannot endure. Another moment and Douglas loses his grip on the rail. Carrie, held fast by the rope of silk about her neck, follows him over the parapet, plunging into the empty cold. In the final throes of their desperation they reach out. Finding only one another, they embrace, clinging fast as they fall, screaming, down into the night.

THE END

There Must Be Evil

BERNARD TAYLOR

In 1887, Elizabeth Berry, an attractive young nurse from the grim Oldham workhouse, found notoriety throughout the nation after the death of her daughter, perceived by many to be the cruellest of murders – performed with an ice-cold callousness that was almost beyond belief. There were many who protested her innocence in the affair, but there were also suspicions surrounding another death related to the nurse: that of her mother. Suddenly Elizabeth Berry's tragic story began to appear darker still. Was she in fact a cold-blooded serial killer?

In his new book, the celebrated and award-winning crime author Bernard Taylor investigates the disturbing life of Elizabeth Berry endured during an era of grinding poverty, when Victorian England was obsessed with the exploits of murderers and forensic science was in its infancy. He takes a fresh look at the demise of Berry's husband and two other young children, deaths that for a long time were thought to be of natural causes.

For the first time we discover the true story behind this infamous case of the first woman to be hanged at Liverpool's Walton Prison, and one of the Victorian period's most harrowing set of homicides.

Paperback, ISBN 9780715650516
£9.99

Perfect Murder

BERNARD TAYLOR AND STEPHEN KNIGHT

Winner of the CWA Gold Dagger for Non-Fiction

From the mysterious death of William Saunders, whose beaten body was discovered in a pond near Penge cricket club, south-east London in 1877, to the spooky demise of Charles Walton whose death is believed to have been linked to witchcraft, unsolved murders litter British history. Authors Bernard Taylor and Stephen Knight, experts in the unravelling of unsolved crimes, re-investigate seven classic cases from the last hundred years.

Creating in lively detail the background to each crime and the course of the police investigation, they reveal clues, interpret evidence and study the characters and motives of the alleged killers. In many instances the authors have unearthed previously undiscovered facts – none more startling than in the case of the lurid Brighton trunk murder of 1934, to which Tony Mancini, initially cleared of the time, confesses his guilt to Stephen Knight.

Perfect Murder is an eye-opening and gripping read, serving as a stark reminder that justice does not always prevail...

Paperback, ISBN 9780715650738
£9.99

Black Fridays

MICHAEL SEARS

Jason Stafford is a former Wall Street hotshot who made some bad moves, paid the price with two years in prison, and is now trying to put his life back together. He's unemployable, until an investment firm asks him to look into possible problems left by a junior trader who died recently in an accident. What he discovers is big – there are problems, all right, the kind that get you killed.

But it's not his only concern. Stafford has another quest as well: to reclaim his five-year-old son from his unstable ex-wife, and then learn just what it means to make a life with him. The things Stafford discovers about himself in the process are every bit as gripping as his investigation, and when the two threads of his life come together the results are unforgettable.

Black Fridays marks the arrival of a remarkable new writer.

'An absorbing first novel, a financial thriller with an unusually emotional heart ... an exciting yet often moving tale'   *The Times*

'*Black Fridays* has it all: superb writing, a riveting plot, and a hero I'm still thinking about days afterward. A must-read!'   Tess Gerritsen

'An exciting and fascinating tale of big money and even bigger crime. More than a gripping procedural, it's a moving, deeply human story'   Joseph Finder

Paperback, ISBN 9780715651155

£7.99

Layer Cake

J. J. CONNOLLY

The basis for the 2004 film starring Daniel Craig, Michael Gambon and Sienna Miller

Layer Cake (the phrase is a metaphor for the many murky levels of the criminal underworld) is set in modern-day London and features a smooth-talking, sophisticated but anonymous drug dealer: 'If you knew my name,' he says, 'you'd be as clever as me.'

His plan is to very, very quietly bankroll enough discreetly laundered cash to retire young and extremely comfortably. Operating under the polished veneer of a legitimate businessman, his mantra is to keep a low profile and run a tight ship until it's time to bail. And when the old-school crime boss, Jimmy Price, asks him to find his pal's wayward daughter, our narrator spots his opportunity to make a final very lucrative score and ease his path out when.

He agrees to the seemingly innocuous gig – but a dark, twisted, thriller of a story ensues, which takes us from the glitz of the London club scene to the grubbiest reaches of the capital's criminal underworld.

'A storming piece of work ... has a grasp of street argot unparalleled since Kinky Friedman first sashayed out of his from door and nailed a checker straight out of the bat'   *D. J. Taylor*

'Connolly's style is fast and funny and just frightening enough to make you sit up all night finishing the book'   *Independent on Sunday*

'One novel in and Connolly has hit the jackpot, jump-started British crime fiction into the present ... Like good drug fiction you're given glamour and squalor, a voyeuristic thrill, and the bill'   *Uncut*

Paperback, ISBN 9780715641118

£7.99

Viva La Madness

J. J. CONNOLLY

The authentic voice of British gangster fiction, J.J. Connolly, is back with his trademark razor-sharp dialogue and quick-fire violence. From the London underworld he portrayed so brilliantly in *Layer Cake*, the plot of *Viva la Madness* goes international, with transatlantic drug deals, money laundering and high-tech electronic fraud, described with uncanny believability.

The anonymous hero of *Layer Cake* is pulled back into the drug game before he can enjoy a sunny retirement. From living the high life in the Caribbean to a dangerous existence in London, with Venezuelan drug cartels toting machine-guns in Mayfair, the story moves from violence and farce to criminal insanity.

'Masterful plotting – double-crosses abound – a cracking pace and some truly excellent set pieces including a chase through the London underground all lead up to a wham-bam ending. Fast, furious, funny and highly recommended for fans of *Layer Cake* and new readers alike'   *Guardian*

'The novel has its predecessor's driving energy ... and the protagonist's disparate colleagues are terrific characters'   *Sunday Times*

'Connolly's style is fast and funny and just frightening enough to make you sit up all night'   *Independent on Sunday*

Paperback, ISBN 9780715643655
£7.99